SHADOW REAPER

AN URBAN FANTASY

ANN GIMPEL

CONTENTS

Shadow Reaper — 1

Book Description, Shadow Reaper — 3

Books in the Gatekeeper Series — 5

Author's Note — 7

1. Chapter One, Cait — 9

2. Chapter Two, Liam — 25

3. Chapter Three, Cait — 39

4. Chapter Four, Liam — 55

5. Chapter Five, Cait — 71

6. Chapter Six, Liam — 87

7. Chapter Seven, Cait — 101

8. Chapter Eight, Liam — 115

9. Chapter Nine, Cait — 129

10. Chapter Ten, Liam — 143

11. Chapter Eleven, Cait — 159

12. Chapter Twelve, Liam — 173

13. Chapter Thirteen, Cait — 189

14. Chapter Fourteen, Liam — 205

15. Chapter Fifteen, Cait — 221

16. Chapter Sixteen, Liam — 237

17. Chapter Seventeen, Cait — 253

18. Chapter Eighteen, Liam — 269

19. Chapter Nineteen, Cait — 287

Book Description, Rebel Reaper — 303

Rebel Reaper, Chapter One, Cait — 305

About the Author — 321

Also by Ann Gimpel — 323

SHADOW REAPER

GATEKEEPER SERIES, BOOK ONE

An Urban Fantasy

By

Ann Gimpel

Tumble off reality's edge into myth, magic, and Death

The dead are restless, and a whole lot less cooperative than they have been. That was true even before I drew the short straw and ended up with Vampire duty.

Since then, Reaping has taken way more time. So much, I'm worried I'll lose all the clients from the career that actually feeds me. I run a small private pilot school. It pays most of the bills and means I don't have to keep regular hours.

Death wants me to remain in one piece. She's bailed me out often enough, she's all but ordered me to find other employment. I just smile and nod after our little talks, and then I climb back into a cockpit.

Our last toe-to-toe didn't go so well. She went and assigned Vampires to me. That's when Reaping turned into a million-hour-a-week job. I can almost hear the Reaper who was stuck with them before, laughing his head off.

I shepherd souls to the other side. Vampires have zero

interest in leaving, but I have a quota to fill. Means I have to trick them, but it didn't work for long. They're onto me. Damn Death, anyway. She painted a target on my back, and now the Vamps are out for blood.

In more ways than one.

BOOKS IN THE GATEKEEPER SERIES

Shadow Reaper, Book One
Rebel Reaper, Book Two
Untamed Reaper, Book Three

AUTHOR'S NOTE

After a million dragon books, I'm branching out. Good to cross train that muse of mine. The concept of the Grim Reaper has fascinated me for years. I used to work for a residency program where I taught bedside manners to newly minted doctors. A few of them were quite sensitive to supernatural phenomena, and they'd come into my office and talk with me about sensing Death's presence before a patient passed.

They'd also talk with me about the numinous aspect of both birth and death.

Fast forward the clock a few years to *Supernatural*. Sam and Dean dealt with both Death and Reapers—until Dean killed off Death in I believe season ten. Then it's mostly Reapers.

A Reaper tale has been running around in my mind for quite a while. I hope you enjoy the Gatekeeper Series.

CHAPTER ONE, CAIT

The screen on my crappy monitor looked blurrier than usual, but it might have been my vision. No sleep these past few nights had to be taking a toll. I rubbed grit out of my eyes and shut them, promising myself it would only be for a couple of seconds. Then I had to get back to last month's books.

They weren't looking good. I'd spent more on mechanic bills and aviation fuel than I'd made. Big surprise. To teach flying, I have to actually be here. Not off chasing Vampires. A sigh started in my chest and burbled out my mouth before I could stop it. Sighing is for wimps.

I'm more of a take-charge type. Or maybe I'm deluding myself.

A pair of ghosts drifted through the far wall, making a beeline right for me. They were on the youngish side, maybe late forties when their lives had been cut out from under them. I'm a Reaper, and souls who have yet to cross are drawn to me like the proverbial moth to a flame. It's a scent thing, kind of like pheromones, except keyed to crossing the veil rather than for sex.

They say hearing is the last sense to go. Nope. It's smell.

I stood and flapped my hands at the approaching pair. "Find another Reaper. I've been reassigned."

"But we're here," the man protested.

"Here," the woman echoed.

They were only a few feet away. A closer look revealed bullet holes in both their foreheads. Crap. Had they been victimized by another mass murderer?

"Please," the man said. "Winnie and me, we—"

"Nope." I turned both hands palms out. "Determining where you end up is above my pay grade. Sorry you're dead, but telling me how it happened is a waste of your time."

At this point, acting as a conduit was simpler than arguing. I covered the remaining distance between us and opened my arms. The duo didn't require further instructions. They walked into my embrace, first one then the other, more than ready to depart this portion of their existence. As I held them, they passed through me.

My Reaper side channeled the dark forever of death, and a chill I knew all too well shot from my toes to my head. If I'd had any hopes of finishing my bookwork, it just went up in smoke. Or ice chips. Reaping is hard work. There are several of us, but never enough to go around.

Fuck it.

I sat back down. Next I pushed the keyboard aside, folded my arms on my dusty desk, and laid my head on top of them. A fifteen-minute nap would do me wonders. Maybe after I finished the books, I'd clean my office. Customers offered pilots latitude when it came to neatness, but I'm not sure I'd climb into an airplane with someone whose workplace looked quite as down-at-the-heels as mine.

Carrick Sky Sports is located in a small Quonset hut right next to the hangar housing my three planes. The hangar was a whole lot cleaner than my digs, but then so were the planes.

I took care of them. They were my babies. Thoughts of airplanes and Vampires and Reaping whirled through my tired brain before I finally nodded off.

A staunch knock startled me so badly, I nearly tumbled out of my chair. It skidded back a few inches, leaving me fighting not to end up on my ass.

"Cait Carrick?" a deep male voice inquired.

I had yet to get a visual on the speaker. At least he wasn't dead. Their voices lacked resonance.

"Yeah. Um, yes. That would be me." I stuffed my feet under my body and stood, turning until I faced the single door into my office. I'm tall, so tall I'm used to looking down at everyone, including men, but the dude who stood there was at least six foot four, topping me by a good two inches.

Faded Levis encased his long legs. Torn trail runners might have been black once, but they'd faded to gray. A battered leather vest and frayed blue-plaid shirt covered his torso. Fair hair was long enough for him to have gathered it behind his head into a ragged braid. He had an interesting face, all planes and angles with a square chin and sharp cheekbones, but his most unusual feature was his eyes. I suppose they were hazel, but in the light streaming through the door behind him, they glowed like burnished copper.

"Sorry to disturb you." He grinned rakishly. "I tried knocking softer, but you were really out of it."

I swallowed back annoyance. I'd be damned if I'd stand here while a total stranger blithely assessed my physical state.

"And you are?" I raised my eyebrows.

"Liam. Liam Hunter." He glided toward me, hand extended.

Something about him bothered me, but I couldn't home in on what it was. I tucked my hands behind my back. "Sorry," I mumbled, "I've got grease all over me. What can I do for you?"

"They say you're the best flight instructor around." His smile, which had slipped a few notches, bloomed again.

"Who's they?" I winced. I should just have said "thank you" and let it be.

"Why all the pilots down at *The Tailwind*."

It was a small bar and grill at the far end of the airstrip I used. Most days, they served breakfast and lunch. Weekends, they served dinner. While I knew all the local pilots, I wasn't aware they ever talked up my skills. Most of them were pretty old-school. Chauvinistic enough to believe women belonged in the kitchen—or the bedroom—rather than in an airplane.

I'd dealt with a lot of flak a decade ago when I opened my business. Once the guys figured out I wasn't a flash in the pan, they dialed back the harassment but never totally accepted me.

What to do about the dude standing three feet away?

He had an expectant look on his face, as if he'd offered up the aeronautical equivalent of "Open Sesame." If I didn't have so many unpaid bills, I'd have chased him out of my office. On the other hand, I didn't want to share a cockpit with someone who started out on the wrong foot by lying to me.

I pushed my shoulders straighter. If I'd gotten any mileage out of my nap, it wasn't readily apparent. "Um, look, Mr. Hunter—if that's even your name—the other pilots would never steer business my way. Either you play this again from the top, or we have nothing to talk about."

His smile developed a definite sheepish cast. "That transparent, huh?"

I nodded and waited, too tired to spar with him. Night would fall soon enough, and then I'd be back to herding Vampires. Death wanted them in Hell, but they were a slimy, sleazy lot with a huge investment in remaining on Earth.

There it was. My problem in a nutshell. Their motivation in staying topside was significantly more pressing than my need to move them across the veil. I'd quit if I could, but Reapers are born into Reaping.

And we live for a very long time.

The thought of chasing down Vampires until the moon fell out of the sky depressed the living fuck out of me.

"Ms. Carrick?"

I started. I hadn't exactly forgotten Mr. False Name, but he'd moved away from dead-center on my radar. He kicked the door shut. A surge of magic flickered around him, turning the air as blurry as my monitor had been.

"You're right about me being tired," I told him. "If you're about to cut the crap and tell me who you are and why you're here, we'll both be money ahead."

The angles in his face grew more pronounced, his fingers more elongated, the copper cast to his eyes deeper, shinier.

I narrowed my eyes. "Sidhe or Fae. Am I right?"

"Aye, Ms. Carrick. I'm Daoine Sidhe. Liam is a modernization of my name, and my family name is Warwick." His accent had shifted from pure American to a lilting Irish brogue, or maybe it was Scottish. Never could tell them apart.

Breath hissed through my teeth. At least he'd offered his true name. The teensy jolt I'd gotten from the other one hadn't bothered me this time. "You scarcely need my airplanes. You can teleport."

The corners of his generous mouth twisted into a wry expression. "You know about us?"

No point dancing around what I was. I was certain he knew, and my soul-herding skills were why he was here. "I went to Reaper school. We have to get passing grades before Death turns us loose."

He furled a blond brow. "Fascinating. I had no idea."

"How about if you tell me why you're here? Then you can leave. I have work to do." A quick glance through my single window told me time was about to betray me. Sunset would be in maybe an hour. With it would come the Vampire horde blood-bent on my destruction.

Or my assimilation, to be more precise.

He frowned. "You're about to have company. I shall return later."

Before I could tell him not to bother coming back, the place he'd stood was empty. I could still feel the beat of his soul, but damn if he hadn't vanished before my eyes.

I stared at the door. I might not know Mr. Warwick, but I trusted his paranormal ability. Sure enough, a knock was followed by a swoosh as the door flew open. Kiko Tanaka strode inside, dark hair billowing around her head like a cloud. She's my closest friend, and another pilot when she's not busy being a pharmacist. Her Japanese heritage is evident in her slight figure and dark, almond-shaped eyes.

"Not late, am I?" She grinned at me. It lightened her features and made her look about sixteen.

I must have appeared blank because she added, "Remember? You promised me an under-the-hood check ride."

Heat rose to my cheeks. "Sorry. I didn't exactly forget. But it's okay. I have time."

"Are you sure?" Kiko asked. "You're looking a little ragged around the edges."

"Yeah. I'm sure. I'm good for a check ride." To avoid more commentary about how trashed I appeared, I strode to the board and snapped up keys for the Cessna 172. Like I said, I have three airplanes, a Cessna 152 trainer, the 172, and a Piper Seneca. The Piper is a twin-engine jobbie. It costs me five hundred bucks an hour to keep it in the air, so I rarely fly the old girl. She's left over from when I used to have a contract for air freight runs. Then she made sense because she has a great payload.

I really should sell her, but I don't have the heart. Like I said, the planes are my babies.

We left the Quonset hut with Kiko chattering a mile a minute about a hunky dude she'd met the night before. I kicked back and let her manage the preflight checklist. She's efficient. No wasted motion. She even remembered to grab the cushion that made up for her short arms and legs.

She took the left seat; I settled into the right as she nosed the Cessna out of the hangar. I love the moment when a plane is barreling down a runway, gaining the momentum it needs for its wings to carry it skyward. Once we were upstairs, Kiko tugged a hood over her head and proceeded to follow my instructions using the instrument panel rather than her eyes.

We're both IFR certified, which means instrument flight rules. It's the step that comes after VFR. All pilots have to be able to manage their planes under visual flight rules, or they don't get to fly anything.

Didn't take long before we were circling to land. Kiko did a great job, flared at just the right time, and the plane settled gently to the tarmac, right on the numbers at its eastern end.

"Do you want her back inside?" Kiko asked. Her hood lay across her lap. She'd removed it on our final approach.

I shook my head. "Think I'll take her back up for a bit."

She taxied the plane off the runway and patted my thigh. "If there's anything I can do, just holler."

"Thank you." What I didn't say was that talking about my particular problem wouldn't solve anything. She offered up her logbook, and I initialed our check ride.

"I'll leave a check on your desk," Kiko told me. Pushing the door open, she climbed down. I handed her pillow outside before I switched sides of the plane. She knows what

I am, but not about my Vampire-herding assignment. I'm not about to tell her—or anyone else, either.

Magic came out of the closet about fifty years ago, but the presence of supernaturals makes most mortals really uncomfortable. If it had only been one variety, things might have gone smoother, but when it became apparent the dude next door could be a witch or a shifter or a Druid or one of the Fae, a backlash developed.

Humans still aren't certain Vampires are real. The fuckers are masters at hiding the corpses they've drained. And the newly turned ones are kept on a very short leash.

Over time, the friction between mortals and magic had done nothing but grow worse. Lots of anger and hatred on both sides of the fence. This group, Humans Rule, has been a particular thorn in my side. Mostly, I keep a low profile and stay out of everyone's way, though.

I have enough problems without turning into a crusader for magic wielders and our rights.

I nosed the Cessna back into the air, glorying in the feel of the plane as I put her through her paces. She's a good compromise. Light, reasonably fuel efficient—for an airplane—and responsive. The sky to the west lit with what was shaping up to be a glorious sunset. On a whim, I flew into it, chasing the colors across the Olympic Peninsula.

When I finally turned back to the east and set the three-axis autopilot to take me home, I considered how to spend the coming evening. Really only two choices. I could barricade myself into my houseboat on Lake Union.

A fortunate choice of residences since Vampires hate water.

Or I could go hunting. Problem was, I'm about out of tricks. Vampires are very old. Even older than me, for the most part. With age comes shrewdness. Because they all talk with each other in some perversion of telepathy, I can only use a strategy once. They were onto me. It was either come up with something new or lie low.

By the time my wheels kissed the tarmac, I'd come to a decision. I had to have another sit-down with Death. If she wanted to purge Earth of Vampires, maybe she had some ideas—other than driving the Reaper assigned to them nuts. The guy before me had done pretty much nothing. It's not like Death can fire us.

I considered my options as I taxied off the runway and into my hangar. I could follow the other Reaper's example, but it went against the grain. I'm not lazy. Beyond that, I do not like to lose. At anything.

Right now, I was slightly ahead. Majorly ahead, actually. I'd shunted an even dozen Vamps to their rightful spot, presumably in Hell. The way it works is this. I'm a gateway, a link between Earth and Death's domain. The dead pass through me, but I have no jurisdiction over their destination.

Better if I don't know.

I can't imagine a Vampire ending up in the good spot, though.

I buttoned up the plane and pulled the hangar door shut. It creaked on its rollers, and I added spraying them with silicone to my endless to-do list. Once the hangar was locked, I trotted to the Quonset hut. I was feeling better. Flying always lifted my spirits.

And I had a direction scoped out. My next heart-to-heart

with Death had to happen soon. I'd make some notes, to be sure I didn't miss anything, and then I'd reach out to her.

It was full dark when I unlocked my office and walked through the door, clicking on the overheads as I passed the bank of switches. I returned the Cessna's keys to their hook on the board. Kiko's money was dead center on my desk. If I hadn't been so cash-strapped, I'd have told her the check ride was on the house, but av gas wasn't cheap. Last week it topped six bucks a gallon, and we'd burned through seventy dollars' worth before my solo indulgence flight.

My monitor had long since blacked out as my computer went into sleep mode. I considered returning to my bookwork but didn't feel like it. The bad news would hold till tomorrow. Even without hard figures, I had choices to make. Either I freed up enough time to make *Carrick Sky Sports* profitable again, or I'd have to sell my planes. Hangar rent was two thousand dollars a month. Upkeep on the planes another thousand—if I was lucky.

Normally, it was doable. Flight lessons were expensive. And I could always bid to fly freight with the Piper Seneca again. But to do those things, I needed time. And a decent night's sleep every night. Not sleeping because I was on Vampire patrol was the linchpin that was killing me.

I rolled my eyes. What an unfortunate turn of phrase. I was only about six months into Vampire patrol, and I was sick of it.

Maybe thinking about the Undead drew them, but the lights flickered, and the chill of grave dirt descended on my head like a ton of bricks. Thank all the gods I had a moment's warning. It was enough for me to dash to the locker where I keep my street clothes and grab the saber I'd bought for just these occasions.

It had cost me an obscene amount of money, but the blade is a mix of silver and iron. Perfect for unruly Vamps and not quite as personal as impaling them through the heart with silver stakes. This way, the length of the blade is between us. Stakes would have required me to be right up next to the loathsome fuckers.

I swung the blade, ready for damn near anything. I'd taken a few lessons in swordsmanship once I bought the saber. Those were a bitch to find. It's not the Middle Ages anymore. Not too many knights errant wandering about running schools for wanna-be warriors.

My death-sense intensified. The smell of rot pervaded my office. Could they come in without an invitation? The lore suggested otherwise, but I'd run across the occasional Vampire in broad daylight, so the rulebook didn't seem to apply any longer.

Sure enough, one sashayed through a wall. I didn't bother looking at him. They're all hunks. And they all reek of decay. Another followed him. And another, until half a dozen formed a semicircle around me. I'd been savvy enough to place a wall behind me, or I'd have been surrounded.

Smart fuckers. They understood my blade would end them, so they kept just beyond its path. I glared. They glared back. Every time I made a move, they jumped nimbly out of my way. They're fast. Superhuman speed and strength comes along with the blood-spell that turns them.

Dawn might end my predicament, but I did not want to

spend the next nine hours staring down the maw of a Vampire horde. More were joining the ones already here. Naturally. A telepathic summons must have gone out. My throat was dry, my breathing shallow. They'd planned this, probably just been waiting for a night when I was stupid enough to be in my office after the sun went down.

I raised my mind voice and shrieked, *"Death!"*

"She can't help you." A blond who could have been a cover model for GQ leered at me.

"You'll like us. Once you're one of us." A woman with long russet hair smiled, displaying her fangs.

Yeah. That is so not going to happen. I can't teleport, though. The floor wasn't about to open up and swallow me. If I charged forward, blade swinging, I might behead a few, but not before one of them sank his fangs into my neck.

I've been in bad spots before, but not quite this difficult. Better to go down fighting than cowering, though. With a pivot in what I hoped was an unexpected direction, I drove the point of my saber through a Vampire chest. It wasn't a silver stake, but it should work the same way.

The Vampire shuddered and collapsed. Where its body had been was a pile of moldering bones. I didn't even have to bother freeing my blade. The circle around me backed up a foot or so.

My breath came in ragged pants. I swung about and skewered another one. This Vamp was younger. Blood spurted from it, blackish ichor that outdid any charnel pit for stink.

Motion from the corner of my eye was the only warning I

got. Swinging blind, I beheaded the Vamp trying to close on me from one side. Bones clattered as he hit the floor.

They could do this all night. I couldn't. I was already woozy from six months of barely sleeping. Where was Death? She'd always come before when I called her. I'm a Reaper, not a soldier. Reaping is usually peaceful.

I silenced my mind. Feeling sorry for myself—or expecting help to materialize—were dead ends. At least it was late enough, no mortals were likely to show up. I didn't want to be the cause of anyone joining the ranks of the Undead.

Time passed. I stabbed, swung, stabbed some more. My head hurt. My hands hurt. My eyes were giving me trouble, refusing to focus. I can build wards, but not against the dead. It would be counterproductive since I'm supposed to be a beacon for them.

A burst of furious Old Gaelic battered my ears. Great. A Celtic Vampire. Just peachy. Had this bunch summoned the Undead version of someone like Sir Lancelot? I narrowed my eyes, but my vision was a joke. Blurry and caught up in the half-light common to the dead, I couldn't see a thing.

"Move over, Ms. Carrick," a familiar voice ordered just before a man slinging magic burst through a portal. I blinked against the glare arcing from his fingers.

"Liam?"

"Who in the bloody fuck did you expect? Santa Claus?" Intent on beheading Vamps with Sidhe magic, he didn't so much as glance my way.

I admit, I was slow on the uptake, but once it sank in I might not end up turned tonight, I waded into the fray, swinging my saber with renewed energy. Maybe Liam did something, but my lethargy dropped away. Once I had enough oomph to drag all of me back to the land of the living, my vision returned to normal.

My mind was firing on all cylinders again, and I didn't care for its conclusions. Liam wanted something. He must have wanted it pretty damned bad to show up now. Surely, his Sidhe magic told him what he was walking into.

I was grateful, sure I was, but also suspicious as hell. Why did I have the feeling death by Vampire might be preferable to the favor Liam was about to call in?

Tough to refuse someone who'd just saved my bacon. Tough, but not impossible. I cautioned myself to wait. Once we were out of this, I'd keep as open a mind as possible. At least listen to him before I said no.

CHAPTER TWO, LIAM

Cait saw right through my ruse about hiring her to teach me flying. I'd layered my gambit with enough compulsion magic to sink a ship. Apparently, Reapers are immune to Sidhe enchantments. Would have been nice if someone had mentioned that before sending me off on this fool's errand.

Find the Vampire Reaper.

Should have been easy enough.

My instructions had been most specific, but I'd wasted a whole lot of time locating a male who'd smugly informed me he was out from under rounding up Vampires. He'd been quick to point me in Ms. Carrick's direction, though. Didn't even ask who I was or what I wanted.

I could have been the devil incarnate for all he knew. I'd had no idea Death ran such a sloppy ship.

I'm Daoine Sidhe. We are many things, but sloppy isn't one of them. Our well-defined hierarchy has been honed to perfection over the millennia of our existence. I take my orders from the same man I've always reported to. Once he was a king among men—until he tired of their petty maneuverings and games.

Most of us thought he was a fool to try to live in the mortal world to start with, but no one ever listens to decent advice. Regardless, Hollis Whitehall tasked me with locating Cait.

We have a Vampire problem in the Old Country. A big one. For each Undead we dispatch, ten more show up to take his place. They thrive on chaos and dissension. It's swelled their ranks beyond anything any of us ever imagined possible. I have no idea what Hollis thinks the Reaper can do about it, but he was most specific we needed Death's agent on our side in this one.

Back to Cait. I hadn't expected her to be so...striking. She's nearly as tall as I am, with black hair and emerald eyes. Her hair was tucked behind her head, but it's thick and curly with dark red highlights. I tried not to examine her body; women don't like it when you ogle them. Camo-patterned pants hung low on slender hips. A stretchy red top covered shapely shoulders. Not overly curvy, her body projected capable strength. A take-charge attitude radiated from the top of her head to the tips of her scuffed boots.

Once she chopped holes in my ostensible reason for being in her office, I was getting around to a soft-sell-test-the-waters approach. Someone showed up before I got very far, though. Running into humans can be awkward. Not all of them are sensitive to magic, but the ones who are don't like me much. Other magic wielders—witches for example —do a far better job cloaking their skills.

Seemed like my best course of action was to leave, so I did. Since I had a spot of time to kill, I moseyed back toward *The Tailwind*. It's a typical American grease pit, but maybe I'd get more information about Cait. I've never spent any time around Reapers. I had no idea they'd be so independent.

Not that mortals would recognize what she was. They'd have to be dead for her magic to sing to them, but presumably they'd worked with her.

I rolled my mental eyes and arranged a glamour to make me look more human and conceal the bits of power clinging to me. I'd been an arrogant idiot. I should have immersed myself in our library. We maintain an extensive warren of residences at the northerly tip of Donegal, right on the Irish Sea. Our dwellings are invisible to human eyes, and we've lived in the same location since before the Crusades. Our previous domicile was in northern Scotland, buried in the Highlands.

Not that Reapers don't ply their trade in the British Isles, but I've never had reason to parley with the dead and dying. Bottom line: I know next to nothing about Death's minions. I'd assumed I'd teleport across the Atlantic, locate the Reaper in question, and they'd do whatever I requested.

Didn't appear to be shaping up that way, but I can be charming. Maybe that was the approach to try next. Flattery and charm. For now, I'd lift a pint and catch up on local gossip. I set a marker to alert me when Cait was alone again. The moment she was, I'd be out of *The Tailwind* in a flash.

I'd no sooner shouldered the door open than a burley

bald man wearing grease-stained coveralls shouted a brisk hello, followed by, "Shot you down, did she?"

His assumption was disrespectful to me. Flattening him with magic for imagining the worst possible outcome would have been intensely satisfying, but I restrained myself. About fifteen people—all men—were scattered through the diner. Most of them had been here on my earlier trip through. I pasted a smile on my face.

"If you're referring to Ms. Carrick"—I kept my tone even—"she and I never got around to chatting. A friend of hers showed up."

"What exactly were you wanting?" Another man, this one tall and thin but wearing equally stained clothing, asked. Cropped reddish hair followed the bones of his skull. Whiskers, some red but mostly gray, dotted his cheeks and chin.

What was it with Americans? Were they allergic to washing machines? Or was wearing filthy clothes a new status symbol? "Flying lessons," I replied.

"I can teach you." He jumped out of his chair and loped to where I stood, hand extended.

I didn't shake it. His nails were rimmed with grease.

"Thanks for the offer, mate," I told him.

Oblivious to my dismissal, he plowed ahead. "I've got way more certificates than she does. Newer planes too."

Words weren't doing it, so I nodded his way and turned for the bar with its collection of stools bolted to the floor. To soften my rejection, I gestured at a tired-looking blonde behind the counter and said, "Two beers please, miss. One for me and the other for him." I jerked a thumb behind me.

She trotted to a cold case and pulled two amber bottles out. I scrabbled in my pockets for unfamiliar money. We traded, and she looked happier when I told her to keep the change. Surely five dollars wouldn't make much difference on either side of the fence.

I expected Mr. Flight Instructor with a Million Certificates to collect his beer. Instead he said, "Thanks, but I'm on call. Can't drink and fly."

I twisted until I had him in a line of sight and said, "Then you can't very well offer lessons."

He perked up. "Sure I can. They get priority. I'd rustle up another pilot to watch my air ambulance service."

I slid onto a barstool and twisted the cap on one of the beers, reading Budweiser on its label. Not a brand I'd heard of. My first taste told me I was damned lucky not to be familiar with it. Warmed-over piss wouldn't have tasted much worse. The beer was cold, but you get the idea.

I hunched my shoulders, hoping to simply let conversation flow over me. Didn't work. Both men, the burly one and his lean counterpart, grabbed the stools on either side of me.

"So why do you want Cait Carrick to teach you to fly?" the lean man asked.

I shrugged and muttered, "Heard she's good."

"Odd is what she is," the bigger man said.

I spared him a glance. "Odd, how?" I'd come in here to gather information. I might hear something that would help me lure her to my cause.

"She might be sick or something," he said. "These last

few months, she's been looking worse and worse. Like she stopped sleeping."

"We were thinking maybe cancer," the other man tossed in.

Something about his tone caught my attention. "You sound delighted."

He had the grace to turn bright red. "Uh, not exactly, but if she got too sick to fly, she'd have to sell her planes, and…"

I loosened my grip on the beer bottle before I shattered it. "Aye, and you'd be there like a bloody vulture, eh? Keen to pick up the pieces."

His expression hardened. "Look, buddy. Sounds like you're not from here. You've got all those fucking social programs that pay for everything. It's tough making a go of things in the States. Flying is a hard business."

I bit back my annoyance and a strong urge to plant my fist in the center of his face. Pretty soon he'd be telling me about his hungry children and impoverished grandmother. "Was she odd before she started looking haggard?" I fed the tiniest bit of magic into my question, hoping it would net me an answer.

"I've always appreciated Cait." The blonde waitress had obviously been eavesdropping. "I don't like it when you guys trash talk her." She turned her next words my way. "She's her own woman, Cait is. Independent. She loves to fly, and so she made it happen for herself."

No one said anything after that. Maybe the waitress and her words had shamed the criticism out of the men. Regardless, it was clear Cait didn't have many friends at this small airstrip south of Seattle. After half my beer, I couldn't choke any more down.

I'd just made my way past the swinging doors into full-blown dark when the magical sensor I'd keyed to Cait's energy pinged a note that told me she'd returned. Too risky to teleport in clear view of the diner, so I strode toward her hangar a quarter mile away. The distinctive feel of Vampire buffeted me, and I fought a sinking feeling.

I wasn't the only one on the hunt for her.

Shrouded by darkness, I slid between two hangars to conceal winking out of plain view and teleported the rest of the way. By the time I got there, Cait was surrounded by Vamps with more arriving by the minute. They're a bitch to kill. Takes a lot of magic, and even then some of them don't stay down. It's why Hollis sent me for the Reaper: to make double damned sure they passed through a one-way gate to the other side.

Back in the day, I was a warrior, but times have changed. A lot. Still, some skills never die. Excitement coursed through me as I jumped into the fray. Every time I polished off one of those unholy bastards, satisfaction filled me. It took Cait a moment to recover, but then she started swinging her blade again. Silver and iron aren't exactly my friends, either, but so long as she didn't chop through me, we'd be good.

I built a ward. A strong one. Should have done it straight away, but maybe I'm rustier than I thought. "There," I shouted at Cait. "No more can get in."

She didn't take her eyes off the two Vamps closing on her from both sides. I shot one straight through its undead heart with lethal magic. She beheaded the other. Her breath came fast; she had to be working far harder than me since my primary weapon is magic.

I can run my stores down, but it takes a long time.

An eerie sensation bore down on me. I ignored it. My ward was bombproof. Nothing could penetrate it. Yeah. One more thing to be wrong about. If I didn't watch it, this mission would take a humiliating chunk out of my confidence.

The space between Cait and me and the Vampires burst outward. A leggy woman dressed in skintight leather waltzed through. Silver hair swung around her, hanging to her knees. Ice chips clattered as they shot from her hands.

"Off with you." She made shooing motions with both hands. They had the opposite effect of what I anticipated. Moans and screams rose from the ten Vamps still in Cait's office. They were clearly fighting the call, but one after another they flowed into the newcomer's outstretched arms.

Death.

The woman who looked like a college ingenue must be Death. Her eyes were silver-gray, and she stood an inch or so taller than me, courtesy of high-heeled black leather boots.

"It's about fucking time," Cait shouted.

"Watch your language!" Death absorbed the last of the Vampires. "Finish the ones on the floor. Once that's done, I'll take care of the bones."

After aiming an eat-shit-and-die look at her boss, Cait made her way from one pile of bones to the next. As she touched each, I saw what was left of Vampire souls flow into her. I assumed they marched right out the other side and across the veil that separated the land of the living from the realm of the dead.

Straightening after she'd dispatched the last Vampire, Cait crossed her arms beneath her breasts. "I called you hours ago," she said to Death.

Death marched to where she stood and faced her. "Maybe an hour. You always did have a tendency to exaggerate."

"Oh I do, huh?" Cait tossed her shoulders back. "I can't do this anymore. Find another patsy."

"But dear, you've barely begun. Hold up for a moment." Death swung her arms wide. A burst of magic—heavy on fire and air—rolled through the room. When it cleared, the bones had vanished.

"I have to eat," Cait pointed out. "I can't work when I'm up every night. In truth, I can't do much of anything. I'm tired. And the Vamps are onto me." She turned her hands palms up. "I'm flat out of tricks. If you have ideas for how to get rid of them, I'm all ears, but they're out for blood. Mine. Unless you want a Reaper who's been turned, we need to do something different."

My respect for Cait expanded by leaps and bounds. I should have told Hollis to get another lackey when he proposed this project, but I'm too well trained. Too invested in being polite. Ha! I could learn something from the Reaper.

Death turned her attention on me. When she did, I noticed her eyes weren't exactly silver. They held a cavalcade of images. Maybe the life stories of the recently departed dead? I didn't know her well enough to ask.

"Humph. Sidhe, eh? What are you doing here with my Reaper?"

I extended a hand. "Liam Warwick. Nice to meet—"

"I don't give a crap what your name is. What are you doing here?"

My eyes widened. I was used to being treated with deference, or at least courtesy. Death and I played by different rulebooks. I'd also assumed Hollis had at least told Death what we planned. The Reapers were her purview. She had a say in how they were utilized.

As I've mentioned, charm has been one of my fallbacks. I laid it on as thickly as I dared. It's not easy being male these days. Women used to appreciate us. Not anymore. I bowed, a little, not a lot. No point being too obsequious.

"Hollis Whitehall sends his regards," I began.

Death screwed her face into a mask of annoyance. "I might vaguely remember him, but I do not need his regards." Breath hissed from her. "What I do need to know is what the Sidhe have cooked up that has to do with my Reaper. You being here can't be coincidental."

Unfamiliar magic speared me. It stung like a bitch. "Stop that," I blustered. "No need to be rude."

She tapped one booted foot on the wooden floor. "Yeah. There is. I have asked you the same question twice and have yet to receive a credible answer."

Cursing Hollis eleven ways from Faery, I said, "We have a Vampire problem at our ancestral residence, and—"

"I should have known," Cait interrupted me. "Fuck! Vampires. Vampires. Vampires. I am so bloody fucking done with Vampires, it's pathetic. I'm grateful to you for helping me today, but the last thing I want to do is jump feet-first into another fire."

Death was staring at me, an incredulous look stamped into her patrician features. She no longer resembled an ingenue. Maybe she'd dropped a glamour, or maybe she could alter her appearance at will. Regardless, where before she'd been attractive, now she was stately—and ancient.

And angry.

"Hollis sent you to remove one of my Reapers from her post. Really?" Death's tone was glacial.

"I, um, assumed he'd covered it with you." I was still trying for diplomacy.

"He assuredly did not." Done with me, Death turned her attention back to Cait. "How about if I give you a couple of weeks off."

Dark hair danced around Cait's shoulders as she shook her head. "No. It's either run my business or chase Vampires. Give them another target—or better yet, write them off. They made their choice when they drank from the Vamp who drained them." An eloquent shrug held a let-them-eat-cake air.

We appeared to have moved to a bargaining phase. I can barter with the best of them. "How about this?" I smiled brightly.

"How about if you hold your tongue?" Death retorted.

I ignored her. I'm immortal. Not much she can do to me. "If you let us borrow Cait to deal with our Vampire problem, the Sidhe will commit to"—I thought fast. If I offered too much, the other Sidhe would excoriate me—"a few months of assistance dealing with the Vampire problem."

Hurrying on, I swept my arms wide. "I did a credible job assisting Cait this evening. Think what forty or fifty Sidhe could manage. Paired with Reapers, of course. To ensure the Undead actually cross the veil."

I avoided wincing and waited. My compatriots would not be pleased, even after I was done explaining it was the only way to get our own Reaper on loan. Damn Hollis, anyway. He should have known better than to try to make this a stealth operation.

Cait repositioned herself so she faced both of us. "I am definitely not a bargaining chip." Even chillier that Death's, her voice could have frozen Hell's surface.

Death zeroed in on me with her eerie eyes. "Five years," she said in a flat tone. "At least twenty-five Sidhe working for me for the next five years." After a brief pause, she added, "Take it or leave it."

"What is wrong with you?" Cait shrieked. "You can't make deals for me."

"Of course I can," Death corrected her. "You've let modern life go to your head, sweetie. Pretend it's the Middle Ages, or the Dark Ages. You work for me. It means I assign tasks and you fulfill them."

"Hah! The last Reaper didn't do shit about Vampires."

"You'll notice he was reassigned," Death countered.

"Lucky him. He tossed the dice and won."

Death closed on Cait. When she was about a foot away, she said, "He's what took me so long to get here. I fed him to the Vampires he refused to deal with. He's in the same section of Hell where they are." She dusted her long-fingered hands together. "Now, about the Sidhe's proposal..."

"You're just saying that," Cait muttered.

Death turned to me. "Test my words, Sidhe. All of you faery-folk have truth-seeking ability."

"Already did," I said. "You spoke true."

Of course I'd tested her words. Assuming she was referring to the same Reaper who'd pointed me in Cait's direction, he'd been very much alive and present yesterday.

A riot of emotion passed over Cait's face. Disgust. Fury. Hopelessness. "I'd rather stay here than be forced into an agreement that smacks of feudalism."

"Stay here and herd Vampires across the veil?" Death obviously sought clarification.

Cait nodded dully. "I've figured it out this far. Maybe I'll come up with something else."

"Spend a month with the Sidhe," Death said, "and I will reassign you."

Cait narrowed her eyes. "A month as in thirty days? Earth days, not some other convention from a different world."

Death nodded. "Thirty Earth days."

"I'm not certain I can get my kin to agree to five years," I said, wanting to make certain Death understood this was far from a done deal.

She flapped a hand my way. "Go find out. Cait and I will wait. We have some catching up to do."

A groan burst from Cait. "Christ. All I want is to go home and go to bed."

"Aye, and I want a world where humans aren't a bigoted bunch of asses," Death said.

"Not all of them are," Cait murmured.

"It's a problem, though, and it's growing by the day..."

Seemed like as good an opportunity as I was going to get to leave. I built a hasty teleport spell and set the coordinates for Northern Ireland. Wouldn't take me long to journey there and return. Maybe Hollis would be humiliated enough by his lapses to bite on the bait.

I hoped so. The prospect of spending a month with Cait was enticing. She fascinated me, and then reality intruded, kicking me in the guts. She'd looked like a cornered animal. Death might sweeten the pie enough to get her to agree to assist the Sidhe, but she'd drag her feet the whole way.

And run like hell as soon as the agreed-upon period of what she perceived as servitude was over.

CHAPTER THREE, CAIT

My legs weren't feeling all that swift. Before I fell on my ass, I stumbled to my rolling desk chair and fell into it. Swinging it around, I stared at Death. She met my gaze with her usual implacable demeanor.

"You may as well ask," she said after a few minutes had ticked past.

I nodded. Even that small motion cost me, and I rubbed my forehead with a hand. "How many others of us have you, uh, done away with?"

"You're worried about Jake? The Reaper I sent to Hell?" Death knit her silver brows together.

"Not especially. I never liked him. But Vampires are the worst, and I suppose I feel his pain. I've never minded being a Reaper. Until now." I dropped my hand into my lap. There. I'd said it again. Told Death I wished I could be relieved of my duties too, but not in quite as dramatic a manner.

"He isn't dead," she said. "But I will leave him in Hell

long enough to light a fire under him—pun fully intended. Imagine what a terrible tangle everything would end up if none of you obeyed my directives." She strode across my office until she was close to me and grabbed the chair I have for my customers. Turning it, she folded her tall form until she sat across from me.

I wasn't sure what to say. I thought I knew Death as well as any of us did, but she'd just revealed a vindictive side. One where punishment for disobedience was swift and unpleasant.

"Vampires got your tongue?" She angled her head to one side and swept a hank of hair off my dirty floor. "Really, dear. Can't you afford cleaning help?"

I unclenched my jaws. "No. I can't. Airplanes are expensive. I spent more than I've earned these last three months. Why, you might ask? Because I'm too tired to do much more than drag my ass in here every morning. Advertising has fallen off the charts. So has a whole lot of other shit."

She shrugged. "Reaping is your primary job, child. Why would you expect otherwise?"

Hot words crowded against the back of my throat. That's the problem with ancient immortals. They live in a world that no longer exists. We'd never had quite this frank a conversation before, though, so I arranged my palms across my thighs and leaned forward.

"The world has changed. A lot. A couple of centuries ago, people's families were so grateful for my services, they left me food. Well, more like vegetables and fruit and chickens or part of a deer or a bear. I had to prepare it, but I never went hungry. I also never had to worry about a dwelling. Someone always provided a vacant cottage for me."

"Aye?" Death crooked two fingers my way.

"Aye." I echoed. "Everything went to hell in the later part of the 1800s. People stopped believing in magic. The food offerings went away. So did a place to live. Where people had sought me out to ease their dying kin across the veil, now they no longer trusted me. Death happened in hospitals, not homes."

I squeezed my eyes shut for a moment, hoping to ease the ache behind them. My vision swam in a blurry haze as I opened them. Death hadn't said anything, so I kept talking. Maybe I'd get through to her.

"I limped along until after the first World War. After that, I couldn't do it anymore. I was starving and wet and cold. I had to find a job. And I've had a bunch of them since then." Swinging an arm outward, I added, "This is the first job I've actually liked, but if I can't put more time into *Carrick Sky Sports* I'm going to have to sell my planes."

"You could move back to the Old Country." Death folded her hands in her lap, clearly pleased she'd come up with a solution.

"It's worse there."

"But you can't know that. You've been here for the past hundred plus years."

A reluctant smile forced its way past my resolve to be angry. "I exchange information with people. Used to be on the phone. Now we text or use email." I hesitated for a moment before asking, "Don't you talk with any of us? I mean really talk beyond slinging assignments around?"

She shook a long-nailed index finger in my face. "Respect, child."

I blew out a tight breath. "Sorry."

"Better. I do not 'sling' assignments. A great deal of thought goes into which of you works which area. Let's talk about Vampires, shall we?"

A sinking feeling twisted my empty stomach into a sour knot. I knew that tone, or I thought I did. "We could," I mumbled. "But why would we want to?" I bent sideways, reached behind me, and opened my lower desk drawer. The one where I kept an assortment of energy bars. I grabbed the first one my fingers closed around. Didn't matter what it was. I needed fuel.

"Want one?" I waved a Luna Bar in Death's direction.

She crinkled her nose. I took it as a no and ripped the wrapper open.

"What do you know about Vampires?" Death sidestepped my barbed query about why we'd want to pollute the atmosphere by hauling the Undead into a conversation. Apparently, we were going to talk about them whether I wanted to or not. I lurched out of my chair and poured myself a cup of cold coffee.

Back in my seat, coffee and snack in hand, I said, "Not a whole lot. They figured out a way to remain on Earth after death by living on blood. Some legends suggest they eat food too. Sunlight is a killer for them. They swell their ranks by offering Vampirism to humans when they're vulnerable and 90 percent dead."

"What else?" Death pressed.

"Uh, they're all drop-dead stunning, with superhuman

strength and speed. They communicate telepathically, but I'm not sure what other magic they command."

"What does it feel like when they pass through you?" she persisted.

I tossed the empty Luna Bar wrapper in the trash and set my cup down. Damn. I'd inhaled the energy bar. Maybe I should grab another. Winding my hands together in my lap, I thought about Death's question. It made me uncomfortable, and I could always eat more later.

"They're different from newly dead humans," I said at last. "Mortals are still warm and pliant. Light shines through them, and their souls glow blue. Vampires leave a smoky taste in the back of my throat, and they kind of cling rather than passing straight across the barrier. Their souls are in tatters, and whether they'll actually leave or not always feels like a crapshoot."

I shook myself, chilled by the memory. The moment when I wasn't certain whether a Vamp would give up and let go was downright creepy. Would they get stuck within the web of my power if they refused to keep on going?

I never wanted to find out.

"I shall tell you where Vampires originated," Death said. "So you have a better understanding of them. They are monsters, to be sure, but they weren't always. It will take a while for Sidhe-boy to return. He and Hollis will go at it like a pack of wild dogs, but I'm confident I'll win this round. Meanwhile, listen and learn. 'Tisn't often I'm in a chatty mood."

My thoughts turned to Liam, although I'll be damned if I knew why. I had his number. Men like him were a carryover from earlier times, an era when they snapped their fingers and women flocked to do their bidding. He was Daoine Sidhe, so I could probably expand "women" to include "everyone."

At the top of the magical heap, the Daoine were Sidhe royalty. Their magic was unparalleled, and they took advantage of it to maintain their position. By comparison, Reapers sat near the bottom of every magical pyramid. We were one-trick ponies. Shepherds of the dead. Nothing more than that. I couldn't teleport or use telepathy—except to call Death—or even kindle a mage light.

And forget about casting spells.

Death had begun talking. I shut off my jumbled thoughts and focused on what she was saying.

"Only a Vampire can create another Vampire. Logic suggests the history of Vampires began with a single creature, who then created the others. But how did the first Vampire come to be?" Death quirked a silver brow.

It was a good question, but I had no light to shed on the topic, so I just looked expectantly at her, waiting for her to go on.

"Not surprisingly, the first Vampire started life as a human man. His name was Ambrogio. An Italian-born adventurer, he traveled to Delphi where a series of blessings and curses transformed him into history's first Vampire.

"Back in those days, humans mingled with the gods. Ambrogio was arrogant, and he failed to fall to his knees and bow before Apollo and his chariot. In a fit of rage, Apollo cursed Ambrogio so his skin would burn should sunlight ever touch it again.

"Needless to say, Ambrogio tested this a few times, and nearly died. His bad luck continued when he ended up gambling away his soul to Hades, god of the underworld, and a close friend of mine."

"Not so much bad luck," I muttered, "but horrible judgment."

"Aye," Death agreed. "That too. In any event, Ambrogio's next curse arrived via Apollo's sister, Artemis, goddess of the moon and hunting. He made a grab for her breasts—or perhaps it was her ass. Regardless, she cursed Ambrogio so his skin would burn if he touched silver."

"Gah. What an idiot." I rolled my eyes. "The stupidity of men never fails to amaze me."

"Makes two of us." Death came as close to smiling as I'd ever seen before she took up her tale again.

"Ambrogio's fortunes improved after that. Artemis may have felt guilty. She couldn't retract her curse, but she gifted Ambrogio with immortality. He would carry his curses—his skin burning from sunlight or silver—but he would live forever in his current form. Artemis also gave him the speed and strength to become a hunter whose skills were second only to her own."

"Ha!" I broke in. "Bet he did more than grope her."

"My guess as well," Death agreed, the same almost-smile in place.

"Where did blood come into things?" Fascinated by the tale, I slugged back what was left of my coffee and leaned forward a bit more.

"Ambrogio hunted swans and used their blood to pen love letters to various ladies, Artemis among them. This next is lore—and it may not be true—but he licked his fingers and got a huge jolt the moment blood touched his tongue. From then on, he hungered for blood, craved it. Human was best, but absent that, he fed from animals.

"Each feeding quieted the craving, but not for very long. All too soon, he ended up on the hunt once more. One day, he lost control of himself. He'd bedded a lissome wench. When she fell into a sated sleep, her neck was exposed. Ambrogio was overcome. He dug his fangs into her jugular vein and drank and drank."

I wrapped my arms around myself against the sudden cold that had turned my blood to sludge. "When did he develop fangs? First time you've mentioned them."

"Not sure," Death replied. "The lore isn't clear on that point. They just appear."

"Is there more to this tale?" I vacillated between a sick fascination and a need for her to be done. Vampires had a huge creep factor whether they were physically here or not. My office still stank of them.

"Aye, a bit more. The young woman woke. Instead of screaming, she begged Ambrogio to make her like him. I suppose he was flying blind, but he understood she hovered at the gateway to the underworld. His reasoning is easy to follow. If losing blood was her undoing, perhaps adding some might bring her back. He ripped open his wrist with a fang and held it to her mouth."

"The rest is history," I said, not bothering to modulate my sarcasm. Or my disgust.

"It is, indeed." Death nodded. "I know the last part is true because one of my Reapers witnessed it."

"If your motive in telling me this tale was to give me a soft spot for Vampires—" I began.

"It wasn't. But understanding your enemy is critical to determining how to win any battle. Vampires weren't much of a problem until the last fifty years or so. The unrest sweeping Earth has had...unexpected effects. It's strengthened their magic and led them on killing sprees.

"Before, they only fed to assuage their hunger and swell their ranks. Vampires are far from stupid. They understand most societies can only support so many of them, so they weren't in a rush to make more."

"New Vampires are a management problem, aren't they?" I eyed Death.

"Aye, that they are. It takes years, often many, before they learn to control their blood lust. Remember the problems Ambrogio ran into at the front end of his transformation?" Once I nodded, she continued. "All Vampires face the same problem, but it's worse for them now. Their line has become corrupt, diluted."

"Can we wipe them out. Forever?"

She screwed her face into a grimace. "We don't have much choice. If we leave even one, they'll just start the whole shit-show all over again."

I'd been watching her carefully. "What aren't you saying?"

She bobbed her head briskly. "Good girl. You've always had potential. Talent you insist on wasting with your ridiculous fixation on airplanes."

"It is not a ridiculous fixation." I bristled and sat straighter in my chair. Part of me knew she was baiting me, tossing me a different focal point so I wouldn't perseverate on my last question. I shook my head. "Not going to work. What did you leave out?"

She rose and paced in a tight circle before stopping a few feet away. "Earth contains many points of dynamic balance. For everything evil, something good counterbalances it. Over the years since Ambrogio got himself upside down with the god and goddess who cursed him, Vampiric wickedness has been balanced by human decency and integrity."

Death fell silent and skewered me with her bizarre eyes. People's deaths replayed over and over through the ever-changing collage of her irises, but it was unsettling to watch.

She didn't have to connect the dots. Understanding crashed over me. "Humans haven't exactly put their best foot forward lately," I said haltingly as I searched for a collection of words that might gloss over the truth.

Death nodded, encouraging me to go on.

"Some mortals are still all right"—I chewed my lower lip —"but the percentage is shrinking. If we kill off all the Vampires, it removes the balance. Right? There won't be anything to stop millions of mortals from fully embracing the worst of themselves. And others."

"Aye. I believe that's correct." Lines spiraled outward from the corners of Death's eyes. "Even knowing such might be true, we have no choice."

"If we killed off most of the Vamps, it would take time for them to replenish their ranks." I was clutching at straws, but it appeared we were in a lose-lose situation. Damned if we slaughtered the Vamps. Damned if we didn't.

"It would buy us time," Death said. "Probably far less than you're anticipating. They'd be furious at the reduction in their ranks."

"And hellbent on securing retribution," I muttered. It didn't take very long to make a Vampire. And they'd no longer be worried about controlling the newly formed ones. The implications were staggering.

"Christ. We're fucked," I said.

"When no good choices present themselves, we select the least onerous one."

I pushed to my feet. My legs felt stronger. I had no bloody idea why unless the coffee and Lara Bar had kicked in. "You sound like one of my college philosophy professors."

She shook her finger at me again, but without much conviction. "We exist to serve a purpose. If Earth runs up against a juncture where no more people require our services, we too shall fade."

Privately, I thought that might not be such a bad thing. What I said was, "Surely, we're not the only ones with skin in this game."

Death frowned. "What do you mean?"

"Liam is off trying to convince the Sidhe to help. What about the Fae? Or witches? Or shifters and Druids? Lot of magic-wielders out there." I wasn't all that concerned about a few million fewer humans. Earth might be a better place. I was invested in maintaining magic, though. We magical types were here first. Humans were nothing but an afterthought, but they'd never believed it.

"We shall see how this plays out." Death paused to take a breath. "The primary stumbling block will be convincing mortals they have to join forces with us. Believe in magic again."

"Never going to happen," I said flatly. "You probably don't watch the news or pick it up from the Internet, but the Humans Rule movement has been growing by leaps and bounds. Their whole bully pulpit is how much they hate and distrust anyone with a scrap of magic. I've been expecting them to start marching witches to the gallows again."

Death's eyes widened; she sat straighter in her chair. "You must be exaggerating."

I shook my head. "I'm not. Where are you when you're not with one of your Reapers?"

"With the dead. I told you Hades is a friend. So is Arawn."

I tiptoed through a potential minefield when I said, "If any of the other gods and goddesses are still around, you might want to gather forces and spend time on Earth. Nothing like seeing a thing firsthand."

Waiting for the explosion I was certain would follow, I stood my ground. In Death's world, she handed out orders, and we followed them. Turnabout wasn't part of the game.

She regarded me out of eyes so ancient they sent shivers down my back. Sadness swirled around her, turning the air a dull gray. She looked so bereft, I considered hugging her, but in all our long years of working together, we'd never touched.

Somehow, I intuited now wasn't the time to begin. She might not even be corporeal. The woman sitting across from me could be a cunningly crafted projection.

"It doesn't seem like Liam is going to come back anytime

soon," I said. "How about we go for a ride?" If I couldn't offer comfort, my airplanes were the next best thing. In my book, anyway.

Death turned her head and stared at me as if I'd lost my mind. "What kind of ride?"

I offered a sheepish smile. "Let me take you up in an airplane. Maybe you'll fall in love."

"Ha. I doubt it. Teleporting—"

I took a chance and interrupted. "I know you can move yourself from Point A to Point B without much effort. This is different. Humor me."

The Death I knew would have spat in my face and vanished. The goddess standing across from me did neither of those things. It told me my assessment about her feeling hopeless had been accurate.

"All right," she said. "At least this time if the contraption keeping those wings in the sky fails, I'll be right there to whisk you to safety."

"There is that." I started for the door, stopping by the board to grab the Piper Seneca's ignition set. Death would be my passenger. This was a time to go big or go home. Besides, it had been a while since I'd flown the twin-engine craft. Good to get its fluids warm and flowing.

The mild sexual analogy made the corners of my mouth twitch. Flying was a great substitute for my absolute and utter lack of male companionship. The planes were always ready when I was. I didn't have to coddle them, and they made me happy.

More than I could say about any man.

Death followed me out of the Quonset hut and around to

the hangar. Once we were inside, she kindled a mage light and strode to the Piper. "This one." She extended her arm.

I jangled the keys. "Yup. I thought you'd like her."

She followed me around the plane as I completed a perfunctory preflight. After her sixth question about what I was doing, I relaxed into my primary comfort zone: airplanes.

She'd just tossed an unimaginable weight into my lap with her disclosure about Vampires and mortals and balance points, but for now I shunted it to a distant place.

We were going flying. Everything else would still be waiting like a big fat spider squatting over a kill after we returned. Liam would be back by then—maybe.

"What if the Sidhe refuse?" I nosed the Piper out of the hangar, enjoying the purr of the twin engines. Death hadn't bothered to hook her shoulder harness, and I didn't nag about it. Wasn't as if she needed one.

"Think positive, dear." Death patted the instrument panel. "Tell me what each of these things are for."

I ran two fingers down identical banks of instrumentation and began a familiar lecture. Death might have been reluctant at first, but she was warming to sharing my enthusiasm for planes.

Maybe she needed a diversion too. She hadn't exactly answered my question about moving forward absent the Sidhe. "Here we go," I announced and opened the throttle.

My responsive darling shot down the runway, and we were airborne. From now until we landed, it would only be us and the Piper. Wind beneath our wings, and a glorious sunrise shaping up to the east.

Somehow, the night had gotten away from me. One more without a shred of sleep. I didn't feel all that bad. Maybe I was adapting to my nocturnal existence.

"My turn," Death announced and grabbed the yoke on her side.

I laughed and dropped my hands to my lap. "Grows on you, huh?"

She didn't answer, but the smile that had almost escaped back in the Quonset hut bloomed on her stark features.

CHAPTER FOUR, LIAM

"You're a stubborn bastard," I shouted in Hollis's face. He developed the insubstantial aspect that told me he was about to teleport away. I put a damned quick stop to that with magic of my own. "Not so fast you lily-livered coward. I can't believe you didn't bother to tell Death you planned to abduct one of her Reapers."

"Deucedly inconvenient she showed up." Hollis said in a voice totally devoid of inflection. How the hell he managed it was anyone's guess. Every line of his body radiated fury. He wanted to leave but couldn't break past the circle I'd hastily scribed around him.

"Even if she hadn't dropped in on the Vampire fight"—I kept on keeping on before Hollis dismantled my spell —"Cait would no more have come with me than she'd have signed up for Purgatory."

"For Danu's sake, spare me." Hollis sounded annoyed

this time. "You're not without resources, Liam. You could have ensorcelled her."

I choked on incredulity. "Really? Just dragged her here by her hair and deposited her in Northern Ireland. How well do you think that would have gone? Were you also planning to hold her in chains? She'd have called Death, who would have showed up and been furious with us."

"I thought Reapers didn't have magic beyond the obvious."

"They don't," I sputtered, "but she can communicate with her mistress."

"And you know this how?" Looking every inch the aristocrat he fancied himself, Hollis arched a black brow. He'd never moved past dressing in nineteenth century garb. Tan riding pants encased his hips, their bottoms brushing boots so shiny you could almost see your reflection. A creamy linen shirt with flared sleeves was topped by a brown tweed smoking jacket. His skin was paler than usual and provided stark contrast to his impeccably barbered black hair and dark blue eyes. Clean-shaven as was his wont, his cheeks bore faint marks from his morning razor.

Most of us employed magic for our various grooming needs, but not Hollis. I'd always suspected he valued long moments staring at his perfect face in the mirror.

"Liam?" Hollis flapped a hand my way.

"I know they have ways of talking because Cait's first words to Death were that she'd called for help hours ago."

"I see." Hollis thinned his mouth into a line.

I narrowed my eyes. Guess I wasn't the only one who

hadn't bothered to read up on Reapers. "Regardless, we can have the Reaper for a month—"

"In exchange for twenty-five of us killing Vampires for five years." Hollis sent a pointed look skittering my way. "I'm not deaf, nor is aught amiss with my memory. That's the worst bargain I've heard in centuries. I'm disappointed you couldn't do better."

I swept a hand downward to dismantle my casting. I no longer gave a fiddler's damn if Hollis took himself straight to Hell. "None of this is my fault. It was your idea."

"I expected you'd do a spot of research before you—"

"Uh-uh. Your decision. Your responsibility." I cut my flow of words. I sounded like a spoiled youth blaming everyone around me for something that had turned into a travesty.

His sour expression deepened. "Death knows something."

"She probably knows a whole lot of things. Which one are you referring to? And then I'll be on my way."

"To where?" He ran a hand through his perfectly coiffed curls.

"Back to Ms. Carrick and her mistress. They're expecting a reply."

"Eh. They'll figure out soon enough it's a nay."

My hand doubled into a fist, but I caught myself before I punched him. "No. Just no. What we did before was rude. Let's not amplify our sins. Besides, no one says I can't offer my assistance, even absent that of my kinsmen." The peculiar rotten stench of the Undead wafted from somewhere. My nostrils flared, and I turned toward where it was coming from.

Hollis pinched the bridge of his nose before extending his arms. Power arced from his fingers. "The slimy, unprincipled maggots appear to have returned."

"But it's daylight," I protested. "Around noon. Since when—?"

"Since now, apparently. I'm going to remove the illusion shielding us, and then we're going to kill whatever is out there."

"Um, mate. They're already dead."

"Semantics. This time, we're going to boot them so far past the veil the next thing they see is the back wall of Hell."

I'd already been in one Vampire battle. It hadn't been going all that well. Until Death showed up and exerted a magnetic pull they couldn't resist. I closed a hand around Hollis's upper arm.

"We need more of us."

"Gone soft, have you?"

My grip tightened enough, Hollis grunted with annoyance. He's always been a persistent fucker. "This isn't Merry Old England where you played at being a knight. If Vamps are out and about in daylight, we need more magic than the two of us command."

"I did not play at being a warrior."

"Aye, and nor have I gone soft." Tired of sparring, I raised my mind voice and summoned whomever was close enough to hear me. My skin prickled from Hollis's magic, and the astringent scent of Sidhe magic surrounded me.

I may have called in the cavalry, but Hollis had decided not to wait. The perpetual mist swirling around our domicile drew back, leaving us exposed. A bevy of shouts mingled with horrified screams. I figured our sudden appearance had shocked whatever mortals were wandering the streets of Malin, a rustic village at the northern end of Inishowen peninsula. With its cobblestone streets and buildings left from an earlier era, it was normally a bastion of charm.

Turned out my assumption we'd surprised Malin's human inhabitants was far more benign than the reality.

My eyesight is different surrounded by Sidhe enchantment. It takes time for the harsher wavelengths common to the mortal world to sort themselves into a pattern that makes sense. Once that happened, I wished it hadn't. Bodies lay at unnatural angles. White as the ghosts they'd become, they'd clearly been drained of blood.

Off to one side, a youngish man was slurping greedily from a Vamp's wrist. Fury rolled through me, displacing horror. At least twenty mortals were dead. The wail of sirens alarmed me. Unless the constables had silver-laced bullets, they'd be the next victims. If other humans had been milling about Kilkenny Green, they'd had the good sense to run like hell.

A brisk swoosh told me my call-to-arms had been answered. An even dozen Sidhe swarmed through the mist and came to an abrupt halt. Before anyone complained about being summoned, I pushed power through my outstretched fingers and flattened the Vamp trying to transform the human he'd like as not drained. That was how it worked: drain the victim and then offer blood to turn them.

Except Vampires hadn't been especially interested in augmenting their ranks for a very long time. Something had changed, and I'd bet my shorts Death knew about it. After all, the dead were her purview.

As I'd hoped, the other Sidhe picked up on my example. Magic arced every which way. Vamps fell by the wayside, but most bounced right back to their feet. Them already being dead was quite the impediment. We needed Reapers to send them packing.

None of us possessed the type of magic that would pierce the veil surrounding the realms of the dead.

I admit I wasn't paying all that close attention, but when a heavy weight landed on me and drove me to the ground, I was shocked. Usually, my reflexes are far sharper than that.

I bucked and writhed and twisted, but the Vampire was stronger than he had a right to be. The stench of rotten meat decaying under a tropical sun filled my nostrils until I was certain I'd never get it out of my clothes. Something sharp nicked my neck.

It was the wakeup call I needed. A quick jolt of a different mix of magic teleported me out from under Fang-boy. I ended up standing next to where he crouched, flame-red hair spread around where I'd been lying. Switching magics isn't quick, but I propelled the process forward and sent the biggest blast of lethal magic I could rustle up right into the abomination's back.

I didn't stop there, either. I carved my power down his spine, opening him like a filleted fish. The stink made my eyes water and my stomach protest, but I kept my power flowing. Good thing I'd asked for help. Every one of us was fully engaged. I hadn't counted the Vamps, but they were pouring into the usually peaceful green from somewhere.

In broad daylight, but I already mentioned that. I've heard of Daywalkers, but they're supposed to be rarer than hen's teeth.

Once I got out of this, I'd scour the library for everything I could find about the Undead. Reapers too. We could use one, but our local Reaper was nowhere to be found. I couldn't recall his name. Might have been Malcom or Michael. M-something to be sure. I would have called him, but they didn't report to the Sidhe.

There were mortals here, though. Humans who required escort across the veil. Their souls glowed in soft shades of blue and teal, hovering above their ravaged bodies. Some were crying and moving through one another as they tried to hold onto who they'd been. And each other.

Normally, I don't pay much heed to humans and their affairs, but my heart went out to them. The days of the Sidhe holding ourselves apart had just ended. Even if my kin didn't agree, I'd be hornswoggled if I stood by and let evil mow through innocents. I'd already decided to provide whatever help I could to Cait Carrick. This wasn't any different.

The Vampire I'd all but drawn and quartered was trying to get up.

How? His body lay in pieces, but it was pulling together before my eyes. Even with Sidhe power dialed to the nth degree I couldn't heal myself that fast. Was it worth wasting more magic on him?

Probably not, but I did anyway. Principle of the thing and all.

Where was our Reaper? The dead were crying piteously. They were fortunate they hadn't been turned, but I was certain they wouldn't see it that way. I kept a stream of destructive magic flowing at my victim. This time, I broke his ribcage down the middle. He flopped back onto the ground, scrabbling at the dirt with cracked and broken nails.

Vampires were vermin. Their souls were riddled with rot. Whatever held them together only provided the appearance of a human body. The air thickened with the scents of Vampire decay and Sidhe magic. Our power varies, but mostly its smell reminds me of a forest after a strong rainstorm.

Hollis sidestepped to where I stood over the red-haired Vampire. "We are not winning."

I didn't bother to spare him a sidelong glance. "Really, mate? What tipped you off?"

"Your sarcasm isn't helping."

Screams, grunts, and curses rolled around us. I did look at Hollis then. He'd lost his *Gentleman's Quarterly* grandeur. His trousers and waistcoat sported long rips; dirt and blood streaked their surface—and his face.

"Ideas?" He gritted the word out. It had to have cost him. He hated to admit he needed help.

I nodded grimly. "Aye. One, but it won't be pleasant." I sorted out a thread of power and sent it on a mission. Two longswords clattered to the cobblestones between Hollis and me.

He took a step back. "But those are silver."

"And iron, crafted by our smiths from an earlier time."

"I recognize them well enough. No need for a history lecture." Hollis's tone was chilly, and he made no move to pick up a saber.

"Fine. Be a coward," I muttered and ground my teeth in anticipation of pain as I hefted one of the swords. The hilts had been bound in leather to soften the brunt of touching the silver and iron alloy, but my palms began to ache immediately. Soon they'd be a mass of blisters.

I had to move fast. And I did. Blade swinging, I beheaded Vamps as fast as I got to them. Motion from one side caught my eye. Unbelievingly, Hollis had snatched up the other blade.

Guess he couldn't stand the hit to his image. Cowardice isn't pretty no matter how you spruce it up with excuses. About twenty Vamps later, they oozed out of sight as quickly as they'd shown up. I dropped the blade, but the hilt was slick with my blood.

Most of the ones we'd killed were nothing but piles of bones. A few of the younger ones had left lumps of putrefying flesh. The other Sidhe were in the process of rounding all the remains into a central heap. They'd call magefire to obliterate the carnage. I aimed some of my dwindling magic supply at my abraded palms. Bone showed through in two places.

The ring of steel on stone told me Hollis's blade lay near mine on the ground. I walked to where he stood. "Thanks for the help."

"Don't mention it," he said stiffly. "Where in the fuck is our Reaper?"

It was a decent question, but one I lacked an answer to. Power barreled through the green, followed by the sucking vortex of a bonfire. At least the Vampire remains would vanish without a trace.

A soft song, notes trilling up and down the scale, brought my head around. The Reaper who worked this region strode between the Church and a crumbling castle. He's been the local Reaper for as long as I can remember, and he's always reminded me of the second coming of Christ with his flowing blond hair, chest-length beard, and bright blue eyes.

Today his long legs were encased in ragged jeans, and he wore an ancient fisherman's sweater. He glowed faintly, but what drew the dead was his scent. He smelled of heather and wildflowers. Something about it held the promise of better times to come. All the disembodied souls that had been milling about zeroed in on him.

He opened his arms, and they flowed into them and through the portal he provided between Earth and what came next. I exhaled sharply. At least the current problem was winding down.

"Better late than never," Hollis muttered. He turned his right hand palm up. It looked as bad as mine.

"I'm returning to where I left Ms. Carrick and Death," I told him.

He grunted something unintelligible, and I focused on him. "Having second thoughts about Death's offer?"

"Second thoughts, aye, but not about that."

He fell silent. Impatience made the pain in my hand throb worse. "Planning to tell me? Or is it a secret?"

The air around his hand began to glisten as he

summoned a healing spell. He pushed his shoulders straighter and stared me down. "You won't care much for this, what with your Sir Galahad proclivities, but I believe our time on Earth has drawn to a close."

My eyes widened. "You're going to gather our kin and make a run for where?"

He shrugged. "Does it even matter?"

I gripped his upper arm with my uninjured hand. "Aye, mate. It matters a great deal. We've coexisted with humankind for something like two thousand years. Over that time, we've dealt with many manifestations of evil."

I paused for emphasis. "And we've always won. What is it about Vampires that's turned you into a craven?"

He bristled, but didn't refute my statement. Instead, he said, "I prefer peace."

"Me too, but guess what? So do the humans. If we run off, who will stand between them and events like today's?"

Hollis ticked a list off on his fingers. "Witches. Druids. Fae. The odd shifter. It's not like we're the only ones with magic. Let someone else take a turn on the front lines."

I let go of him and dragged my fingers through my hair, moving it out of my face. "Magic wasn't the ticket today. Silver did the trick, and mortals are far better wielding it than we'll ever be. But they need someone to teach them."

"Doesn't have to be us."

"What in the name of the gods has happened to you?" I demanded and grasped his arm again. Power still flickered around his hand, fixing the burnt, broken places. When he didn't answer, I went on. "You sent me to find another

Reaper—the Vampire specialist one. Did you plan to just dump this entire problem in her lap?"

Color stained his fair cheeks, so I intuited the answer was yes.

"What were we going to be doing while Ms. Carrick hunted Vampires? Serving high tea?"

"Shut up," he sputtered and tried to wrench out of my grip.

I held fast and added magic for good measure. Although I've always discounted intuitions, considering them more of a female trait, something pushed me to delve into Hollis's mind. I wasn't gentle. If I had been, he'd have driven me out at the first touch of my power invading his private places.

Blinding insight boiled through me, followed by equally blinding rage. Heedless of my not-yet-healed hand, I doubled up my fist and pounded it into his nose. The crack of breaking bones was satisfying, but not nearly enough. Nothing would be sufficient punishment for what Hollis had done. I hit him again. And again. Breaking both cheekbones.

"Get him off me," Hollis squealed. The bite of his magic bored into me, but I ignored it.

"What in the fuck are you doing?" Krin yelled. Several Sidhe, male and female, joined him and dragged me off Hollis. Krin has always been a friend, and his dark eyes were both angry and troubled. His red-gold hair was cut short, and he was clean-shaven. Like me, he preferred Levis and nondescript shirts.

"Hollis sold the Reaper out," I shouted. "Sold her to the Vampires. It's why they all showed up here. To capture the Reaper—" I stopped to catch a decent breath.

"What in Danu's name are you talking about?" Krin was still yelling.

More truth dawned. Hollis hadn't told anyone about my assignment. And now I understood why.

"Hollis sent me to the States to bring a special Reaper here," I informed Krin and the others. "The one who deals with Vampires. Whoever he parlayed with assumed I'd be the good little errand boy I usually am and return here with the Reaper in tow."

"Why didn't you?" another Sidhe asked.

"Because Death put a crimp in things. Hollis hadn't bothered to clear his little plot with her, and she wasn't pleased. No one commandeers her Reapers. Not without her permission."

"Ye're insane." Hollis had switched to Gaelic.

"I am not." I wrenched myself free from the pile of Sidhe hanging onto me. "Look for yourselves. Dig deep, though. Hollis's secrets are far from the surface of his mind."

Sidhe faces took on dour casts. The ones still grappling to catch me left off. "Bind him," I told my fellows.

"Who did ye bargain with?" Krin bellowed into Hollis's ruined face, spittle flying into his wounds.

Aye. I hadn't gotten that far. I wanted to know too. I took a few steps back from the circle that had formed around Hollis. How long had he been a traitor to our people? What inducements had lured him? A lingering glance at Hollis told me he'd never answer any of us.

Not willingly.

I flexed the fingers of my injured hand. Punching Hollis

hadn't done me any good, but neither had it worsened my hurt places.

"Are you all right?" Dena strode to my side. One of our elders, healing power ran strong in her.

"Aye. Thank you for asking." I jerked my chin at Hollis and the other Sidhe. "Tell everyone I've gone back to the States. I left Death and the Reaper Hollis tried to trick waiting for a formal reply from the Sidhe."

"What was the question?" Dena arched a dark brow. Black hair fell to shoulder level in tight curls. Her dark skin and equally dark eyes conferred a mysterious appearance. She preferred robes. Today, they were a deep emerald, providing a stark contrast to her skin and hair.

I hunted for a condensed version. "Hollis sent me to collect the Reaper assigned to Vampires. Death agreed to loan her to us for one month in exchange for twenty-five of Sidhe working to eradicate Vampires for five years."

Dena's brow edged higher. "We stand against evil anyway. Seems like a decent enough trade to me. I say you return and accept it. I shall square things with the others."

"Hollis refused," I growled.

"Aye, and now we understand why." Dena smiled coolly. She curled her fingers around the wrist of my hurt hand. Soothing power flooded my palm. After I blinked a few times, the flesh had knitted back together.

"Thank you." I inclined my head.

"No need."

I readied a travel spell. "You do realize I'll have to tell Death the truth," I said to Dena.

"I wouldn't expect any less of you." She patted my arm. "May the goddess bless your journey, Liam."

"Whatever you do"—I leveled my gaze at her—"do not let Hollis shinny out of your clutches. Death may wish to question him."

"Now there's something I'd like to witness." Her smile developed vicious edges. It was the last thing I saw before my spell swept me away.

CHAPTER FIVE, CAIT

The Piper Seneca was long since returned to her cozy hangar. Death and I had retreated to the Quonset hut where I dragged sleeping bags out of a chest and arranged them on the floor. Death might not require sleep, but I did. It was obvious I wasn't going to return to my houseboat anytime soon. I had questions, lots of them, but I wasn't in any kind of shape to absorb information.

As soon as I hung the Seneca's keys back on the board, I made a pillow from my leather flight jacket and arranged my body over one of the sleeping bags. I considered taking off my boots, but given how yesterday had gone, I might have to move quickly.

I left them on and shut my eyes. Death crouched next to me and placed two fingers on my forehead. Before I could ask what she was up to, I fell into blackness.

When my eyes fluttered open, the muted light of afternoon shone through my single window. It faces west, so on days when the sun shows up, its fading rays illuminate my office. Kinda pretty if you ignore the dust bunnies winking from every corner.

Death sat in my chair, typing at my keyboard. I swallowed surprise she was conversant enough with electronics to use them, but keeping up with the modern world was a prerequisite for understanding it. I must have groaned as I rolled to a sit because Death left off whatever she was doing and spun the chair until she faced me.

"Feeling better?" She arched a gray brow. She'd braided her long hair out of the way while I was sleeping.

I nodded. "Lots." Everything came rushing back. "The Sidhe. He's not back yet, huh?"

"Nay, but we shall be seeing him soon. My Reaper from that area reported in."

I crossed my legs beneath me. "And?"

"I believe I'll let Liam tell us his version of that particular bit of reality." Before I could protest, she hurried on, "If you're hungry, we could order something."

My stomach growled at the thought of food; my mouth flooded with saliva. Had it been that long since I'd had more than an energy bar? Yes. Breakfast yesterday was only a distant memory.

"I thought so." She smiled, and I did a doubletake. Smiling and Death were not cozy bedfellows. "I took the liberty of ordering for us. Should be here soon. It's nearly time for the evening meal."

"Thank you." I unfolded my legs and stood. After a quick trip through my small bathroom where I washed my filthy hands and face, I felt ready to float a question or two. I had no expectations Death would answer me. I've been one of her Reapers forever, but we've never been friends.

Friends presumes some level of equality between people, and we've never had anything like that. She creates assignments. I accept them. Turning them down has never been an option. In truth, until she dumped Vamps in my lap, it never occurred to me to complain. About anything.

I accepted being a Reaper once I discovered the dead flocked to me. I was still a young child then, so it was an easier mouthful to swallow and digest. Children believe in magic, or the possibility of supernatural phenomena. It's only as they grow up that cultures drum it out of them.

Hell, the era I came from, everyone believed in magic.

I ran soap and water over my hands one more time. When I dried them on a paper towel, they didn't leave dirty tracks. Ready as I was likely to be, I let myself out of the john and walked to my desk. Meanwhile, food had arrived, and Death handed me a crinkly paper sack that smelled amazing. French fries and some kind of sandwich, maybe a burger.

I dragged the second chair over and sat.

"Go ahead and eat," Death urged.

I eyed the second paper bag. "Aren't you hungry?"

"Not in the same way you are. I don't require food. If you finish yours and have had sufficient, then I'll eat mine. Otherwise, you can have it."

Gratitude tightened my throat. "I'm sure this will be fine. Go ahead and enjoy yours. I'd appreciate the company." Reaching into the sack, I stuffed a few French fries into my mouth and then unwrapped what turned out to be a chicken burger. It was incredibly yummy. Death and I ate in silence until the only thing left was wrappers.

I got up and pulled a Coke from my small refrigerator. "Want one?"

"Sure."

I tossed the can Death's way; she caught it on the fly. Dusk was ceding to night, and Liam still wasn't back.

"Do you have any idea when the Sidhe will return?" I wiped my mouth and fingers on a napkin before cracking the tab on my soda.

"Soon."

I took a slug of Coke. The caffeine-sugar mix headed straight for my bloodstream in a welcome rush. "Why'd you assign me Vampires?" I blurted. No reason to waltz around things. Either she'd tell me. Or not.

Death leveled her silver-gray eyes at me, the ever-shifting imagery as unsettling as ever. "Because you'd take it seriously."

I waited, hoping for more, and not getting anything. "Um, I get it that Jake was kind of a deadbeat, but how about the others?"

"What others?"

I frowned. Was Death being purposefully obtuse. "Hasn't there always been one of us assigned to Vampires?"

"Not always," she replied carefully.

If she'd been anyone except Death, I'd have crooked two fingers her way and told her to stop dancing around the point.

"You've been alive for quite a while," she said. "What do you remember?"

Back in my court, eh? I took another slurp from my Coke. When I set it down, I said, "I recall two Reapers before Jake who dealt with Vampires, but it wasn't an exclusive assignment."

She nodded and folded long-fingered hands in her lap. "Correct."

The implications were obvious. "Vampires have—?" Had what? Spread? Increased their numbers? Become more aggressive?

"All of the above," Death said, a rough note in her deep voice. "But we covered that ground when I offered up their history."

So we had. Clear enough she enjoyed full access to my thoughts. "How does that work, anyway?" I asked.

"Which thing?" She narrowed her eyes my way.

"Your connection with Reapers."

"At any given moment, I know where all of you are, what you're doing, and what you're thinking."

My eyes probably widened at the unexpected disclosure. I'd assumed she could zero in on each of us as she chose, but to process information from what was likely hundreds of us on a continual basis was impressive. No wonder my computer hadn't posed problems for her.

Her brain was like an information superhighway managing incoming bits of data without any RAM-limitations standing in her way.

"How many of us are there?" I stammered.

She shrugged. "Enough to do the job, but Jake did leave us one short."

I killed what was left of the soda and gathered up the

remains of our meal, carrying everything outside to the recycling bins. My lips curved in a wry smile. Nice that the airstrip had made a small ecological commitment. Nothing was worse than airplanes. They had a far bigger carbon impact than cars, and that was saying a lot.

As if to mock me, several big passenger jets swooshed over my head, probably on their way to or from the nearby international airport. Too bad the Humans Rule fuckers couldn't take on a project that actually meant something, instead of hassling those like me.

I was on my way back inside when the distinctive smell of Sidhe power smacked me head-on. Finally. Liam was back. Once we'd heard him out, I could get back to things and...

Yeah, right. The only things I'd be getting back to were Vampires. I raked my gaze over my Quonset hut with its *Carrick Sky Sports* sign. I had a feeling my aeronautics business wasn't long for this world. Death had been entirely forthcoming about Vampire history. What she hadn't said was one word about releasing me from my current assignment.

Nope. She was definitely grooming me. Hence the meal and standing by while I basically passed out, courtesy of a push from her magic. It was what she'd been doing when she touched my forehead: spelling me to sleep.

I gave it a couple more minutes and strolled inside, leaving the door propped open to encourage the cool night air to enter. It smelled sweet, a good counterpart to oil, grease, and electronics.

Liam was, indeed, back. He'd lost the polished aspect

from earlier. Hair fell around his shoulders. His face was streaked with grime and blood, but beyond that, his expression could have carved glass. Before he'd looked beautiful. The basic lines were still there. Of course they were, but this time his character overshadowed his physical traits. Something had happened, and it had shaken him deeply.

He was bowing before Death, a full, from-the-waist affair. "My sincere apologies," he said before he straightened. "While I figured out Hollis hadn't talked with you before I left here, our problems run deeper than that."

"Do tell." Death's tone was silk and vinegar.

I made my way around Liam and stood next to where Death still sat in my saggy office chair. He nodded tersely in my direction. "Thank all the gods you didn't come with me."

I cast him a pointed look from beneath lowered brows. "Even if Death hadn't shown up, I still wouldn't have accompanied you." I kept my tone even but wanted to make certain he wasn't under any illusions about his power to manipulate me. "I take my orders from Death, not the Sidhe."

"Thanks for the vote of confidence, sweetie." Death touched my leg briefly before getting to her feet. "Go on," she urged, aiming her words at Liam.

A muscle twitched along his jawline. "No simple way to say this. I am ashamed of my kinsman, but Hollis dealt with someone—perhaps Vampires or perhaps whoever is in charge of them. His goal was to trap Cait."

Liam's eyes—more green than copper—bored into me.

"If you'd come along with me, you'd have run dead into a Vampire attack. In broad daylight, no less."

"They shouldn't be functional in the daytime," I muttered and kicked my shoulders straighter. "Why are you so certain I'd have lost? You appear to have survived."

He had the grace to look away. Patches of color formed on his whiskered cheeks.

"Let me make certain I have this straight," Death spoke up. "Your kinsman, Hollis, instructed you to drop my Reaper into the midst of a Vampire attack."

Liam nodded. "Aye. Once we dispatched enough Vamps the others hightailed it out of there, something didn't feel right to me, so I dug into Hollis's mind. I was quick about it, or he'd have warded himself against me."

"Who hired him?" Death inserted spaces between the words.

"I don't know. The rest of the Sidhe are grilling him, but at the point I left, it wasn't looking promising." Liam's face twisted with what might have been embarrassment, foreign territory for most Sidhe.

"The other part of my message," Liam plowed on, "is we will accept your deal. We will provide Sidhe for five years in exchange for Cait's assistance."

Death clasped her hands behind her and paced in a rough ellipse. When she came to a halt, she stood nose-to-nose with Liam. "You told me the truth, something I already knew from Maxwell."

"Who's he?" Liam asked, followed by, "Never mind. Must be the Reaper who showed up collecting souls from the fallen mortals."

My ears perked up. We Reapers all knew one another. Not well, of course. But we do recognize one another's names. Maxwell was a bit on the stuffy side. I'd always chalked it up to him never leaving the Old Country.

"You didn't mention that part." I aimed my words at Liam.

He nodded slowly. "You're correct. I left it out in the interest of expediency. Vampires mowed through at least twenty humans before we stopped them."

"How'd you intervene ?" I asked.

"How else? We beheaded them with magical blades imbued with silver and iron."

Death frowned. "Maxwell didn't reveal that part. How it is you're not injured."

"I was," Liam told her. "Sidhe magic is useful for more than deception." He fisted a hand and punched the air, clearly still bitter.

"Given what's happened," Death said, "my offer is no longer viable."

"I understand," Liam replied. "I wouldn't want to work with us, either. Who knows if others have been corrupted, and—"

"Silence," Death thundered in her outdoor voice. One that made my ears hurt. "We are going to the Sidhe stronghold. I would talk with Hollis."

I glanced from her to Liam and back again. "Fine for you," I muttered. "I don't teleport."

"No, but I can bring you with me," Death said.

I looked around at my rather barren office. If I left, when would I return? Would I return at all was a better question, and it made me uncomfortable. I'd carved out a life for myself. None of us Reaped fulltime. It was a side occupation. If I stopped paying hangar rent, what would happen to my airplanes? How about my houseboat? I owned it, but the slip was a monthly rental as well.

Death turned and dropped a hand on my shoulder. My head snapped up, and she snared me with her strange eyes. "You can say no."

"If I do?"

She shrugged. "Nothing changes. You cozy up with your airplanes and keep on Reaping. I enjoyed my ride in your aircraft enough, I might stop nagging you to give up flying."

"Vampires?" I sought clarification, hoping to hell she'd dump them on someone else.

"They'd still be your responsibility. I said nothing changes. Usually, you're quicker on the uptake than that."

I cringed under her censure. No shit, nothing had changed. We may have shared a meal. She might have watched over me while I slept, but I still reported to her. I felt the full force of her attention. And Liam's.

"Can't take the pressure. I'm going for a walk. Be back in ten with an answer." Before either of them could toss arguments or inducements on the table, I snatched up my leather jacket and strode out the door.

Good thing I'd left my boots on. It saved me from an awkward few minutes pulling them on and lacing them up. Slipping my arms into my fur-lined flight jacket, I zipped it to the chin. It never gets terribly chilly in the Pacific Northwest, but my soul was freezing.

It would be so much simpler if I could leverage teleport

magic. That way, I could leave for a short time and return just as quickly. If I ended up in Ireland, my only option to return home would be a commercial flight. Or Death or Liam taking pity on me.

I wasn't at all certain about him. Death and I were linked. He and I weren't, so whether his magic would extend to ferrying me via journey spells was a big unknown.

Fuck. My entire life was feeling like a big unknown.

Breath steamed through my teeth, and I'd balled my hands into fists so hard my nails chopped into my palms. I forced myself to unfurl them and got a handle on my breathing. My heart beat so hard, I was surprised it didn't make a leap out my mouth.

I felt like screaming, but I was being an idiot. And a weak, selfish, immature one at that. I'd done better controlling myself at fifteen than I was right this minute. No one owed me shit. Least of all Death. From her perspective, being one of her Reapers was a huge honor.

In the grand scheme of everything, my planes and my business weren't important. Years would pass. The planes would end up in a boneyard. I'd move on to another business, maybe one I liked better, but I doubted it. Regardless, I would continue, emphasis on the *I* part. The trappings I surrounded myself with were transitory.

My rapid pace had slowed.

Balanced against the specter of Vampires who'd found a way to walk in daylight, my anguish at maybe losing my pet airplanes paled to insignificance. The other problem I hadn't done more than pay lip service to was Humans Rule. They needed to be dismantled before they did more damage than they'd already done to those with magic.

Those like me.

Didn't matter if they were under the unfortunate illusion supernatural phenomena were a threat. We could make it a far bigger threat if they didn't back down. A bitter taste coated my tongue. A few more incidents like today's slaughter in Ireland, and Humans Rule would become far more aggressive. I remembered mobs from earlier times. Innocents always bore the brunt of their mass hysteria.

Hard to argue with Humans Rule's reasoning, though. Some supernaturals were a bona fide threat to them. It was why they needed the rest of us to step in…

A wisp of rot made my nostrils flare. When I looked up, I'd just passed a bank of rubbish bins. Whew. They were supposed to smell like that. I had no idea how much time had passed, but I should turn around, head back to the Quonset hut. My dash into the night had helped, and I'd mostly made up my mind.

I'd go to the Sidhe stronghold with Death. And Liam. Maybe Irish Vampires weren't aware of the tricks I'd come up with to lure them over the veil. Even if they were, Death was still stronger than they were. I'd deal with the fallout to *Carrick Sky Sports* after I returned.

If I had to start over, well I've done that more times than I can count. Once more won't make any difference. The rotten smell grew stronger. Not the dumpsters, after all. I recognized grave stench and dialed in my psychic view, the ability that allows me to view shades. The blue-black of night faded to crumbled gray as the boundary between Earth and the realm of the dead came into view.

Not sure why I expected to see a bevy of rebel ghosts, ones who'd refused to leave. What kind of Pollyanna world do I live in? Ghosts are a nuisance, but when wind howled around me, I understood I'd been snared.

And not by ghosts.

Infuriated by their earlier rout, Vampires crawled out of hidey-holes until they surrounded me, fangs gleaming in the half-light of the nether world. "Shoo." I made flapping motions. "It's night. Go feed from something."

"Did Death fire you?" a blond Vamp, who looked as if he'd been about ten when he died, jeered.

"In a manner of speaking." I held my breath. Would they believe me? The only interest they had in me was because I was assigned to push them beyond Earth's barrier.

And make certain they never returned.

My guts twisted with apprehension. Where had this batch come from? I was obviously their target. My precipitous dash into the night hadn't been one of my brightest ideas. I opened my channel to Death but then slammed it shut. I'd be damned if I yelped for assistance at the first sign of trouble.

"What do you want?" I folded my arms under my breasts and enhanced the lumens on my Reaper magic. My entourage developed a sickly green glow.

"You. Who else?" A Marilyn Monroe-clone replied.

"Why?" Maybe I'd learn something. At the least, I'd buy time to maybe find a way out of my predicament.

"Join us," a man with smooth dark hair exhorted. If he

hadn't smelled so bad, he might have had a chance of capturing my attention. Vamps left pretty behind long ago. They're all gorgeous. It's how they lure their victims. Not sure why humans aren't repelled by their stench.

"Afraid my dance card is full," I quipped.

He glided toward me and gripped my arm. I twisted away. He wasn't very strong. Was this batch some of the ones I'd chased toward Hell? Unfortunately, the direction I feinted tossed me squarely into two others. I fell through their insubstantial bodies.

It gave me all the information I needed. These Vamps had passed into some weird limbo. No longer corporeal, they hadn't yet been shepherded to Hell. This had to be some kind of forward guard, deployed to keep me busy. I wasn't about to wait for the main event to show up.

"It's been great." I offered a mock salute and sprinted through the mass of Vampire shades. Places my body brushed against them made me feel unclean, as if I'd touched something revolting.

Light from the Quonset hut split the night. Damn it anyway. It was farther away than I'd expected. I must have walked for way more than the few minutes I planned to be out here.

No longer battling false pride, I yelled for Death and Liam.

They shot out of the door like gazelles. One minute they were framed in the doorway, the next they flanked me, and I quit running. The ghost Vamps had tried to cull me from the herd. They'd failed.

"I'll come with you," I gasped around lungs laboring to

get enough air to breathe and talk. As an afterthought, I jettisoned my psychic view, and the world jolted back to the way night is supposed to look.

Death didn't question me. Neither did Liam. Good thing. What would I have said? Vampires are out to get me, and I don't want you to leave me here alone? It was the truth, but it shamed me. I'd been alone for hundreds of years. And I'd be alone again.

But not while I was a walking, open-invitation for Vampires to capture and turn me.

"Do you have to lock anything up?" Liam was asking.

I nodded and jogged ahead, all business. No reason to linger. I gathered my shoulder bag and locked both hangar and office. After turning the window sign to "Closed," I altered my magic so Death's travel spell would include me. This wasn't my first time teleporting.

"Any chance I could learn to do this without your help?" I mumbled.

"Maybe. If you ask nicely."

"I just did."

"Mmph. Quiet. I have to pay attention, or we could end up at the North Pole," she told me.

Privately, I thought it wasn't such a bad locale. At least there weren't any Vampires there.

CHAPTER SIX, LIAM

*D*eath's insistence on accompanying me back to the Old Country had been a surprise. Since she'd clearly had advance warning of everything that came out of my mouth, I suppose she'd been testing me. Making certain I didn't whitewash the truth, so the Side didn't appear quite so tarnished.

How far had the rot spread?

Was Hollis the only traitor?

We'd had a few fallen Sidhe, emphasis on few. It was an unusual enough occurrence, I remembered most of them. As my journey spell wound down, I decided to make a trip to the dungeon level of the *Dreaming* at my earliest opportunity. It was where we imprisoned rogue Sidhe since there was no way to end them.

I didn't see how they could have escaped—unless they'd had help. Hollis's defection had shaken me to my roots. If stodgy, straight-arrow Hollis had a hidden dark side, all bets were off.

Before, the prospect of spending time with Cait had been enticing. It still was, but my priorities had shifted. I still battled creeping guilt that I'd nearly chucked her into the center of the attack I'd had to fight my way out of. She'd made a good point, though, when she questioned me.

Having observed her skills, I fully understood she had a better-than-even chance of holding her own in any Vampire battle. The edges of my spell developed an insubstantial appearance, and I warded myself. Smart of me. Malin's rustic buildings and cobblestone streets rose around me. Kilkenny Green swarmed with medical personnel and local gendarmes.

The skies were a deep gunmetal shade as they spit rain. Good. It would wash the bloodstains away. Most of them. A man in soaked navy-blue scrubs rose to his feet from where he'd been crouched next to a corpse. A stethoscope was draped around his neck, and his red hair was plastered to his skull.

He shook his head and trudged to a waiting ambulance. "They're all dead, lass. Transport them to the morgue."

"Sorry, Doc." The ambulance driver, a middle-aged woman with brown hair going gray, touched his shoulder. She lowered her voice, but we Sidhe have excellent hearing. "Is it what they say?" She made the sign of the cross.

The doctor angled his blue eyes at her. "Probably a wild animal. Don't go spreading rumors."

"Got it," she said tersely and ran to the back of her vehicle to drag its double doors open.

I looked around for Death and Cait, but either they weren't here yet, or they'd come out in a slightly different location. Perhaps Death had wanted to include Maxwell in Hollis's interrogation. I try not to second-guess deities, mostly because I'm usually wrong.

The squeal of tires on wet stones snapped my head around. All four doors of a black sedan swooshed open, and half a dozen men leapt out. All of them wore shirts blazoned with the Humans Rule logo of a man with raised arms standing on top of a mountain. The figure was red on a deep blue background, and the design striking in its simplicity.

The Sidhe had joked among ourselves not to look too closely at the mountain since it was probably comprised of every animal that had ever existed from amoeba on up. No jokes today, though. The men were furious, screaming about Vampires attacking humans.

They split up and ran to the gendarmes, shouting and demanding justice.

Justice for humans, that is. No one gave a crap about magic-wielders. Except us.

Death chose that moment to plop into the center of the green with both Maxwell and Cait by her side. Either she didn't think to conceal herself and the Reapers, or she didn't give a fuck.

I voted for the latter.

Frightened squawks rose from everyone who'd seen them burst from nothingness. Moments later, the Humans Rule gang transferred their attention to Death. Except they had no way of knowing who she was. I smelled their fear, but they didn't let it stop them.

Back to her college ingenue look—if ingenues wore battle leathers and had silver eyes—Death held up a hand. Power arced from her, and all six of the men stopped in their tracks. She may have relieved them of forward motion, but curses blatted from their throats. Mostly in Gaelic, they invoked all manner of spirits to save them.

Ironic, since Humans Rule was supposedly anti-magic. But then, superstition is hardwired into humans, whether they wish it or no.

"Do you want to lose your tongues as well?" Death inquired acidly. "Silence."

Everyone ranged around Kilkenny Green had stopped what they were doing. All eyes were on Death and her small contingent. I remained invisible; no reason to alter it. For one thing, the villagers would recognize me. Many of us often wandered beyond the illusion separating our domicile from Malin. I'd shared meals and brew with locals for hundreds of years.

The brew had improved, while the meals had not.

The only sounds were raindrops splattering down. Death nodded once, perhaps in approval. "I am Death," she said. "I rarely show myself to mortals. Know that I am as outraged as you about today's tragedy in your village. You must lay aside your fears and work with those who command magic. We will defeat darkness, but only if we join forces."

A mild shockwave rolled over me as my ward disintegrated. Guess Death had seen right through it, but I hadn't been trying to shield myself from her.

"Some of you will recognize Liam," she went on and

pointed right at me. "He and other Sidhe also live within this village. They are your allies, as are all with true magic."

"Vampires killed those people." A Humans Rule man located his vocal chords.

"Aye," another chimed in. "Magic is an abomination."

The group began to chant, "Humans Rule. Humans first. Humans Rule. Death to magic."

"Silence," Death thundered again. "If you would obliterate magic, you've signed your own death warrants."

I felt the weave of her magic extend to the men's mouths and grimaced. Her forcing their hand wouldn't help. Mortals presumed many things, including the supremacy of their free will. Death had temporarily suspended both their ability to move and their ability to speak. Unless she also wiped memories—or killed outright, which seemed unlikely —the Humans Rule crowd would leverage today's experience to whip their fellows into a frenzy.

No one was paying any attention to me. All eyes were on the men with their red-and-blue logoed shirts struggling against invisible bonds.

"I shall leave you to tend to your dead," Death said. "Their souls are with me."

I waited, but she was wise enough not to mention the sorting process that sent the wicked straight to Hell. The power sputtering around the men winked out. Death strode toward me with Cait and Maxwell.

"I don't see why you need me," Maxwell was saying. "Vampires are in Cait's court."

Death didn't bother to answer him. Instead, she hooked a

hand beneath my arm. "Take us to wherever your kinsman is."

I understood well enough. She was done here and ready to interrogate Hollis. I called magic to part the mists keeping the Sidhes' domain hidden from the rest of Malin, and then stepped aside while Death and her Reapers walked through. Additional power cloaked my actions. It probably wasn't necessary. The mortals milling about the green had their hands full between the dead and Death's impromptu visit.

The Humans Rule contingent hadn't even waited until we vanished from sight to start proselytizing. Bits and pieces of sentences drifted my way. "Abominations," and, "You heard her. She said we're as good as dead," were followed by, "Och, Liam ain't such a bad fellow."

I rolled my eyes, glad I hadn't alienated the villagers.

"Leave the portal open," Death commanded.

"Not a good idea," I murmured.

She turned to me. "They know you're here now," she said. "One of the reasons that ridiculous bunch of jackasses gained such a big toehold is because you've insisted on holding yourselves apart. Of remaining the purview of faery stories and weird television shows."

"She's right," Cait said. "People fear us because our existence is buried beneath layers of misconception. My closest friends know what I am. Kind of. Sort of. They don't ask too many questions, or any at all. They care about me, but they're careful not to dig too deep." She blew out a heavy breath. "I suppose they're afraid if they had all the nitty-gritty dirt, they'd have to change their minds about being my friends."

"Speaking of minds, I'm keeping mine open," Maxwell muttered. "Although 'tis a wee bit simpler if only the dead see me for what I am."

I glanced at the open gateway unsure whether I could close it if I wanted to. Revealing our location, a far older section of Malin than humans knew existed, was scarcely my decision. The other Sidhe had to agree. I tried for diplomacy. "You raise good points," I told Death and Cait. "I shall bring the issue up for our Council, and we'll put it to a vote."

Before Death could argue, I withdrew my power, surprised when the illusion snapped back into place without a hitch. A low growl told me Death was not pleased by my decision.

"You're as bad as they are," she sniped at me.

"Scarcely." I bristled.

"You don't like or trust them any more than they like or trust you," she retorted. "Until one of you concedes, I see little hope for either side. Where is your perfidious kinsman?"

Anger roared through me. She might be a goddess, but she didn't have a right to ram her imperious attitude down my throat. To avoid saying something I was certain I'd regret, I set off at a quick clip. It wasn't raining on our side of the veil, but then it rarely did. Our spells kept the UK's notoriously poor weather in check. My boot soles beat a tattoo on the uneven stones lining the streets.

No cars in the Sidhe side of Malin, although we did keep horses and carriages. Medieval-style structures rose on both sides of us. Many were a blend of illusion and reality. We didn't require much space, and quite a few of the original buildings were in a serious state of disrepair. Built of rough-hewn timber, fieldstones, and mortar, the ones still standing hadn't changed in the last 500 years.

If the Sidhe have a weakness, it's that we like nice things. Graceful possessions that please the eye. And the spirit. It was why watching Hollis squirm wasn't anything I was looking forward to. Or my promised visit to the dungeons in the *Dreaming*.

Necessary evils, but I'd be glad once they were behind me.

I led the way into the building where we held our Council meetings, and then up several flights of stairs. The smells characteristic of old buildings—damp and sugary—filled my nostrils. A broad hall ended at tall double doors. The flicker and flare of power told me they'd been sealed.

"Pfft." Death sliced a hand across the juncture where the latch was. The door popped open, and she strode through.

Someone shouted, "Halt."

Aye, like that was going to make a dent in Death's outrage.

"We may as well go inside." Cait prodded me, and I realized I was standing square in the doorway.

"Wonder if I could get away with leaving," Maxwell mumbled.

Cait swung her head to stare at him. "What do you think?" Her voice was a lot louder than his had been.

"Bad idea, eh, lass?"

"Death made a special stop to collect you, and—"

He shook his head. "Not leaving. Souls do pile up, though."

"Try working in a spot like mine," she retorted. "One where there are more than a few thousand residents."

"They're not your problem any longer," he observed.

"Wanna bet? The dead still find me. No one cares I've been reassigned." Turning on her heel, she marched into our meeting room and Council chamber. Back in the day, it had served as a courtroom, complete with a magistrate. Primitive cells were a few levels down.

Because the room was large with intact windows and a high ceiling, we'd turned it to our needs. Rows of wooden seats faced a central dais. Jury boxes sat on both sides. When I caught sight of Hollis, I stopped dead. Apparently, he'd tried to make a break for it.

The antique iron cage that had once held mortals considered too dangerous to corral with manacles had been dragged from its corner. I had no idea how my kin had shuffled Hollis into it, gotten the gate shut, and sealed it with magic, but someone had taken care of everything.

We employ a few human servants. Perhaps they'd been pressed into action.

Hollis huddled on the floor of the cage, arms wrapped around his knees. I might have felt sorry for him if I weren't so angry. Krin and Dena fired questions at him. All he did was stare back, a vacuous expression on his face.

"My turn." Death sounded almost cheerful.

"Who are—" Dena began before inclining her head. "Welcome, my lady. I wish the circumstances were more favorable."

"My desire as well." Death nodded Dena's way and

pushed between her and Krin. They backed up to offer her space to work.

She certainly hadn't requested my assistance, but that's never stopped me before. I positioned myself off to one side. "He's gone into trance," I said flatly.

"Cowardly piece of scum." Death skinned her lips back from her teeth. "Never did like him."

I started to offer pointers to drag his mind back from whatever he'd barricaded it behind when Death began to chant. Low. Sweet. Hypnotic. Hollis developed an insubstantial aspect, color sheeted around him, and an iridescent patch hovered in the vicinity of his chest.

He opened his dark eyes and stared at Death. "Fine," he growled. "Finish it."

Surprise thwacked me in the ribs as understanding bloomed. The iridescent place was his Sidhe soul. Death had neatly detached it from his magical center.

Laughter rolled from Death, harsh and unforgiving. "I don't think so," she said once she was done laughing. "You're the last one who deserves an easy death."

The rumble of conversations swept around the room. We were immortal. If there was a way to kill us, I hadn't heard of it. Presumably, neither had anyone else. If we had, the Sidhe traitors languishing in the Dreaming would be long gone.

"Who is behind the Vampire uprising and their newfound ability to operate in daylight?" Death kept power flowing until it circled Hollis and drove a visible wedge between him and his soul.

"What's in it for me?" Hollis tried for jaunty but came off as desperate and pathetic. He'd made the biggest mistake of his long life, but he wasn't a fool. He understood his fall from grace was absolute. No Side would willingly suffer his company after this.

Death shrugged. "You changed sides once."

"Aye, but they welcomed me." Breath steamed from between his teeth. "I loathe Vampires as much as the next Sidhe, but I believe in their, erm, worldview."

"What might that be?" I asked.

"The days when mortals and those like us could coexist are done. Back when mankind were steeped in superstition, our détente worked out well enough. Men have changed. They worship electronics, science. We're no longer valued."

"The Vampires don't seem to be going anywhere," Cait pointed out. "Damned convenient for them if they can be rid of the Sidhe and witches and all the other magic-wielders. Kind of leaves the field wide open for them to gorge themselves on mortals."

"Not my problem," Hollis said. His nostrils flared. "I don't expect any of you to believe me, but I acted in the Sidhes' interests. We need to relocate to a spot we can live in peace. A place where what happens on Earth is no longer of concern."

"I don't recall you bringing this up for all of us to discuss or vote on," Krin said coldly.

"I was getting around to it," Hollis replied. "As soon as the Reaper was out of the way, I'd have—"

"Watch what you say in my presence," Death snarled. "My Reapers are dear to me. Who did you bargain with?"

"I shall not say," he snarled back.

Death deepened the wedge between his soul and his body. "Last chance," she told him.

"If you kill him," I said, "we'll never find out."

"Listen to Liam," Hollis wheezed. Clearly, whatever Death was doing was causing him pain.

A burst of unfamiliar magic crashed into the room. It was unsettling enough I warded myself and the two Reapers.

"Thanks, mate." Maxwell tipped his chin my way.

Without turning her head, Death said, "Selene. I figured you'd show up sooner or later."

Perhaps naming her made her visible, but an aristocratic woman shimmered into view. Scraps of golden cloth barely covered the swell of breasts and ass. Her hair was deep blue with copper highlights, and her eyes glittered like chips of obsidian. A scepter graced one hand, glowing with colorful gems set along its length.

The first of the moon goddesses eyed Death. "You won't win." She raised her staff and Hollis's soul exploded, leaving a glistening trail in its wake. He slumped to the bottom of the cage.

"Who is she?" Cait hissed next to my ear.

"An ancient Greek goddess worshipped by Vampires. She's taken care of them since Ambrogio's time."

"Nice to visit," Selene purred.

"Not so fast," Death thundered. The steel behind her words made no difference at all.

With a flash of bouncing breasts, Selene vanished as precipitously as she'd arrived with Death right behind her.

"No need for me to cool my heels any longer," Maxwell mumbled. Turning, he hustled out the open door.

"Damn it," Cait cursed. "Now I'm stuck here."

I should have kept my thoughts to myself, but it wasn't happening. "Instead of feeling sorry for yourself," I told Cait, "find ways to help."

"I'm a Reaper, not a Sidhe warrior. Best way for me to 'help' is to find my own way home."

"Liam!" Krin yelled my way. "Get over here. We have decisions to make." I got it. My place was with my kinsmen. We had a war to plan—once we figured out who the enemy was. Selene's involvement was a clue, but not a very good one.

I glanced to where Cait had been standing, but she was nearly to the door walking with long, purposeful strides.

"Come back," I yelled after her. She kept right on going.

I didn't blame her. Eventually, I'd get around to apologizing, but right now I had other priorities. Like stemming the Vampire hordes before they whipped mortals into a worse state than they were already in. Nothing more efficient than runaway fear to light a fire under folks.

Selene had always been a minor goddess. She couldn't have masterminded the Vampire uprising. After a final look at Cait's retreating back, I trotted to Krin, Dena, and the others. Over the next few hours—or perhaps days—I was determined to come up with more answers than we had right now.

I'd give Cait a spot of time to cool down, and then I'd use magic to find her.

CHAPTER SEVEN, CAIT

Goddamn Liam to Hell and back a million times over. He had no fucking right to criticize me. I was stuck. In Ireland, and nowhere near someplace convenient like Dublin. Nope. I was in the bloody sticks in Northern Ireland. I'd have to change money to pounds and figure out when the busses ran.

Next time I'd follow my first instincts.

Forget this Polly-Do-Good routine. Death had dangled teleport power in my face, but when the rubber met the tarmac, she'd raced off after the hussy dressed in so little she'd have been chased off most public beaches.

Once I exited the building, I broke into a lope and kept going until I was past the illusion shielding the Sidhes' part of Malin. I'd no sooner broken through than souls converged on me. Three of them, two women and a man. Clearly victims from earlier, they had puncture marks over their neck veins.

"Help us," the man whispered.

"Aye, for the love of Mary, help us," one of the women echoed.

Where the hell was Maxwell? This was his turf, not mine. He'd been right ahead of me, but at the moment he wasn't anywhere to be seen. The dead had chosen me because I was the only game in town. Why hadn't they nabbed him when he walked this same route? My vision shifted to the half-light of the ghosts' world, and I opened my arms. Unlike most transitions, the first one nearly flattened me.

What the unholy hell?

Before I could slam my grave vision shut, another ghost barreled through me. Pain shot along my limbs. In all the years I've been Reaping, acting as a portal has never hurt me before.

"Hold up." I put as much force as I could behind my words. And withdrew the power that turned me into a gateway.

"But I'm still here." The last of the ghosts sounded confused.

I felt for her, but I wasn't willing to risk any more Reaping in this spot. My legs vibrated as if I'd stumbled across a high voltage wire. My hands weren't much better.

I turned to leave. The ghost tried to grab me, but her hand went right through my arm. Of course it did. I might be able to see ghosts, but they're no longer corporeal.

"Call Maxwell," I told her. "He's your Reaper."

"But he's not here," she insisted.

"He will be if you call for him," I said and hurried away.

The dead have very short attention spans. Once I was gone, she wouldn't remember talking with me. Hopefully.

Nothing else was unfolding like I wanted it to. No reason for this to, either. After an anxious few minutes, I determined she wasn't chasing me. Excellent, I'd take any win I could, no matter how small.

I didn't have any idea where I was going, but the village was small. Eventually, I had to find the train station. Or a bus depot. I clenched my jaw in a tight line. Getting home would set me back thousands. And a couple of days—if everything went well.

"Never should have come," I muttered. Maybe Liam had been right. I was feeling sorry for myself, but this was his turf, not mine. I flexed my hands. The odd sensation was abating. Had some bizarre manifestation of Vampire toxin remained in the ghosts?

I shivered and slipped a noose around my imagination. Next I'd be convinced the Vamps had planted those three ghosts specifically to trip me up. Out of nowhere, a headache pounded behind my eyes. I blinked, but my vision developed the grayed-out aspect from when I share the world the dead inhabit.

Aw crap.

Now was not the time for my body to do something weird. I was in a strange place. No one knew me. I had my cell phone in my bag, but it wouldn't work here since I hadn't had time to add an international calling plan. If I could find an Internet café, maybe I could finesse lining up airline tickets with the laptop that also lived in my shoulder bag...

A sputtery groan emerged from my throat. Who was I kidding? All that required time, and whatever I might have was slipping away fast. I was feeling worse with each passing moment, and it wasn't my imagination.

Or me indulging in self-pity.

Nope. Unfortunately, this was all too real.

I shook my head, but the Malin from a few minutes ago remained stubbornly absent. What I saw was the realm of the dead. Vague forms moved to and fro, but they ignored me. It argued they were still alive because the dead were drawn to me, no matter which world I was in.

Other Reapers have had issues returning from the non-living side of the veil, but it had never been a problem for me. Until now. I sank to a crouch and rubbed my temples, willing myself to remember the remedy. There was one. Death had covered it in Reaper school.

Christ on a bloody crutch, but that had been eons ago. No wonder my memory wasn't cooperating. The longer I hunkered next to a bench, the farther I sank into the half-light of the in-between spot. The place shades passed into once they'd walked through me. Presumably, other guides showed up and ferried them to their final resting place.

The time to act was passing quickly. I did recall that part. Death had been abundantly clear this wasn't a spot Reapers could remain without risking never finding a way back. Our minds would blur, and a desire to simply drift would supersede everything.

Fear coated my tongue with a metallic taste I identified as adrenaline. It lit a fire under me, and I gave up trying to remember long-ago lessons. I wasn't without resources, and

I'd use what I had, goddammit. With my breath coming in panting gasps, I built a ward.

Time was outstripping my puny efforts. Even though my hands shook, I was careful. Checking and double-checking each element, I delicately wove shielding. Once it was done, I draped it over myself and drew it tight. Somewhere along the way, I'd gotten my feet under me. Moments dribbled by, probably more than I thought because I was only an angstrom from a full-blown panic attack.

Those three ghosts had to have been one more salvo, attempt number forty-seven—or five hundred—on the Vampires' part, to rid themselves of me. What if I'd allowed the third one to pass through me? I didn't care for the answer. My reluctance to allow her passage was probably the only thing that had saved me from annihilation.

I told myself to keep breathing. At least the gray, crumbling world of the dead wasn't growing clearer. It might have faded slightly, but it could be my imagination. Hope is a funny thing. I've imagined instruments in various aircraft carrying far more optimistic messages than what was really there.

"Come on," I muttered and visualized my protective cloak propelling me forward. Out of this no-man's land and back to Earth. I may have cursed my fortune being in Ireland, but I'd have given my right hand to be back in Malin. The real one, not this travesty of what the hamlet had been hundreds of years ago.

"Visualize it and make it happen." I was still talking out loud. One of the first tenets of magic is to hold the result you want front and center. I started at ground level and built an image of the medieval church that anchored one end of the town square. Perhaps it retained some of the religious fervor of those who'd prayed there, but my primitive magic finally worked.

I wasn't proud. I'd take help from any quarter at all. Even one that wished everyone like me would burn in Hell. The place I'd been burst outward, leaving me panting and shaking on legs that threatened to give out at any moment. I staggered over to a bench.

No one could see me because my warding was absolute. Probably just as well. The townspeople hadn't had a very good day so far. Last thing they needed was for me to bound out of nowhere. I waited for a break in the knots of people before I dismantled my ward.

Light was fading from the day, and I wasn't in any better position than I'd been in when I bolted from the Sidhe stronghold.

"Are you all right, lass?" a male voice asked.

"Yeah. I'm okay."

The speaker came into view. Youngish and dressed in faded jeans and a brown woolen shirt topped by a vest, he tipped his chin my way and walked on.

Good. I wasn't in a conversational mood. Malin was small enough, I was surprised the teenager hadn't commented on me being American, but perhaps tourism had established a presence here.

Before any other Good Samaritans could take a crack at me, I stood and walked back the way I'd come. Time to eat humble pie and see if the Sidhe could put me up for the evening. Perhaps tomorrow one of them could drive me to someplace big enough to have an airport. Or jump me there with magic. I hadn't seen a single vehicle once I crossed the mists separating the Sidhe domain from the remainder of Malin.

Remembering the portal, I slowed my steps. Would it allow me through? Could I even locate it again without help? My heartrate, which had finally resumed its normal rhythm, lurched higher again. Sheesh. What was wrong with me? Normally, I was unflappable.

My near brush with being trapped in the nether world had shaken me worse than I suspected. I reached the place where I remembered Liam opening a gateway. A nondescript side street led to what appeared to be the oldest sector of the village.

I stared at the structures nearest me, and then at the cobblestones, seeking clues. Nothing popped out. I pinched the bridge of my nose between my thumb and forefinger. I'd reasoned my way out of my last predicament. Perhaps it boded well for figuring out how to get back into Sidheland.

Dusk had fallen. With it, the few people wandering the streets had vanished. Smart. I didn't blame them. Vampires walked at night.

Apparently, in the daytime too.

"Nothing's changed," I reminded myself, still mumbling out loud. "I'm still their favorite target."

I clutched my shoulder bag closer. Maybe I should hole up at an inn. I'd seen a few on my walkabout through the village. The more I thought about it, the better I liked the idea of getting myself off the streets before full dark.

Vampires couldn't come into buildings—unless they were invited.

I screwed my face into a frown. They supposedly couldn't operate in daylight, either. That had proven to be a myth. Was the threshold-crossing legend any more accurate? And then I remembered how they'd surged into my office.

A series of shivers racked me. I might not care for what my memory had dredged up, but neither could I pretend it wasn't real.

Feeling like an idiot, I cupped my hands around my mouth and shouted, "Liam."

No one was out and about to think I'd gone nuts, but I still labored under the illusion I should solve my own problems. And I would. If Liam didn't hear me—and there was no reason why he should—I'd backtrack to the nearest inn and rent a room.

Damn it, anyway. If *Carrick Sky Sports* hadn't been hovering on the brink of financial ruin before, my impromptu trip to Ireland would be its death knell.

Don't think about it, I told myself and called Liam's name twice more.

Maybe it was something with threes because he came striding along the side street I'd been staring down.

"Cait." He loped to my side. "I'm so sorry about earlier. Sometimes my mouth gets the better of me."

My lips formed a lopsided smile. "You have that problem too, eh? I was trying to find my way into your realm."

"It would never have happened. You lack our magic, and it provides the only key." He stopped long enough to take a measured breath. "Would you like to return to our domain?"

"Either that or a hotel," I said and glanced over a shoulder. "It's getting dark. The Vamps took another shot at me, using ghosts as bait."

Liam's handsome face darkened until he looked grim and foreboding. Hooking a hand beneath one of my elbows, he barked a few words in Gaelic. The portal I remembered from earlier flared into being, and we walked through its arches.

"What happened?" he asked as we moved along narrow, twisting streets.

I sketched out my run-in with the ghosts—and my unexpected journey through the wasteland I associated with the dead.

A low growl reflected both anger and concern as Liam listened to how I'd managed to escape. Before he could chastise me, I added, "Leaving here in a huff was stupid and highhanded. I won't make that mistake again."

"I'm relieved you recognize it." His words held a formal edge. "Come inside and have something to eat." He held a door open for me. This structure was across the road from where we'd been earlier.

I hesitated at the lintel. "I appreciate the offer. Would it be possible for someone to help me get to Dublin tomorrow?"

"Why there?"

"I need an airport. I have to get home somehow."

"Mmph. You'd be better off in London, but I can see you home."

My tired eyes widened. "You can include me in a journey spell?"

He nodded. "Probably. I have to check to make certain your magic won't sabotage mine, but there's no reason why it wouldn't be compatible." His stern expression softened. "How about if we worry about that tomorrow?"

I didn't have much left in me for worry or anything else, so I nodded and walked inside. In contrast to the building's rough exterior, the interior was cozy. One large room held a kitchen affair at one end including a rustic wooden table with four chairs. Either the Sidhe had figured how to funnel electricity into their hobbit-hole, or they ran appliances with magic because a refrigerator and stove sat on either side of a sink. Gleaming rows of copper pans hung from an overhead rack.

Liam bustled to the kitchen and stirred a large pot bubbling on the stove. I guess I was worse off than I thought. Once I connected the dots that dinner was nearly ready, I smelled something like a beef and whiskey stew. It made my mouth water. Usually, the scent of food would have tipped me off before the visual did.

As he worked on dinner, I took in the remainder of the room. A living area and study occupied the rest of it, complete with comfy sofas, an elaborate desk carved out of some lush, dark wood, and a computer setup. Clinched my impression about electricity being available, although the thought of the Sidhe having their own Wi-Fi network was amusing as hell.

I shook myself from head to toe and crossed the room, leaving my shoulder bag atop a chair. "Can I help?" I asked.

He glanced at me over one shoulder. "Sure. Grab whatever you want to drink from the cold box."

"What do you want?"

"Whatever you're having will be fine."

I opened the stainless steel door and surveyed a surprisingly robust selection of beer along with a normal complement of foodstuffs. Not familiar with Irish brands, I grabbed a couple of likely candidates and plopped them on the table. Next, I began opening cabinets, hunting for dinnerware to set the table.

"Next one over," he told me. "When you're done, you can slice up a wee bit of bread and then we'll be ready to eat."

I was grateful he wasn't overly chatty. I located an opener hanging on one wall and removed the caps from both brews. He brought a tureen of stew to the table and ladled some into both my bowl and his own. For the next little while, we ate in silence. I wanted to know what had happened after Selene killed Hollis, but it could wait until my belly was full.

As my blood sugar rose out of the basement to something approximating normal, I started to feel more balanced, like I wasn't hanging on by the thinnest of margins.

"Thank you. This was really excellent." I stopped there and set down my spoon. It was refreshing to find a man who knew his way around a kitchen, but it wasn't like Liam was my date.

"There's more stew." He gestured at the tureen.

"I'm good for now." I bit my lower lip, debating whether to give voice to the question burning brightest, but I had to know. "Um, can Vampires get in here?"

"Not that I know of, but they're not supposed to be able to walk in daytime, either."

"Any idea what it means that they can?" I took another slug of beer and emptied the bottle. Because I was pretty sure Liam wouldn't mind, I got up and grabbed two more, removing the caps when I passed the opener.

"Thanks." He picked up the fresh beer and drank from it. "To answer your question, none of us have any idea why the Vampires are stronger. We were hoping Death would show up with information from Selene."

I'd been banking on the same thing, but apparently she had yet to return. "She might not come back here," I cautioned him.

"Aye, I know that. You're probably onto something about those ghosts," he said in a thoughtful tone.

"What do you mean?"

"You mentioned that Maxwell was only a few steps in front of you. Granted, I'm far from an expert on you Reapers, but it seems to me most ghosts would gravitate toward the first Reaper to offer them passage."

"Either that, or he's in cahoots with the Vampires," I muttered.

"What would be in it for him?" Liam arched his fair brows.

"Yeah. Good point. Probably not much." I rolled my shoulders back. "Not feeling very trusting of anyone right about now. How'd the rest of your day go?"

Liam nodded and took another sip from his bottle. "I was waiting for you to ask. I'd have brought it up while we were eating, but you looked as if you needed a break—from everything."

"Did you know I'd return?"

He smiled. It turned his striking face to something profanely gorgeous. I felt like a dolt, but I couldn't look away. "Preordination isn't one of my skills," he murmured. "I hoped you'd find your way back here because I behaved badly, but I wouldn't have bet on it."

"Speaking the truth isn't behaving badly," I told him. "I was being a twit. The mob scene with the Vampires rattled me, and then that slutty goddess dropping in out of nowhere didn't help."

Liam laughed, rich and low. When he replied, he'd switched to Gaelic. "Och, lass, doonae judge her by today's standards. She ran about naked for millennia."

My turn to quirk a brow. "You know her?"

He nodded. "Her and most of the others in various pantheons." His tone turned serious, and he reverted to English. "Up until recently, Selene was a very minor goddess. Other moon goddesses—like Artemis and Arianrhod—supplanted her."

"Why are you thinking she's taken a step up in the world?"

"Let me start at the beginning. Shall we get these dishes out of the way and then move to more comfortable seating?"

"Works for me." I pushed to my feet and piled the dishes, carrying my stack to the sink.

Liam plopped a lid on the remains of the stew and placed the pot in the refrigerator. I'd started washing dishes when he moved to my side and murmured a few words in Gaelic. The bowls and silverware slithered from my grip. Food vanished from their surface, and they arranged themselves in a nearby drainer while I stood staring at them.

"Can you teach me how to do that?"

He chuckled. "Probably not. I could do everything with magic, but some pursuits—like cooking—please me, so I manage them the old-fashioned way. Care for a spot of port?"

I nodded. Between my full belly and a slight buzz from two beers, I truly felt like myself again. The world was still a shitstorm, but I'd latched onto my self-confidence. I walked to an easy chair that sat cattycorner to one of the couches. It would allow us to talk without worrying about the mechanics of actually sitting next to one another.

Liam was deucedly attractive.

He apologized, a small voice in my head reminded me.

Maybe so, but words were cheap. Better keep this relationship on the up and up. All business. I assumed his bedroom was upstairs, but I could sack out on one of these couches. It would work for a night.

He settled across from me and handed me a snifter of port. It smelled divine. Rich and oaky and full of the mysteries of a lush forest.

"I'll be as brief as I can," he said. "Both of us could use rest."

I started to ask if Sidhe actually slept, but decided not to. It was a personal question, and I'd just given myself a pep talk about keeping things between us all business.

"First thing I did once all of you left," he said, "was pay a visit to the *Dreaming...*"

CHAPTER EIGHT, LIAM

A Few Hours Earlier

Death hadn't shown any sign of returning. Presumably, Cait understood her mistress far better than I did. For all I knew, Death had connected with her Reaper and sent her home. As hours had passed, I'd been certain Cait was long gone—either via magic or on an airplane winging toward Seattle. I'd considered hunting for her, but I'd been busy until just before the frantic note in her voice snagged my attention.

I came on the run when I heard her calling from beyond the mists keeping the Sidhe domicile separate from Malin. Either she knew to call my name three times, or she'd stumbled onto the right thing to do. Regardless, I was relieved she was still nearby.

More than relieved, if I were honest.

When I got a look at her, it took all my considerable self-discipline not to sweep her into my arms and force her beyond the mist. Her expression was drawn, haggard. Lines cut into her forehead and around her eyes. The aftereffects of whatever had happened in the span of time since she'd left gave her beauty a haunting aspect.

No matter what she'd been through, she was proud—and independent. If I announced she was coming with me, it wouldn't go down well. Like as not, she'd decide the local hotel she'd mentioned was a better bet than me.

Rather than clucking over her, I started right off with the apology I'd vowed to offer up. It seemed to do the trick because she accepted my invitation to return to the Sidhe realm. Don't judge me. I meant every word of my "I'm sorries." If I'd been aiming to manipulate Cait, it had been when I'd accused her of being selfish.

Then I'd been convinced every soul with magic—from Brownies on up—owed that power to the Sidhe and our emerging campaign to beat the Vampires back to the shadows they'd come from. If Selene was backing their play, it meant she had help. Always one of the minor deities, she'd never have taken on a project like urging Vampires to grow their ranks absent help from at least one of the other gods.

Beyond Vampires, the bloody Humans Rule movement had developed legs. Even in Malin, the crowds at their rallies were growing larger. A few more massacres like the one earlier today, and Humans Rule could well become unstoppable. I knew something about mob mentality, and it wasn't pretty.

With Cait ensconced in my home, I kept mostly quiet as I finished the supper I'd begun before her arrival. We had a pleasant, if rather silent, meal, but by the end of it her color had returned and a bit of her pluck. Still, I didn't make assumptions.

I asked her if she wanted a recap of my day. I'd already heard about hers, and it infuriated me. I'd flirted with telling her she had to quit Reaping entirely until this whole thing blew over. But that would have been overstepping my purview by a huge amount.

Death needed to know what had occurred. Cait would make certain she was up to speed, but it needed to happen sooner rather than later. I had questions. Like how frequently she actually saw Death, but it was none of my affair. Cait was skittish. I had a feeling she'd bolt if I grilled her with questions verging on the personal. Regardless, I had plenty to share without lecturing her about how to do her job or what to tell her mistress.

"What happened in the *Dreaming*?" Cait set her snifter on a table and laced her fingers around a knee as she bent slightly toward me.

"Sorry. I was figuring out where to begin. What do you know about the *Dreaming*?"

She shrugged. "Probably the mortals' version. It's the land of the faeries."

I nodded. "Much like our realm here in Inishowen, the *Dreaming* is separated from Earth by a series of veils. Certain magics are required to pass through them, but they aren't warded in the same way as this place." I swung an arm to signify the whole of our settlement.

"Immortality has...drawbacks. When we tire of our endless lives, many of us retreat to the *Dreaming* and remain for varying lengths of time. Until we're ready to face returning to Earth."

"What's it like there?" Interest flared in the depths of her green eyes.

"Different for each of us. It's a magical land and it senses our needs—and fulfills them. In that way, it's both soothing and dangerous. I've always taken care not to overstay my welcome."

A furrow formed between her brows. "Why, exactly?"

"Because anywhere else can't come close. Imagine a land where your every desire is fulfilled the moment it occurs to you. It's..." I hesitated, hunting for a description that would fit. "Seductive, but it erodes your will to accomplish anything worthwhile. A few of my kin journeyed there and never left."

"I see. It does sound appealing in a *Stepford Wives* kind of way. Go on."

I sipped at my snifter, letting the port roll around on my tongue before I swallowed it. Such an excellent vintage, but I was stalling. "Next bit of Sidhe lore," I continued, "is about the Leanan-Sidhe."

Her frown deepened. "Never heard of them. Leanan means darling, doesn't it?"

"Aye, or loved one. I never figured out why they were named such, but labels don't matter." I pressed my lips into a tight line. Admitting what would come next was hard. Sidhe have an investment in perfection. I'm certain the same fixation extended to the Leanan-Sidhe, but they'd crossed many lines.

There wasn't any easy way to soften what I needed to tell her, so I blurted it out. "They're Vampires."

Cait slumped back against her chair. She couldn't have looked more thunderstruck if I'd told her a friend had died. "You're kidding, right?"

"Wish I was. We've always had our own Vamps. Luckily, there were never many of them. They prey on humans as love objects. If the human refuses—and well they should—the Sidhe is bound to them for a year. But if the human acquiesces, as most do, they become a slave to the Sidhe. The bond is marked by blood rituals and continues for one year, after which the mortal is free to leave."

"So they're not precisely turned in the same way as with the other type of Vampire."

"True enough, but they might as well be. Once a Sidhe shares blood with them, there's no escape. Mortals are never the same. Many sink into insanity after their time bonded to a Leanan."

"Can the mortal create more Vampires?"

"If you'd asked a month ago, I'd have answered a definite no. Now, I'm not so sure."

"Mmph. Interesting and creepy, like a grade B horror show."

"Long ago, we tired of the Leanan-Sidhe victimizing humans and put a stop to it. I believed all of them were incarcerated behind layers of impenetrable magic, deep in the *Dreaming*."

"Believed, as in past tense?" Her voice sounded hollow, thin.

"Aye. They've escaped." Breath whistled from between my teeth. "Perhaps holding them was a mistake, although at the time it didn't seem so. They'd taken to joining forces with other Vamps. Betwixt the two types, they were wreaking havoc and sowing fear. We couldn't do much about the garden-variety Vampires, but our Council decreed the Leanan-Sidhe would wait out their immortality in the *Dreaming*."

"How long ago?" Cait's voice still held a strangled quality.

"1400s."

"Wow. Why would they wait till now to make a run for it?"

I leaned forward and placed a hand on her knee. It was an intimate gesture, but she looked distraught, and I wanted to comfort her. She flinched beneath my touch, and I moved my hand.

"We have no idea when they escaped," I said, needing to make that point.

"What? No one ever checked on them?"

I shook my head. "Why would we? We assumed they couldn't run off. In our defense, I did look in on them the first few years, but once I was certain they'd accepted their fate, I quit going. For one thing, the *Dreaming* exerts its own pull. I told you about it."

"Yeah. Your kin who liked it so much they're still there. Too bad the Vampire ones weren't cut from the same cloth."

"Maybe they were." I spoke slowly. "Hard to say what happened. Once I made the discovery they were gone, I had time to think about things. Sidhe aren't the only magical beings who access the *Dreaming*. Anyone with the right combination of enchantment can enter."

"Doesn't matter," she said dully. "Gone is gone, but it explains a lot."

I crooked fingers her way to encourage her to keep talking.

"I'm guessing your Sidhe Vampires aren't allergic to daylight." At my nod, she went on. "Well, they found a way to share that ability with the others. Assuming that's true, they didn't escape all that long ago. The Vampire problem has only grown worse lately."

"I came to the same conclusion, if your definition of lately is the past fifty or so years. Takes time to build anything, good or bad."

She rested an elbow on the arm of her chair and propped her chin on an upraised hand. "Guess I'll be a whole lot more selective which of the dead I allow through. What do the rest of the Sidhe think? I'm assuming you talked with them."

"We are in agreement on one objective."

She eyed me from under lowered brows. "And that is?"

"We have to locate the Leanan-Sidhe and return them to the *Dreaming*."

"What's the point? If they got out once—"

"We would take greater precautions," I cut in, irritated she'd questioned the Council's decision.

"Sorry if I'm not impressed." She sat straighter in her chair and dropped both hands into her lap. "You have places like this to hide from everything. I have to live out there." She punched an index finger in front of her.

I started to tell her she was welcome to remain with the Sidhe, but it was the wrong thing to say. She wasn't looking for shelter. Feeling like I was tiptoeing through an obstacle field, I said, "I understand you'd like your home to be as safe as this one."

"Oh you do, eh? Look, buster, I don't need a therapist."

I'd threaded a soothing spell into my words, but it didn't touch her. Were Reapers immune to Sidhe enchantments? Might come in handy rounding up the rogue Leanans. It also might mean she was out of luck grabbing a ride on one of my journey spells.

"Maybe this is enough for tonight." I drained the dregs of my port. "I have sleeping accommodations upstairs."

"One of these couches works for me. If you have a blanket and could point me to the bathroom, I'll figure things out."

Something in her tone warned me against arguing, telling her she'd be more comfortable in a bed, but I had ulterior motives. I'd been fascinated by her from the moment I laid eyes on her. I wanted her in my bed. Who wouldn't? But she'd jerked away from my touch as if it disgusted her.

All I'd done was pat her knee. No reason to think putting my arms around her would meet with any better results.

"Certainly. The bathroom is just through there." I pointed at a door to the right of the kitchen. "By the time you're done, I'll have a blanket and pillows out for you. " I rose smoothly and carried my glass to the sink.

She stood too. "Thank you. Sorry. I know I sound surly, but I feel guilty taking even a few hours to sleep. There's so much to figure out, and my brain is too fuzzy to do much besides chase its tail. I wish Death would come back."

"Have you called her?"

Cait rolled her eyes. "I thought about it, but not yet. The Sidhe Vampires aren't dead. So she won't have much to contribute."

"She does need to know they're missing, though. And likely in cahoots with Vampires that are part of her responsibility." I left it there. Death was Cait's mistress, not mine. Decisions about whether to call her or not weren't mine, either.

"Yeah. I get that." Cait nodded and turned abruptly, heading for the bathroom.

"Feel free to shower," I called after her.

"What for?" She glanced over one shoulder. "I'd be getting back into the same stinky clothes."

"Don't take this wrong, but I can toss whatever you want washed in the machine. Or you can rinse garments out in the sink, and we can dry them with magic. There's a robe hanging on the inside of the door."

I'd said enough. I walked briskly up the first flight of stairs and reached into the cubby where I keep linens. Extracting a couple of soft blankets and a pillow, I instructed them to land on the couch and walked up two more flights to the second floor of my home. Much like the main floor, it was one large, open chamber. My bed sat under a generous skylight. Armoires and dressers held an assortment of clothing I've collected.

Unlike Hollis, I'd rid myself of everything that screamed "thrift shop specializing in costume-wear" long since. I spent quite a bit of time among mortals, and this way I didn't have to be forever switching out my garments.

I bent to unlace my trail runners. Once they were off, I

unzipped my denim trousers and pushed them down my legs. My leather vest came next, and then the blue-plaid shirt. Everything needed washing—except the vest. Leather and water didn't play well together, so I sent jots of magic at the bloodstains.

I yanked a silk robe off a hook and tied it around my waist. Usually, I wouldn't have bothered, but part of me—a rather substantial part—was hoping Cait would come upstairs.

I muffled a snort. Aye, right. And someday pigs might sprout wings and fly, but it wouldn't be today. Thoughts of Cait sent me to an alcove where I kept a collection of lore books and moldy scrolls. A better-stocked library lived across the street, but I might have enough in the way of source materials to read up on Reapers. If not, I'd teleport to the main library and find what I needed.

It took me a while, but I selected a few promising documents and retired to an old, comfortable leather chair not far from my bed. A mage-light bloomed next to me, illuminating my reading material. Cait's presence altered the feel of my house, but I didn't let myself dwell on it.

On her heather and wildflower and cinnamon scent, or the subtle weave of power that shimmered around her.

A soft laugh pushed its way out. Who was I kidding? I'd had to closet myself one story up to avoid the overwhelming desire to touch her, to run my fingers through the silk of her dark hair. Already halfway hard, my cock finished its transformation and jutted from my lap.

Ready and willing, its presence was a silent rebuke. I couldn't recall the last occasion when I'd bedded a woman.

Like many pursuits, mindless sex had lost its appeal a very long time ago. But I was wasting time. Educating myself about Reapers was far more critical than my nonexistent sex life.

I muffled my arousal with magic and opened one of the books from the stack at my feet. Some of what I discovered surprised me. Reapers were one of the first magic-wielders, and Death a primary deity. Although she went by different names, every culture had a god—or goddess—assigned to the dead.

Unlike the moon goddesses, for example, where more than one existed, Death had no competition. In Earth's early days, when far fewer people roamed its lands, Death had been the portal. She'd shown up at the point of death and shepherded souls across the veil. That strategy had gone up in smoke around the time of the Crusades. Too many dead people for a single entity to manage.

And so, she'd created helpers. The lore was a wee bit fuzzy on how she managed inserting the alteration to produce a Reaper, but she'd come up with something she did to pregnant women. I had no idea if it worked every time, or if it was a trial-and-error process.

I also wasn't certain if Death somehow vetted the unborn to see if they'd be a good fit for her needs. Regardless, the cadre of Reapers had grown over time. Death was conservative, so she was always short-staffed.

I supposed it was better than Reapers falling all over one another.

Satisfied I understood where they'd come from, I grabbed a scroll and hunted for the composition of their magic. I worried I was snooping, but I had to find out the next part. Cait would insist on leaving tomorrow, and I had to know if we could teleport or if I'd have to drive her to an airport.

I'd already decided to buy her ticket if it came to that. She didn't appear to have the resources for a last-minute purchase. Those could run into the thousands. If she balked, I'd couch it as a long-term loan.

The scroll required digging, but I located what I needed. Reaper magic was predominantly earth based with bits of air and water. Not much fire at all. Keeping my place with an index finger, I kept reading the spidery handwritten lines penned in an old version of Welsh.

Once I was done, I picked up another scroll, hunting corroboration for what I'd read. Aye. There it was. This source proposed Reapers were over 90 percent earth in terms of their magic. I frowned. If that was the case, there was no reason I couldn't teach Cait to teleport on her own.

Surely Death understood her minions were capable of journey spells. And a whole lot more too. Cait had said she'd gone to Reaper school, presumably taught by Death. Why hadn't she instructed her Reapers to utilize the full spectrum of their ability?

Had to be a reason. Was I going to upset some cosmic applecart if I spilled the beans?

Small sounds drifted up from downstairs. Was Cait having a hard time getting comfortable?

Uh-uh. I shook a mental finger at myself and my still-hard-despite-my-best-efforts appendage. Cait was a big girl.

She was more than capable of attending to her own comfort without assistance from me.

Twisting, I picked up the notebook I kept near my bed. I could have used an electronic device, but I preferred pen and paper. I'd discovered two important things, and I jotted them down. Cait's magic wouldn't fight mine, so I could whisk her back to Seattle. Because of all her earth-bound magic, she was, indeed, immune to many of my spells. Like the one earlier where I'd tried to calm her. I sketched out a few arcane equations to double-check my assumptions. They all panned out. Contrary to mortals' beliefs, the Sidhe had discovered calculus long before it was a gleam in Isaac Newton's eye.

No doubt about it, Cait could be a powerful ally rounding up the Leanan-Sidhe because they couldn't raise compulsion against her. Maxwell too, if he could be pressed into service. I didn't want to repeat Hollis's error of not keeping Death in the loop, though. Meant I had to figure out how to contact her.

I carried the lore books back to my library and placed them in their slots.

A dull ache in my nether regions told me I'd run out of choices. My cock was done toying with me. If I was going to ignore the perfectly good woman a few steps away, he'd take release any way he could get it. I curved my hand around my hard-on. Sensation sheeted through me as I stroked myself.

When I shut my eyes, images of Cait bombarded me. Cait with dark hair spilling down her rounded breasts. In my fantasy, she was as aroused as me, with distended nipples and color streaking her breasts and high cheekbones. My grip tightened; my hand moved faster.

In an embarrassingly short time, my balls snugged against my body, and semen juddered from my cock. I'd done my damnedest to be silent, but breath thundered through me in gasping pants. I should have built a sound ward, but it was too late now. Rather than deflating, my cock was as hard as if I hadn't just come.

"Too bad," I murmured. "That's all you get."

I cleaned up the mess on my wooden floor with magic and walked slowly to my bed. Tomorrow, I'd make a bid for Cait to remain and help with my rogue kinsmen. We'd see how things went. If she insisted on returning home, I was honor bound to make certain she got there.

The Leanan weren't exactly her problem.

I felt torn. If Cait went back to Seattle, I didn't want her to be alone, but the Sidhe needed me here. While I was wallowing in indecision, reality intruded. Even if I offered to play bodyguard, she might well turn me down cold.

Why wouldn't she? She'd gotten along fine on her own for hundreds of years. Last thing she needed was a pesky Sidhe shadowing her every move.

Not much I could do about anything until morning. I don't need much in the way of actual sleep, but I spun a calming trance and let it sweep me away.

CHAPTER NINE, CAIT

I'd taken Liam up on his suggestion and rinsed out my underwear. My bra and panties hung from hooks in the kitchen. I hoped they'd be dry by morning. It would be embarrassing to ask him to dry them with magic. Meh. They could finish drying on my body, if it came to that. It did feel good to be clean. The soap in his shower had smelled like him, sandalwood and piquant greenery. Now I smelled that way too.

I'd made myself a nest between two blankets so soft they had to be spun from lambswool and plumped the pillow beneath my head. I'd expected sleep to claim me in short order. It had every right to. I was exhausted. Instead, my body was alive, alight with wanting the man sleeping above my head.

Maybe sleeping. I caught the creak of floorboards that suggested otherwise. I gave myself a sharp virtual kick in the pants. What was I going to do? March upstairs and fall into his arms?

He'd make love with me. I was certain of it, but we did not need an additional layer of complexity muddying our relationship. Besides, tomorrow I'd start my trudge back to Seattle. My odds of ever seeing him again were thin.

So? How would that be different from all my other one-night stands? an inner voice snarked.

"There haven't been all that many," I murmured. I don't usually answer myself, but in this case I wanted to set the record straight.

Something about being here, in the Sidhes' realm, surrounded by Sidhe enchantment, had altered my judgment. Liam's magic had a timeless feel, comforting and stimulating by turns.

Other than my stint at Reaper school, I've never spent much time among others with magic. Death likes us to work alone. I've often thought we'd be more efficient in twos or even threes, but it's not my circus. Anyway, since nearly all of my companions are mortals, my bed partners have been too. I'm sure most of them sensed something different about me. Maybe at some atavistic level they knew someone like me would greet them at the end of their lives, and it creeped them out.

Regardless, none of my boy toys lasted more than a few months.

I had a feeling Liam would be different, and not necessarily in good ways. We might be spectacular together, but the inevitable breakup would be equally spectacular. I had no idea if the Sidhe mated outside their own kinship circles. Reapers didn't mate at all from my observation.

Death liked us available. Families and, goddess forbid, children would put a big crimp in that.

I rearranged my body under the blanket. Its soft fibers caressed me, adding to my lust problem. More floor-creaking from above. The feel of Liam's power shifted, became multidimensional. Was he setting a trap for me? Had the whole dinner been an elaborate front—?

Got to get hold of myself. Front for what?

We were batting on the same team. It would be like sabotaging a preflight, so the plane went down with both of us in it. Waves of sensuality rolled through the house. Tinged with magic, they elicited pictures of beautiful naked men with distended cocks. Long hair, gleaming eyes. Perfect bodies. Long-legged and lean, just the way I liked them.

My hand found its way between my legs. I was slick with heat and need, and I teased my nub with my fingers. My other hand rested on a breast, and I pinched my nipple hard enough to make me gasp with pleasure. Frigging myself felt perverse, but I was past the point of exerting common sense. I had to come. Had to. Heat ignited my nerve endings, and a climax spooled in my belly. Just a little more rubbing, and I crested, tumbling down the other side as spasms racked me with delight.

I stuffed a corner of the blanket into my mouth so I wouldn't cry out.

By the time my breathing was back to normal, whatever had caught me up in its sexual lightshow was gone. Had I imagined it?

Didn't matter. I felt myself slipping into sleep. I might have dozed, but if I did, it wasn't for very long. I know Death's feel, her scent, her magic. She thumped down a couple of feet from the couch.

"Up with you. We have work to do."

I groaned and rolled until I faced her. She stood, hands on hips, staring down at me. For once, she wasn't wearing her neutral expression. If I read her right, she was worried. She clapped her hands smartly. "Come on. Is your hearing going?"

Still swathed in blankets, I maneuvered until I was in a cross-legged sit and focused my gritty eyes on her. "I'm tired," I muttered.

"So am I. You don't see me slacking off."

Anger boiled through me, but I did feel less like a zombie. "I am not slacking off. I've had a miserable day. Vampires are out for my blood." I took a measured breath and blew it out. "Because of you."

"So?" She arched a silver brow. "No one promised you Reaping would be easy all of the time."

"It's never easy, but it used to be tolerable," I retorted.

The clatter of feet on stairs brought my head around. Liam, all gorgeous six foot four or so of him stood at the far end of the room. A black silken robe clung to his broad shoulders and stopped at mid-thigh. Damn but he had great legs. His fair hair hung around him in thick, unruly curls.

I swallowed around a suddenly dry throat. No one had a right to look as appealing as he did.

"Excellent." Liam strode toward Death. "We need to talk, and this saves me hunting you down."

"You weren't part of my plans," Death retorted. "I came to collect my Reaper."

"But we need her," Liam protested. "And others if you can spare them."

"Really? Why might that be?" Death tapped one booted foot. It made percussive sounds on the wooden floor, not unlike a runaway metronome.

"How about if I put on tea for us?" Liam oozed charm. I started to tell him not to waste his magic on Death, but she shocked me.

"I'd love a spot of tea." She actually smiled. "Sugar and milk, please."

"Guess I'll get dressed," I muttered and then remembered my soaked panties and bra. Maybe Death could dry them for me. I was also buck naked under the blankets and robe.

"I'll just run upstairs and give you a moment to get yourself decent," Liam told me and vanished. He hadn't used the stairs, so he must have teleported.

I pushed my way out of my blanket fort and loped to where I'd left my underthings. "Could you dry these?" I asked Death.

"Were you planning on staying?" she smirked. A blast of magic smacked me, and the flimsy garments jumped off their hooks and into my hands. At least they were dry.

I dressed fast, avoiding eye contact, and returned the robe to its hook on the back of the bathroom door. By the time I'd moved to my boots, Liam was back downstairs. He'd donned the same clothes he'd been wearing earlier. After heating water with magic, he tossed aromatic herbs into the bubbling mix. Got to hand it to him, he's got the host-vibe nailed. Soon, three heavy ceramic mugs filled with a frothy beverage materialized on a nearby table.

Unlike Death, I preferred my tea unsullied with add-ons. Liam had somehow intuited my likings without employing words. Or maybe I was reading too much into my black tea. I had a tongue. If I'd wanted milk or sugar, I could ask for them.

He waited until he'd sat across from us to ask, "What happened with Selene?"

"Price for my tea?" Death had grabbed a seat next to me on the couch, and she wrapped her slender fingers around the mug.

"Nay, but knowing would help as we plan our next steps," Liam replied.

Death angled her head to one side regarding both of us. Her first words were aimed at me. "Until we figure things out, no more Reaping."

My eyes widened. "Easier said than done," I mumbled. "Sometimes the newly dead throw themselves my way, and I can't go around warded all the time. I don't have enough magic."

"Guess it means you'll have to pay closer attention," she said smoothly.

A thought occurred to me, one I wasn't a fan of, but it deserved airtime. "Just because I'm not hunting Vampires any longer, it doesn't mean they'll stop trying to wipe their asses with my corpse."

"Which part of paying closer attention wasn't clear, Reaper?" Death's tone was as chilly as the dead she oversaw.

Frankly, it annoyed me. I set my mug down and skewered her with my gaze. Not easy with those eyes of hers. "I was doing fine in the attention department—until you dropped Vampires into my lap. Apparently, you've rethought things."

"Only a foolish commander casts her battle plans in stone," she retorted and turned toward Liam. "Selene hasn't changed. Someone put her up to cooing over her pet Vampires again."

"The Leanan-Sidhe escaped. Was she who freed them?" Liam asked point-blank.

Death regarded him from beneath raised brows. "You're only just now discovering they're loose?"

Liam winced. "The answer would be yes, but you can spare me the lecture."

"Wasn't going to waste my breath. Do you believe Selene had aught to do with your brand of Vampires?"

He shrugged. "I have no idea what level of magic she commands, but my first guess would be she couldn't have penetrated the *Dreaming*, much less located the Leanan-Sidhe."

"Exactly. Which was why I became more...persuasive when she kept smirking and insisting this was all her idea. Pfft"—Death rolled her eyes—"that one couldn't plan a garden party, much less an abduction."

"Did you get her to talk?" Something vicious rode beneath Liam's words.

Death nodded slowly. "She held out longer than I expected, and—"

"Aw, geez. You tortured her?" I broke in, incredulous. In all the time I'd known Death, I'd found her harsh but fair.

She silenced me with a look. "The details are not important. Selene finally got it through her thick head I wasn't going to allow her to leave before she gave me what I wanted."

Liam leaned back against his chair and smiled encouragingly. I should borrow a page from his book and be less abrasive. Information was key, and all I was doing was slowing the process with inane questions.

Death took her time drinking from her mug. When she set it down, she said, "The Infernals have grown bored. Humans no longer leave blood sacrifices because the age of believing in magic has ended. In truth, it's been over for a couple of hundred years, but most of that batch have always been slow on the uptake."

"Thought they'd been quiet," Liam murmured.

Meanwhile, I'd been culling through my memory and coming up with goose eggs. "Before you go on," I said, "who are these Infernals?"

"The bad gods," Death said succinctly.

I raked a hand through my hair. "Aren't most deities on the high-handed side?"

Liam nodded, and Death said, "Of course. Would you expect less of us?"

My mouth twisted wryly. Her use of the inclusive pronoun was a staunch reminder she was a card-carrying member of the pack. I could have shut up, but I needed clarification. "Who exactly are the 'bad gods' in this instance?"

"I was getting to that," Death's tone was pointed, "but you keep interrupting me."

"Sorry," I mumbled, determined to wait until she was done before I posed any more questions.

"Our current problems stem from Tantalus and a group of troublemakers who were never more than minor deities. Perrikus, Majestron Zelia, Adva, D'Chel, Tokhots, and Slototh."

"But they're characters in Marvel Comics," I protested. My five-seconds-ago vow to keep quiet was apparently so much tripe.

"Aye, but those characters were based on the real thing," Liam corrected me. "According to the lore, Thor freed Perrikus, god of infinite power, from the Asgard dungeons. Once freed, he imported the other dark gods to Asgard. Majestron Zelia was his mother and leader of the pack. Adva controlled portals and knowledge. D'Chel was the god of illusion. Tokhots the god of rhyme, and Slototh the god of filth."

"So it's just like in the comic books," I mumbled.

"If you say so. Anyone mind if I continue?" Death banged her mug on the tabletop for emphasis and stared at me. "Where were you during the lore classes in Reaper school?"

"Present enough to pass the tests," I retorted.

"Och. Now I'm who's getting off course," she said. "Tantalus must have run out of mortals to entice. He's just as sex-hungry—and lacking in remorse—as ever, so I'm certain the shortage of mortal women to warm his bed infuriated him. He always was short on patience."

Words fought to escape. I kept them barricaded in my throat. The attraction of the Leanan-Sidhe, who successfully lured humans, was crystal clear. I'd be damned if Tantalus's name rang any bells, but it sounded as if he'd hawk his left ball, if it would buy him the Leanans' ability to seduce women.

"After Tantalus escaped his imprisonment in Tartarus, the gods lacked the heart to track him down," Death continued. "He kept a rather low profile until a chance run-in with Perrikus and his mother, Majestron Zelia."

Death snatched up her tea again, and drained it.

"I can make you another cup," Liam offered.

She shook her head. "According to Selene, she got involved when Tantalus promised to restore her to her earlier glory, when all Vampires worshipped her."

"She actually believed him?" I blurted. At least I'd remembered who he was. One of Jupiter's sons, he'd dismembered his own child and tried to feed him to the other gods in a stew. They'd figured things out before eating the lad and put him back together.

"Selene's never been the brightest star in the sky," Death told me. "I'm not totally clear who broke into the *Dreaming*, but my money is on D'Chel. He can adopt any form he wishes."

"Why not Adva?" Liam asked. "I remember him, and he can create portals out of damn near anything."

"The barn door is open, and the cow long gone. Does it matter who broke the latch?" Death asked. Liam didn't answer.

I looked from one to the other, feeling out of my depth. Reapers are at the bottom of the magical pecking order. Enough talent to do our job, but not one whit more.

"What happens next?" I asked. The history lesson had

been interesting, but we weren't any closer to solving our problems. Or maybe it wasn't even mine anymore. Death had relieved me of Vampire duties. And Reaping too.

"Scratch that question," I said brightly. "This seems like a task for people who have a lot of power. Probably best for me to go home. I can find my own way back, and—"

Death leveled a withering look my way. It effectively silenced me.

Liam drew his fair brows into a thoughtful expression, but he addressed Death rather than me. "About Cait."

"What about her?" Death retorted. "She works for me."

"Not disputing that," Liam said. "Last night I read up on Reapers and their magic, and—"

"Stop right there." Death sputtered.

"Why should I?" Liam's tone rivaled hers with its combination of hubris and disdain.

I felt seriously outclassed but then reminded myself neither of them could fly an airplane. Yeah, they could teleport, but it was like cheating.

"Reapers are mine to deploy as I deem appropriate," Death retorted.

"What the fuck am I missing here?" I looked from one to the other.

"Don't." Death stared at Liam.

"She has a right to know," he said.

"If by she, you mean me," I gritted out and couldn't think of what to say next. I slopped down most of the rest of my tea, hoping to hell it had caffeine in it. I needed a lift.

"You have a lot more power than you realize," Liam told me.

"Pfft." I flapped my hands his way. "If that were true, I'd have figured it out a long time ago."

"Want to take a look at my source materials?" He arched a brow.

Death sprang to her feet. "How dare you?" she shouted in Liam's face.

He stood and faced off with her. Death was taller, but only because of her penchant for high-heeled boots. "Many reasons. *Your* Reapers"—he stressed the word your—"could be a great help capturing the Leanan-Sidhe. As you know, Reapers aren't sensitive to Sidhe magic, so they can't be tricked by compulsion or coercion."

The idea of commanding more magic was heady. While the two of them batted words back and forth, I looked within, assessing my magical reservoir. Not sure quite what I was expecting to unearth, I was vaguely disappointed because it looked the same as it always had. Was it a matter of treating it differently, viewing it differently, asking more from my ability?

I'm a decent truth-vector, and Liam hadn't been lying.

I'd have posed questions, but Death and Liam were snarling at one another. She was shouting something about him not having a right, and his reply was she'd been remiss not to maximize her Reapers' abilities.

One thing that stood out was she hadn't refuted his assertions. Also, they seemed to have forgotten I existed.

I skirted around them. No one paid me the slightest heed as I headed up the stairs intent on locating whatever books or scrolls Liam was referring to. The farther I got up three steep flights, the more Liam's scent and the feel of his magic surrounded me. Midway up the last set of risers, I couldn't have stopped if I'd wanted to.

Remnants of sexual vibrations filled the air, and I understood more than I had about why I'd been so stimulated I had to touch myself. Not that I hadn't known he was attracted to me, but finding actual evidence thrilled me.

Not now. My inner voice was stern, and it was absolutely correct. I shoved all thoughts of Liam to a distant spot and ladled magic over them. I had a task, and it had nothing to do with him.

Actually, it had everything to do with him—but from a knowledge perspective. My runaway lust had no place here. None at all. The stairs ran out, leaving me in another large room. A rumpled bed sat between armoires and dressers. The space was spare, masculine, but appealing in its simplicity.

Liam's scent and his magic surrounded me, welcomed me. I spaded more layers over my desire, muting it, making certain it didn't make a break for it. I didn't want to end up rolling around in his bed, snuffling up his scents as if they were my drug of choice.

Maybe because I'd tapped into my magical center, it pulsed within me and drew me to an alcove containing messy stacks of ancient books and scrolls. They smelled of old leather and vellum, and wow. Were there ever a lot of them.

Where to begin?

My vision shifted to the half-light I've always associated with the nether regions inhabited by the dead. In this instance, though, a couple of books and scrolls took on a soft glow. Somehow, I understood they were the ones Liam had consulted earlier.

Drawing them from their shelves, I sank to the dusty floorboards and maintained what I've always considered my grave vision. So far, it had given me what I needed. I trusted it would guide me to the proper place in the lore materials as well.

I hesitated before flipping the first book open; pages riffled before coming to a stop. Whatever was scribed within them would change my life. I felt it in my bones, and it should have scared me.

It didn't.

Magic has an allure all its own. If I could command more than I did, I wanted every single flicker. Every thread. Every stray bit. Feeling like a greedy bitch, I bent my head and began to read.

CHAPTER TEN, LIAM

$\mathcal{I}$ noticed Cait leaving the room. Good woman. If she was doing what I thought she was, she'd immerse herself in my lore books. Maybe the best way for me to help her would be to keep Death occupied. The cat was out of the bag. No stuffing it back inside.

"I don't intrude in Sidhe affairs," Death growled at me.

"You would if they impacted your Reapers," I told her.

She raised a hand. Magic sliced cleanly through a tapestry I'd had since the 1600s. Her being furious was one thing, but I'd be damned if I'd step politely aside while she destroyed my belongings. I raised my voice for emphasis and said, "No more. I don't come into your home and ruin your possessions."

"What I did with yon wall hanging is exactly what you did with my Reaper."

I resisted a powerful urge to slap her. It wouldn't help anything. Cait viewed herself as an independent agent. As far as Death was concerned, she owned her Reapers. "I'm not making Cait weaker. I'm opening doors so she can realize the full potential of her magic. What I'd like to know is why you saddled all your Reapers with the assumption they can't do anything except serve as portals."

Slowly, very slowly, Death lowered her hand. "I've been at this a while. Probably longer than you've been alive, although years become meaningless for those like us after a few hundred have passed." Breath hissed through her teeth. "When the task of Reaping outstripped my ability to accomplish it, I added those like Cait."

I was familiar with that bit of history, but she was talking. It was better than shouting or shooting up my home with magic.

"The first Reapers had access to the full bounty of their Earth-bound magic." She pursed her mouth into a sour expression. "They fought me at every turn. Made independent decisions that were incompatible with other Reapers. And with me.

"After a few experiments, I settled on a mix that allowed my minions to Reap souls without too many problems cropping up. To anchor them, make certain they all flew in the same direction, I developed a curriculum. My workforce, for want of a better word, had to earn passing grades in Reaper school before I turned them loose."

I digested what she'd said. "You must have cloaked their ability somehow. I can't believe an extra-curious Reaper didn't stumble on all that hidden power."

She stared at me with the equivalent of a Mona Lisa smile in place. "I did, indeed. Wasn't even all that challenging. The school was a brilliant move because I could warn them away from slippery ground."

"Places where they'd have discovered you lied to them?" I curled my lip. That hadn't come out right. It may have been what I meant, but I didn't intend to be quite so blunt. I was absolutely certain she'd had to silence an unruly Reaper or two to maintain order within her ranks. What in Danu's name had she done with them?

I was envisioning a subterranean Reaper prison fortified with magic and iron when a robust blast of magic shot through the room. It had Reaper stamped all over it. Doing an abrupt about-face, I ran for the stairs.

"Too late," Death called after me. "She's gone."

I sent seeking magic up the remaining stairs. Sure enough, Cait must have summoned a journey spell. I stopped on the first landing and trudged back to my living area. "You don't suppose she tried to teleport all the way to Seattle," I said.

"It's precisely what she did." Death skewered me with her odd eyes. "Why would you expect anything different?"

I crossed my arms over my chest. "Let's see. Because it's her first time with that particular magic? Most of us would experiment with a short hop. Maybe from here to a neighboring village and back."

"You learned to make magic work for you when you were very young. Cait is far from young. She views herself as more than fully grown. It would never occur to her to tiptoe around her spells. She's been casting them forever."

"Aye, but this is new," I argued and let my arms fall to my

sides. "Doesn't matter. I'll just make a quick trip to Seattle to make certain she arrives in one piece."

"And if she doesn't materialize?"

Death was baiting me, punishing me for pointing Cait in the direction of my library. I narrowed my eyes. "I'm guessing you have a way of locating her."

"Of course. Her and all the others."

"Is there some reason you haven't gone after her." I rode herd on outrage that wanted out. "You all but told me you're worried about her, and—"

"We learn the most important lessons from our mistakes," she purred, and I wanted to punch her.

"Vampires are out to get her," I retorted. "She's vulnerable when the spell dissipates at her chosen destination." I did a few quick calculations. "It's nighttime in Seattle."

"Tell me things I don't know."

My temper was hanging together by a couple of frayed threads. "I understand you're angry with me for chopping a hole in the charade you've been running. One that was convenient for you and kept your minions fat, dumb, and happy. Cait may or may not tell the others. It doesn't appear you allow them to work together, so the odds of her running into another Reaper aren't terribly high.

"Regardless, I'm leaving. I'll wait for her at her office. If she doesn't show up there, I'll start hunting for her in my own way."

"You haven't asked what I'll be doing."

I ground my teeth until my jaw protested. "Why should

I? You know she's in danger, but you'd rather teach her a lesson than bail her out."

I was done talking. Magic jumped to my call; I built a journey spell. I also performed a quick search for something personal from Cait—in case she wasn't in her workplace, and I had to cast a seeking spell. Blood was unlikely, but I hustled to a glittery place illuminated by my power and snatched up a small ball of hair. Dark as midnight, it had to be hers. Death still stood in my living room, staring at me while the walls dissolved, traded for the gray-black of teleport enchantment.

I was fuming, so angry I was afraid it might skew my chosen exit point. What the hell was wrong with Death? Were her Reapers truly eminently replaceable? I'd had crappy, patronizing instructors in my youth, but none were anything like her.

I made a grab for my equanimity. If I couldn't calm down, I wouldn't be any good to anyone.

Was Cait truly in trouble? Had I exaggerated the dangers of such a lengthy first teleport spell? It hadn't taken her long to glom onto the power that was part of her birthright. She must have heard the argument unfolding beneath her and wanted no part of jumping into the center of it. I was as guilty as Death of treating her as if she were a juicy bone, and we were a couple of starving wolves.

I didn't blame her for leaving.

She might not appreciate me coming after her, but I wouldn't make a nuisance of myself. She owed me nothing—including assistance recapturing my missing kinsmen. I turned my mind to the Vampire problem. The infusion of

Leanan-Sidhe magic had to be what had strengthened Earth's Vampires and given them the ability to walk beneath the sun.

If I was right about that, dealing with the Leanan should take a bite out of the other variety of Vamp. I wasn't certain how to treat with Tantalus and the dark gods. Were they even still a problem?

What was in this for them? Surely, they'd tire of hanging about with the Undead. Vampires were one-dimensional. Two if you counted sex. Beyond their fixation with blood and lust, nothing remained. They couldn't even roll out a decent conversation.

I dug deeper. Chaos fed the dark gods. Vampires too. Earth was a pretty messy place between horrific weather events, mass shootings, overpopulation, and runaway greed. Much as I hated to admit it, the blend was evil's perfectly steeped cup of tea. Pushing all that nasty energy aside would be damned difficult.

Aye, try impossible.

If my memories of the six dark gods was accurate, they'd put up a pitched battle to remain, making everything that much worse.

Too bad we couldn't sic the dark gods on the Humans Rule crowd. It would keep the dark gods busy and decimate one of our many problems.

My spell developed silvery edges. I warded myself just in case people were about. They took a dim view of sorcery that slapped them in the face. My spell had run true. I came out between two buildings quite near *Carrick Sky Sports*, the blackness of a moonless night surrounding me. No one was near, so I let my ward go and hurried toward the Quonset hut.

A subtle seeking spell didn't bring me much information —other than I didn't locate any of the Undead. I also didn't sense Cait. Was there another spot she would have gone besides this one? She'd left before me, so she should be here by now.

Unless the spell had gotten away from her. If that happened, she could be anywhere. Hopefully on Earth, but there were other locales she might have landed. Would she have enough magic left to correct the situation? Teleport spells had a few downsides. If you failed to pay attention, or didn't feed adequate magic into your casting, you could end up lost in the hundreds of corridors stretching around Earth.

I didn't see her as that incompetent, though.

Getting ahead of the game, mate, I told myself. I knew better. Slow and steady could have been my mantra. The other Sidhe had mocked me for my methodical ways, but I'd stuck with them because they were effective.

Looking around, I convinced myself I was alone and made short work of the lock on her door. I could have teleported inside, but this was faster. After I'd kicked the door shut, a mage light bloomed next to me. I kept it low. There was only one window, but it lacked shades or curtains. I rustled through her desk hoping to find another address. Hopefully, the one for her home. I'd thought perhaps she lived here, but it didn't have a homelike feel.

She didn't appear to have much of a filing system at least for paper items. Probably the computer that hummed on the floor was better organized.

Two drawers later, I pulled copies of her pilot's license and her business license from the desk and examined them. Bingo! Two documents, two different addresses. The business license probably held my current location. Meant the other one had to be her domicile.

After a few adjustments, I dialed in another journey spell and headed for where I hoped to hell I'd find Cait. If she wasn't at her home, I'd cast a seeking spell using her hair to kindle it.

Because I was worried, I didn't do a good enough job with my next ward. Muted shrieks told me I'd been seen popping out of nowhere. I ignored them and got my bearings. I was on a pier. Boats extended on all sides of me, but they didn't look as if they ever left the dock.

Interesting. Houseboats. We didn't have many of those in Europe or the UK. I paid out seeking magic again. The few mortals who'd been strolling along the pier or a nearby walkway scattered like pixie dust. Good. Saved a bunch of explanations about why I was wielding power in plain sight of humans. It wasn't exactly illegal, but neither was it sanctioned. If Humans Rule had their way, both of those gray areas would change enabling the authorities to issue citations—and jail time—for what I'd just done.

In for a penny, in for a pound. No one was left to be outraged by visible magic, so I wasn't especially careful with my next arc of seeking enchantment. Relief socked me in the guts, sweet and heady. Cait was inside the boat to my right. I strode down a gangway and knocked on the door.

She pulled it open so fast she must have sensed my arrival, and muttered, "I wondered if you'd show up."

"I'd have been here sooner, except I went to your business first." My mouth wanted to smile, but I didn't let it. Yes, I was happy to see her, but she looked like hell. Dark circles etched beneath her eyes. She'd never done up her hair after her shower; it spilled around her in bunches of fluffy curls. I wanted to scoop her into my arms, tell her I'd keep her safe, but she didn't need a protector. The best way I could help her would be to teach her to cast a wider variety of spells.

She'd changed into dark slacks and a stretchy ivory top with a green sweater tossed over it. The clothing hung on her tall, lanky frame. I hoped she'd made a point of eating since she got home. Magic really took it out of you.

"Well, I'm fine." Her words cut into my thoughts. "I figured things out. Thanks for pointing me in the right direction and all, but—"

I pushed toward her. "Please. Let me come inside. We shouldn't have this conversation out here."

"What conversation?" She arched a dark brow. "I'm home. You have rogue kinsmen to catch."

It was a dismissal, and an obvious one, but I hadn't come all this way for her to walk out of my life. I reminded myself I'd promised not to be a nuisance, but it didn't make much difference. If she out-and-out ordered me to leave, I wouldn't have a choice, but she hadn't.

Not yet, anyway.

"I'm not trying to be obnoxious, but if it weren't for me incurring Death's eternal wrath, you wouldn't have known you had the magic that allowed you to teleport home."

"Really?" She notched her brows higher. "You're playing

the 'you owe me' card?" Cait held up a hand. "Sorry. I'm being a total bitch. Please. Come in. I'm not at my best. No sleep, and when you showed up I was figuring out how to ward my house."

"Against Vampires?"

"What else?" She stood aside, and I stepped over the lintel.

"They really do require an invitation. They can't simply storm the fortress."

She pushed the door shut and threw the deadbolt. "Not my experience at the Quonset hut. They just kind of crept through the walls. So far, my saving grace here has been their antipathy for water, but if they can operate in daylight and ooze through walls, I'm hedging my bets."

I made a face. I hadn't forgotten the Quonset hut battle, but neither had I considered what it meant. Regardless, some protections were prudent. Better safe than sorry and all that rot.

"Let me help you build a ward. Then we can talk." Over the next few minutes, we experimented with how to weave our magic together. It wasn't as intuitive as working with another Sidhe, but the end result was stronger.

"That should do it," I said, assessing the mesh of our reinforcements through my psychic vision.

"Hope we don't find out how bulletproof it is," she muttered and led me from a utilitarian mudroom into a comfortable living area. The floor rocked slightly beneath my feet, reminding me the structure was floating on water. A desk took up one quadrant of the room. Piled high with maps and charts, it reminded me of the helm in old sailing vessels, except I bet her maps went with her flying business. A comfortable sofa cut the room at its midpoint, stretching almost the entire way across. Made of creased beige leather with scattered paisley throw pillows, it looked comfortable. Hassocks were placed at both ends with a coffee table between them.

Two doors ran off the living room. I could see a small kitchen through one of them. The other opened onto a hallway. Presumably where her sleeping quarters and bathroom were.

"How long have you lived on a houseboat?" I asked. "Is this a typical dwelling for Seattle?"

She shrugged and dropped onto one end of the couch. "Probably not 'typical,' but Seattle has a lot of houseboats. It's a cheap way to live. I own the houseboat, so all I have to pay is slip rent. It's way less than an apartment."

Her focus on money surprised me, probably because it was never anything that crossed my mind. The Sidhe had amassed far more than we needed so long ago, no one actually recalled just where our wealth had originated.

"But you have a business, and surely Death provides for you," I said, still trying to understand how she could be in need of money.

Cait did turn to glance at me then. Just before she started to laugh. It wasn't a happy sound, more bitter than mirthful. Fighting a craving to wrap my arms around her, I perched on the far end of the couch. "Sorry," I said a bit stiffly. "Didn't mean to upset you, but I fail to see why you're laughing."

She shook her head and raked both hands through her abundant curls, pushing them behind her shoulders.

"Mostly, I was amused at the absurdity of Death doing anything for any of us. She offers moral support—and shows up if I'm in trouble—but other than that I've been on my own since I left Reaper school. She did house and feed us then."

Cait pressed her mouth into a grim line. "Flying is fiercely competitive. You went to *The Tailwind*, so you met the guys. Most of them operate businesses that are a lot like mine. I used to fly freight to make ends meet. After I got saddled with Vampires, I couldn't do it anymore."

"Why not?"

She made a snorting noise. "Because I can't fly if I haven't had enough sleep. Not with much of a safety margin. I tried to keep up with the freight end of things, but I fell asleep in the cockpit a couple of times. Scared the bejesus out of me. It's not a big deal for flying lessons or check rides because they don't last but an hour or two, and I'm talking most of the time. The freight runs can keep me in the air for ten hours or better."

I picked through what she'd said, hunting for a bottom line. "You're saying *Carrick Sky Sports* is in financial trouble?" At her nod, I went on. "Surely, you could sell the planes, unless they're—" I'd been about to say mortgaged, but she spoke over me.

"No! Never. They're my babies. I love them." She pinched the bridge of her nose between two fingers. "Look. I've thought about maybe selling the twin engine one. She's worth a whole lot, but that would be like giving up."

With her green eyes focused on me, Cait ground out, "All I need is for Death to move me off Vampire duty permanently." She dusted her hands together. "Then my life will get back to normal. I've never had a problem incorporating Reaping with the rest of my life. Until now."

I hoped my expression didn't give me away. Maybe her life would revert to "normal." For a while. She'd outlive anything mechanical—like her airplanes—but I was wise enough not to mention that. It also seemed unlikely Death would reassign her. I kept my mouth shut on that front too.

A corner of her mouth turned downward. "You're quiet. Thanks for not telling me I'm full of shit, that this is the new normal and I'd better suck it up and get used to it."

"Some things don't require words," I murmured.

A flat-screen television was bolted to the wall opposite the couch. Images flared across its screen, but the sound was turned off. Something caught my eye, and I reached for the remote control, intent on hearing what the newscaster was saying. His sandy hair was tousled from the wind, and he wore a rumpled shirt and a tweed blazer. The reporter appeared young, earnest, and cold. His lips had a bluish tinge to them.

Cait moved her gaze from me to the screen. "Crap on a cracker," she mumbled, "they're at it again."

The "they" in this instance were Humans Rule. I flicked the remote off mute, and the man with the mic said, "Lake Union Marina, folks. An active demonstration is in process. Steer clear of this area. Traffic has been rerouted."

Behind him stood a mob of protesters carrying placards and shouting obscenities about, well, about folk like me. Maybe a hundred protesters or more, their signs read things like *Death to Magic* and *Jail Them* and *This is Our City. Take Back Our City* loomed large as well.

"Have there always been this many Humans Rule members here?" I asked, alarmed by the visible display of fear and hatred.

"Depends how you define always," she replied. "The past couple of months, they've upped the ante on their demonstrations, though. There may have been a concerted effort to grow their ranks." She rolled her eyes. "It's not as if they're in the market to recruit me."

I narrowed my eyes, said, "This isn't good," and stopped there. No reason to go into my vivid recollections of other eras and other mobs, all out for magic-wielders' blood.

Cait shook her head. Sadness rolled off her in waves. I couldn't help myself, I skootched closer to where she sat and placed a hand over one of hers. She snatched it back.

"Don't. Comfort would be nice, but it's not real. And it won't last." She twisted until she faced me, tucking one leg under her. "You really should leave. You've got those Leanan-Sidhe to locate. It was kind of you to check up on me, but as you can see, I'm managing."

"Pfft. Hanging on by your fingernails is more like it." I pushed past the anger flaring from her at me stating the obvious. "This isn't anything about you owing me. In truth, I owe you. I'm who kicked the gates to your magic open. It wouldn't be responsible of me to leave without making certain you have the basics to deal with all that extra power."

"Nice try." A laugh—warmer this time—bubbled from her throat. "I like you, Liam, but you need to leave." She made shooing motions with both hands. "I'm expecting Death to drop in any moment."

"Why is that a reason for me to go?"

"The two of you really got into it. She might be in a better mood if you weren't here."

"We more or less buried the hatchet." I blew out a breath and hoped my lie wasn't totally transparent. "Mostly, I was annoyed because she knew you'd ignited teleport magic and didn't show the least inclination to go after you."

"She doesn't have to. She knows exactly where I am twenty-four seven."

I made a face. "Aye, she made certain I understood as much after I announced I was going to check to see you'd arrived home safely."

"Mmph. At least it explains her absence," Cait muttered.

I'd been keeping one eye on the riot expanding on the television screen. "We're on a lake. Is it the same lake as that one?" I nodded toward the TV.

"Yeah."

"How far is this marina place from here?"

"A few blocks. Look. Liam. Just leave. That mob isn't about to come knocking on my door. Vampires are a much bigger threat than—"

"Let's go see what they're up to, shall we?"

Her eyes widened. "What? Why?"

"Always best if you know what your enemy has planned."

"But we do know," she said. "It's right there. They hate us and think we should all end up in a prison camp, preferably in Siberia."

I set my jaw in a tight line. "We know what they want the

public to know," I pointed out. "What if they have bigger plans? Hidden ones?"

"Why is it our job?" she said tiredly. "My plate is overflowing. In case you haven't noticed."

"Because no one else is doing it. We won't be gone long. Just time enough to see if we overhear something useful." I got to my feet and headed for the kitchen. Hopefully, she'd have cheese and biscuits or something we could munch on the way.

I felt her energy, warm and enticing, as she joined me. Snaking a hand forward, she stuffed bread and cheese I'd just sliced into her mouth. After she'd chewed and swallowed, she asked, "What do you have in mind?"

"We pretend to be part of the mob. What else?"

"But they can sense I'm different," she protested. "Surely, it's an even bigger problem for you."

I cracked a grin. "We glamour up."

"Not sure I know how to do that."

"I can teach you. It's much simpler than teleporting." I waited. Would she tell me to run along? Not much I could do about it if she did.

She reached for another piece of bread. "All right. Let's get this plane off the ground."

My grin widened, but I resisted the urge to yip with delight. She hadn't said anything about me leaving. Maybe after we'd finished our sleuthing expedition, we could get a spot of sleep and then teleport back to Ireland...

One step at a time, mate, I cautioned myself.

"I'm waiting." She kicked her shoulders back. "How do I mask what I am?"

We stood at the fringe of the mob, joining in their hate chant at appropriate intervals. The young reporter was long gone. Smart of him because the crowd had grown ugly. Several men brandished clubs and what could have been automatic weapons. I never could tell the difference between the semi- and fully-automatic models, but then I'm not much of a purveyor of firearms. I've seen so much destruction caused by them—purposeful and accidental—they don't hold any allure.

I'd done my damnedest to encourage Liam to leave, but he blocked me—nicely—every time. I wasn't strong enough to strap on a set and order him back to Ireland. Or at least out of my house. The longer he stayed, the less inclined I was to boot him.

I liked him. Probably too much for my own good. The wisest course was no course at all, but a pathetic, little girl part of me had glommed onto his offer of help. I hadn't been lying about my plate having moved well beyond the full point. Problems bombarded me from every side, *Carrick Sky Sports* being the least of them. Vampires sat squarely at the top of the heap. Both the garden-variety type and their Sidhe cousins. Humans Rule were becoming problematic. If they kept growing like crabgrass, it was only a matter of time before they zeroed in on me.

Maybe not them, *per se*, but if a bunch of laws outlawing sorcery were passed, I'd be breaking them every single time a soul passed through me. Mortals had already developed primitive magic detectors, but in a free enterprise system, better ones would emerge.

Death would no doubt be pleased I'd prioritized her Vampire assignment over all the other shit facing me, but she'd never know. I sure as fuck wasn't about to tell her. She could have shunted Vampires to a bunch of us, but she'd chosen to wreck my life. Too bad I couldn't march up to her and quit.

Unfortunately, it didn't work that way.

I'd been shocked when Liam revealed a Sidhe version of Vamps. And pissed no one had bothered to check on their enforced confinement until it was too late, and they'd escaped. I was still absorbing his claim about the Marvel Comics dark gods being more than a product of some writer's imagination.

What else didn't I know? Clearly a whole hell of a lot.

Lake Union Marina was less than half a mile from my home, so we'd walked. Good thing. Traffic was backed up even on my street. If we'd tried to take my extra car—since my SUV was parked at *Carrick Sky Sports*—we'd never have found a parking spot. I was grateful for my leather flight jacket. The temperature hovered just above freezing, and an icy wind cut right through my wool pants.

The throng had grown far more raucous, compared with what we'd seen on my television. I'd expected Liam's glamor to take time to master, but it was simply a slight alteration in the mix of magics I carried. More of an inward facing spell that formed a protective bubble around my skills. One thing we couldn't do much about was my scent—the one that draws wandering souls.

Probably not much chance of running into anyone dead at the demonstration, and even if we did, no one else could see them, so I might get away with allowing them to pass through me. And then I remembered Death's prohibition on Reaping.

Easier said than done. The dead were drawn to me, but I was drawn to them in kind. I've mentioned I was born into Reaping; it's as natural as breathing. I can turn souls down, but it pains me to say no.

A man was walking our way. It didn't occur to me he was heading right for us until his path couldn't lead anywhere else. I studied him. About my height, he looked a bit like an accountant or a stockbroker with an impeccable charcoal tweed three-piece suit, glasses, and dark hair trimmed short. Clean-shaven, he had chilly dark eyes.

Liam was quicker on the uptake than me because he turned to face the man squarely and held out a hand. Touch was riskier than mortals simply laying eyes on us, but I bet the man wouldn't take Liam's extended hand.

I was right, he didn't.

"Who are the two of you?" he growled.

Liam lowered his arm. "Liam Hunter and Cait Carol. I run a talent search agency, *Liam's Lore*. You may have heard of it."

"Can't say as I have," the man continued in a low gravelly tone. "What are you doing here?"

"We want to help," I spoke up and offered a disarming smile.

"We hold membership drives. Show up at one of them so we can validate your names and credentials." He narrowed his eyes at Liam. "You're British."

"Actually, Irish," Liam cut in smoothly, "but I've lived here for many years."

"What's your name?" I asked pleasantly. "So we can list you as a reference when we come to a membership drive. When is the next one, by the way? And where? I might have a client, but I could switch things up if I had enough notice."

"I ask the questions," the man shot back.

"It's only your name, mate," Liam said. "Not as if it's a state secret. And you're who told us about those membership signup places. Why say anything if you didn't want us to go to the next one?"

An unusual vibration snagged the edges of my magic. I started to reach out—it was automatic—but caught myself. The glamour surrounded me, safe and snug, but if I punched through it, all bets were off.

Mr. No-Name's head snapped around. Whatever I'd sensed, he could feel it too. I wasn't sure what that meant since he was mortal and supposedly not particularly sensitive to paranormal emanations. What I'd felt had been pretty damned subtle.

"Where's the next membership signup?" I repeated my earlier question.

He turned his attention back toward me, but his eyes held a fuzzy, unfocused look. I missed my magic. Even the plain old non-enhanced Reaper variety would have been helpful. I wanted to know what was going on with him, what he'd sensed, but my primary weapon was muffled.

Liam gripped my hand. "Come on, darling. It's obvious he's not interested in adding us to his group."

"But you promised me we could be part of Humans Rule." I pouted. "It's why we walked all this way in the cold and dark and—"

A visible shudder passed through the man, but his gaze sharpened. It was like he'd snapped out of a trance—or a telepathic conversation with someone. But humans couldn't engage in mind speech. Did it mean the surly man wasn't human?

Yeah. I needed my magic.

"Our headquarters is down on the waterfront," he said. "Small building between the aquarium and Ivar's."

"Thank you," I cooed, laying it on thick. "All we need now is when to be there."

He slid a phone from his breast pocket, presumably consulting its calendar function, but I couldn't actually see what he was doing. "Next Wednesday night," he said. "Be there at seven and plan for an hour or two."

Liam frowned. "Afraid I've forgotten my phone, mate. But I'm almost certain I have an engagement at that time."

"I don't have my calendar, either." I jumped on the same bandwagon and smiled brightly. "Give us a couple of options. We'll make one of them work. Promise."

Breath rattled through the man's teeth; he dropped the phone back into his pocket. "Read the newspaper, people. We run ongoing ads."

"Gosh"—I did my best to look confused—"as in an actual paper newspaper? Is it in the online version?"

"Christ." He stared at me. "How old are you? Ten?"

I adopted a wounded expression. "Thirty-two, but no one reads newspapers anymore. It's why so many have gone out of business, and—"

Liam had never let go of my hand; his grip tightened. "Not now, dear. Let's get out of the man's way. I'm certain he has better things to do than entertain us."

After adding a few lumens to my smile, I gushed, "Thank you. So nice to meet you—" I inserted a pregnant pause.

"Gregory," he blurted, and then realized he'd fallen for the oldest trick in the book. Even in the feeble light from a nearby streetlight, I saw his cheeks redden before he turned away.

"How to make friends and influence people," Liam whispered in my ear. He tugged on my hand, and we moved away from the still-gathering crowd.

"Never mind that. Something is about to happen." I kept my voice low and my mouth glued to Liam's ear. The vibration I'd felt a little bit ago had intensified until my ears were buzzing, and my skin crawled with apprehension.

He nodded and picked up his pace, but we didn't head toward my houseboat. We traversed alleyways and circled around until we were tucked into shadows well behind the mob. I could probably have leveraged my brand new magic into telepathic speech, but all magic leaves traces. Opting for stealth, I hissed, "What are we doing?"

The feel of his power with its characteristic Sidhe scents of greenery tickled my nostrils. I wasn't certain if the sandalwood undernote was unique to Liam, but it mingled with the greens, creating a mildly astringent blend. He stopped at a wooden door with paint peeling off it and made short work of the lock.

The door creaked on long-unused hinges. As soon as it was open a few inches, I shouldered through it with Liam right behind me. The door swung shut on its own, almost as if it had resented its open state. A deserted shopfront spread before us. From the looks of things, it had once sold marine supplies and trinkets to tourists, but the shelves were mostly devoid of stock.

"How'd you know to pick here?" I asked, taking care to keep my voice very low.

He angled an amused glance in my direction. "Lucky guess."

I was certain it had to be more than that, but he was entitled to magical secrets. Instead of probing, I repeated my question from earlier. "What are we doing?"

"We need to be close enough to eavesdrop," he told me. His voice was so low I got what he was saying via a combination of my ears and lip-reading.

"You just deployed magic. Anyone with even a small sensitivity would have felt it if they were close enough. I think we should leave. Gregory will figure out quick enough we were lying when we don't show up front and center at Humans Rule HQ."

"Who says we're not going there?" Liam lifted a fair brow.

"Why would we? Christ, Liam. We need to focus on the Vampire problem. You haven't forgotten about them. Or have you?"

"What if they're connected?" He hooded his eyes and walked so close his shoulder brushed mine.

"Huh?" Confusion swirled around me.

"When our pal Greg seemed like he'd checked out, someone was talking with him. I'd have listened in, but—"

"I get it," I interrupted. "Same reason I didn't employ my own power." I chewed my lower lip. "I don't understand. Humans Rule is anti-magic. How come one of theirs is using power? For that fact"—I forged onward—"how can mortals utilize any type of magic at all?"

"All good questions. If we aren't discovered, maybe we'll ferret out an answer or two."

I grabbed a whisk broom and swept a clear spot next to one wall. Dust was thick, so this shop had been abandoned quite a while ago. Once I had a place to sit, I lowered myself to the floorboards.

"The odds are in our favor," I mumbled.

"What do you mean?" He folded to a sit next to me, his back supported by the wall.

I held up one finger and said, "I refuse to believe mortals have suddenly turned into a bunch of magical sensitives. If they can respond to paranormal emanations, I bet it's on a primitive level." I extended a second finger. "No one expects us to be here, so no one will be looking in our direction. Greg-baby watched us walk away."

"After you humiliated him," Liam said pointedly.

"No reason for him to be so damned protective of his name."

"Aye, there is. Names have power."

"They do," I agreed, "but only in the hands of those like us. He should have chalked you and me up as a couple with too much time on our hands looking for a little retribution." I clasped my hands in my lap. The shop was cold, and I wished I had a blanket. "Probably everyone who signs on with HR has a bone to pick with a supernatural."

"What if it runs deeper than that?"

"I don't understand."

"If Greg can intercept telepathy, someone must be handing out the promise of magical ability. We need to figure out who the someone is."

"You suspect the Vampires, don't you?"

"They're on the shortlist," Liam agreed. "Right along with the dark gods. Tantalus hasn't gotten his hands dirty since he butchered his son."

"Lovely visual." I shut my eyes for a long moment. When I opened them, I said, "I can understand the allure for Vampires. They trade a little magic in exchange for a food stable. What's in it for Perrikus and that gang?"

"Born troublemakers, and they crave attention. It's been in short supply for a long time."

"Yeah, huh? Since no one believes in them." I thought about it. "Guess they have every right to be angry."

A blast of familiar magic ran through me. "Aw shit." I dropped my head into my hands.

"What's wrong?" Alarm lined Liam's question, and he raised his hands, clearly intent on summoning magic even if it gave away our location.

Death shot through a portal. "What in the name of all the gods are you doing here? Why aren't you chasing down Vampires?" she demanded.

I considered getting to my feet, but it was too much trouble. "You told me to stand down Reaping anyone. Have we gotten to the point where we've dispensed with *hello* or *how are you* or *glad you figured out that teleport spell?*" I inquired acidly.

"You took my suggestion to Reap less far too literally, child," Death retorted.

"How was I supposed to interpret it when you said, 'Until we figure things out, no more Reaping'?"

Rather than answering, she hissed at me.

"Stop it, you two." Liam flowed to his feet and swung to face Death. "You may have just blown our cover." He sounded as friendly as a cornered alley cat. Nothing wrong with his energy, but I felt as if I'd been licking the bottom of an ashtray.

"What cover?" Death settled her hands on her hips.

I unclenched my jaw. Where to start? Another shot of power, this one dripping malevolence, saved me from untangling that Gordian knot.

"What in Hades name was that?" Death twirled toward the direction the disturbance had come from, arms extended and power arcing from her outstretched fingertips.

"You're making it worse," I said, reverting to our private telepathy channel. *"We were hiding, hoping to find out more about the Vampires and Humans Rule."*

"Why didn't you say so?"

"Never had a chance."

The rhythm and cadence of the power glistening around Death changed until the feel of her magic surrounded Liam and me. It was an invisibility casting. I recognized that part, but was it absolute, or did it bleed power the same way a bitch in heat sheds blood?

Dark enchantment passed through the shop again, stopping from time to time. I held myself still, barely breathing, as I willed it to see nothing, find nothing. It had a slimy feel that made me wish for bleach and a scalding bath.

Finally, after a last sweep that lasted longer than I liked, it vanished as quickly as it had come. Despite the cold, a fine sheen of sweat beaded my forehead. More dripped down my sides.

"Can we be done spying for tonight?" I asked.

Death narrowed her eyes. Power already surrounded us, courtesy of her spell. "Take her home," she told Liam. "I'll be along presently."

"What will you be doing?" I lurched to an upright position before I remembered she and I didn't have one of those two-way relationships. The kind where I could ask questions and have any hope of her answering them.

"Clearing this spot so no remnant of us or our power remains. Now go."

Liam's magic encircled me, displacing hers. So exhausted even breathing felt beyond me, I didn't insist I could craft my own transport spell. Absent employing magic, I could have walked—if the night didn't hold Vampires. Something about the wicked, probing spell had Vampire laced into, over, and through it.

A couple of minutes later, my living room formed around us. I sank to the floor, too wiped out to trust my shaky knees.

"Damn it, Cait," Liam demanded. "Why didn't you say something?"

"About?" I tried to wrap a few shreds of dignity around my question.

"Being done in."

"Used to it," I mumbled. My eyes flickered shut. I pried them open with more effort than such a simple activity should have required.

Death popped into view and shook her head. "I can't leave you alone for an hour. If you're not flying airplanes, you're involved in some hare-brained scheme to sabotage Humans Rule."

"Wasn't hare-brained." I slurred my words and slithered until my back rested against the bottom part of the couch.

"We were quite safe," Liam confirmed. "Until you came along. You command a vast spectrum of power."

A satisfied smile bloomed on Death's face. "I do, don't I? Regardless, no one will discover your hiding spot. Tell me why you were there. Don't dress it up."

Liam did a decent job synopsizing his suspicions about the Vamps and Humans Rule. He didn't tell Death about his plan to infiltrate HR, but perhaps she plucked it out of his head. She's a wizard when it comes to mindreading. I gave up keeping anything private during Reaper school.

"Mmph. Interesting," she said after he was done talking. And then she turned to me. "You cannot tell any of the other Reapers."

"About how to access more Earth-bound power?" At her terse nod, I said, "I won't, but only because it's your job."

She shook her head back and forth emphatically. "Been there. Tried that. Didn't work very well."

I rested an elbow on my crossed legs and supported my chin with a hand. "How long ago was that?"

"Hard to say, child. Maybe a millennium."

"The world has changed. A lot. It might work better a second time."

"Why risk it?" Death turned her hands palms up. "I have a system in place that works."

"Does it?" Liam tossed out. "Seems to me you'll need access to all the magic you can round up. If I'm right, and the Vampires are sharing magic with mortals, they've created the equivalent of an army. And that's without the addition of Perrikus and his merry band."

"Unless the Vampires kill those mortals, my purview is limited." Death stared Liam down.

"How dead do they have to be?" Liam countered.

"You're talking in riddles, Sidhe," she retorted.

"For Vampires to infuse magic into mortals, they must be sharing blood. Once a human drinks from a Vampire, they enter the world of the Undead. Seems to me, they'd fall under your aegis at that point."

Death tapped her foot, forehead creased in concentration. "Maybe so. I must consult with Hades and Arawn."

"If they agree with my assessment," Liam pressed, "does it mean you'll unleash your Reapers' power?"

"Some won't want it," Death said with such certainty, I didn't doubt her.

"At least then it will be their choice," I mumbled. Waves of weariness crashed over me. "I have to sleep," I told them and gave up the battle with my drifting eyelids.

The murmur of their voices rose and fell, but I didn't bother figuring out what they were saying. Mostly, I wanted them to shut up so I could have a little peace.

I must have drifted off because the next thing I noticed was Liam lifting me in his arms. He carried me down the hallway and placed me gently on my bed. When he touched my forehead, currents of peace rolled through me.

"Sleep, darling," he murmured. "I'll keep watch."

I started to tell him there was no need. We'd warded the house, and he could go back to Ireland, but my mouth refused to form the words. Telepathy wouldn't rise to my call, either.

It killed me to admit it, mostly because I've always been the original Ms. Independent, but maybe it was good he was staying. The shape I was in, I'd be vulnerable to anything that slithered through my wards. By the time I recognized I was under attack, it would be too late to mount any kind of defense.

My mind was such a confused mess, I was surprised it relinquished its grip on consciousness. The descent into nothingness was fast and absolute. I owed Liam for tonight, and a plate of home-baked cookies wouldn't be nearly enough to discharge the debt.

CHAPTER TWELVE, LIAM

Once I was certain Cait was well and truly asleep, I walked softly out of her bedroom and made my way to the kitchen. It took me a while to find where she kept her skillets, but I made myself a toasted cheese sandwich—two of them, actually—and rustled through the cold box until I found a beer.

Keeping a thread of magic tuned to the hallway—in case Cait woke sooner than I anticipated—I settled at a small table and ate my way down to the ceramic plate I'd filched from the sink and washed. In truth, I was grateful for this small spot of time. I had to figure out which path would be most expedient.

I could return to the Old Country, gather a cadre of Sidhe, and hunt down the Leanan. It wouldn't take long. We're absolute bloodhounds at locating our own once we set our minds to it. But if I did that, it meant leaving Cait alone. I could ask her to come with me, but the other Sidhe would never accept her as part of a warrior band.

So she'd end up hanging around my house. Wandering the village or surrounding countryside on her own had proven to be unsafe. Vampires would attempt to lure her again. Having been trounced a few times, they might resort to clonking her over the head and dragging her somewhere escape might be difficult.

She could make decent use of a spot of downtime honing her magic, courtesy of my spellbooks and suchlike, but she'd chafe at being excluded. The Sidhe are an insular lot. Despite it not being totally accurate, we pride ourselves on our position at the top of the magical heap.

Many, many magic-wielders are more powerful than we are. Blended magic supersedes everything, but it presumes being willing to work with other wizards and sorcerers and witches. We've never been thrilled about sharing anything, and our snobbery was about to come back and slap us silly. We'd be eating humble pie for a long time after the truth about the Leanan-Sidhe leaked out.

And it would.

The magical world didn't agree on much, but one absolute was that each type of sorcery was responsible for controlling its own. We'd failed with the Leanan. If we hadn't been such elitists, someone might have noticed they'd bolted.

I slapped the plate with my hand, an absentminded gesture that reminded me I'd eaten everything. I was still hungry, but dawn was breaking. Once Cait woke, we'd go out for a meal.

"What will it be?" I murmured. "Go or stay?"

Once I cut through everything, those were the two options. I could remain here and work with Cait. Or return to Ireland by myself. I wouldn't subject her to my kinsmen. Hollis was the worst of us, but many others weren't far behind him with their arrogant attitudes.

Perhaps Death was right, and we'd lived behind veils too long.

A healthy dose of reality might be good for us, but to do that, we'd have to drop our illusion and become part of the flow of civilization in Northern Ireland—and elsewhere. The more I thought about it, the deeper my realization spread. Integration with mortals was no longer an option, a luxury. Nay. It had become a necessity. One of the reasons Humans Rule had done such a bang up job fanning the flames of bigotry in our direction was because we'd remained partially hidden, retreating to our hidey holes at the first sign of trouble.

Tough to stand up for yourself when you're invisible.

I dragged a hand down my face, feeling like I'd stumbled onto something we should have realized several hundred years ago. If we hadn't tucked our tails between our legs and faded from sight when the scientific revolution first hit and then exploded, mortals wouldn't have developed such a healthy distrust of us.

Magic-wielders had missed the boat not once, but several times. The initial burst of enthusiasm for all things science had ended in the middle of the seventeenth century, displaced by the Age of Enlightenment. Mankind were like children with new toys. The more they gloried in science, the deeper the wedge between them and us grew.

We looked down our magical noses at what we viewed as a pathetic effort on the part of mankind. They were better off when they'd allowed magic into their lives. We were certainly superior healers, better at damn near everything that didn't involve iron.

Aye. Iron.

Another reason we'd faded from view. None of us except witches could stand the stuff. It played hell with our magical ability. Once modern smelting methods evolved, the use of iron proliferated until the air was permeated with its nasty stench.

I narrowed my eyes in thought. I was still certain I was onto something important with us finding a way to reintegrate ourselves into mortal society. It might not be as straightforward as I'd envisioned, though.

I drained the last of my beer. A rather insipid brew by Irish standards, but drinkable. Better than the one I'd had at *The Tailwind*. It had truly been rotgut.

Daylight streamed through the houseboat's many windows. Apparently, I'd been sitting far longer than I thought. Pushing to my feet, I walked back toward Cait's bedroom to see how she was doing. Careful not to disturb her, I stopped in the doorway and drank her in.

She'd turned onto her side, dark hair fanned around her like a cloud. Her mouth was partly open, and the soft sound of her breathing filled the small space. She still wore her leather coat. I should have pried it off her and tucked the blankets around her shoulders.

She'd wanted me to go. I'd plucked the thought from her mind, but she'd been too knackered for me to leave her by herself. Her jacket had been the least of my concerns when I'd spelled her to sleep. Not that she wouldn't have found her own way there, but my method was faster.

And it had spared us the conversation where she pushed me out of her home. If she had, I'd have remained nearby. She was a proud woman and independent as they came. Knowing I was watching over her wouldn't sit well, mostly because she didn't view herself in need of rescuing.

Maybe I wasn't offering her enough credit in the self-sufficiency department. She'd managed a long journey spell her first try—with zero assistance. Protecting women was hardwired into me, though. And Cait wasn't just any woman...

Best not to go there.

She stirred and rolled onto her back. "I'm not going to turn into foam on the sea if you take your eyes off me," she murmured and tucked her hands beneath her head, elbows akimbo.

I covered the space to the bed intent on spelling her back to sleep. "Rest," I murmured. "Not time to get up yet." Compulsion threaded into my suggestion, but it didn't work with her.

She opened her green eyes. "It's daytime. I'm good. I've slept long enough. Were you standing in the doorway the whole time?"

I laughed. "Oh hell no. I made myself something to eat and drank one of your beers."

"Good. Glad you made yourself at home." She pushed

higher, leaning against the wooden headboard. "I'm going to clean up, put on fresh clothes, and then we need to have a chat."

A chat, huh? What did she mean by that? Was this when she patted my hand, thanked me, and told me she'd maybe see me in a few weeks?

Sidestepping the chat topic, I asked, "Are you hungry?"

A smile began in her eyes and found its way to her full mouth. "Ravenous. You're a phenomenal cook, but I don't have much in the way of ingredients."

"I'll find us something out there." I jerked my chin in the direction of the houseboat's outer wall.

"There's a good breakfast place a couple blocks north of here on Count Street," she told me. "They do takeout. I often stop there on my way to the airfield."

My next words were a cheap shot, totally pathetic, but I glommed onto her mention of the airfield. "Could you take me flying sometime?" I held my breath. She had to see right through my gambit, recognize it for a bald-faced attempt to remain by her side.

She frowned until twin furrows cut at right angles to her brows. "Sure. Any excuse to take a plane up, but don't we have bigger fish to fry?"

I've always been a master at masking my emotions, and I blessed my long years of practice with bland expressions. "We do, but maybe next time we end up at the airfield...?" I left it open-ended.

"Why the attraction? You teleport."

"Aye, but it's totally different. I can't see anything between my departure and destination sites."

Her generous mouth curved into a smile. "Flying is like nothing else. The moment when the wheels leave the ground and air catches the wings leaves me breathless every single time.

I smiled back, wanting to leave her breathless—every single time—but for far different reasons. Warmth flooded my groin, and my cock began to thicken. Before it got totally out of control—and tented the front of my trousers—I turned to leave.

"Back in a bit with breakfast. Any preferences?"

"Surprise me. Oh, and don't bother with coffee. I'll put on a pot. Do you have U.S. money?" she called after me.

"Nay, but I have plastic. Works everywhere."

I chinked a hole in the ward and let myself out the front door. Luckily, a deeply recessed porch stretched a couple of meters, masking my movements as I patched the protections surrounding Cait's houseboat. I put more effort into it than my usual "good enough" standards.

When I could no longer sense her energy within, I decided I'd done the best I could. A quick jaunt along the porch and up the slanting gangway deposited me on a busy street. Probably normal morning traffic glut, but it hadn't looked all that different last night when we'd walked to the marina.

Wasn't likely I'd run into anyone who might recognize me from the previous evening, but just in case I crafted a quick glamour. Nothing elaborate, only a slight alteration to soften the planes of my face and make me appear shorter and more rotund. Lacking a mirror to check the result, I assumed I'd done a decent job and strode north in search of Court Street.

I will say one thing for most American cities. They overdo the whole street names thing. Signs are obvious and easy to read.

Many spots in Europe and the UK travel incognito. You couldn't locate a street sign if you tried. Even magic doesn't do the trick. Either you're familiar with a neighborhood—or not. Maps help, but even they're not absolute. The morning was lovely. Crisp and clear with a sun that flirted with fluffy white clouds. Another thing about living in Ireland—or anywhere in the UK—is I truly appreciate sunlight. Because I don't see it very often.

Everywhere I looked, people had their heads buried in phones or tablets. I avoided rolling my eyes. No need for such accoutrements in the Sidhe compound. So far, I'd avoided the electronic blitz, but if I remained here for long, I'd have to cave in and purchase something. Still determined to infiltrate Humans Rule, I assumed someone would want my phone number. It would be a huge red flag if I said I didn't own a phone.

Even the homeless had cell phones.

A sign proclaiming Court Street flashed by in my peripheral vision. I backtracked and glanced the length of it on both sides of my cross street. Which way to go? Food smells wafted from myriad places. Cait hadn't exactly given me the name of her favored café. Nor had I asked, more's the pity.

A vague sense of discomfort pricked me; I shook it off. Both sides of Court Street bustled with activity. Even if something sinister was examining me, no one would be so bold as to strike in the midst of a busy morning.

Thoughts of Cait alone in her houseboat catapulted me into action. I'd get us breakfast from the first promising spot. Hopefully, the service would be snappy. Adopting a brisk pace, I crossed with the blessing of a green light and angled down Court Street assessing potential eateries on both sides of the thoroughfare.

It's amazing what I can accomplish without magic. I discarded several possibilities because of stale grease smells, but one tiny spot across the way caught my attention. Flower boxes in the windows added splashes of brightness. Not bothering with returning to the corner, I wove between honking cars to get to the *Daily Grind*.

After a quick look at the posted menu, I ducked inside and ordered two omelets with everything. To go.

"Coffee, sir?" a frazzled black-haired waitress asked.

"Nay. Just the entrees, please."

She smiled. It lighted her expression, made her appear almost youthful again. "You're from England."

Not invested in correcting her—she looked as if her life was hard enough—I nodded pleasantly and handed over a credit card, making certain my hand brushed hers. A spark of healing magic flared, visible only to me. I hoped it was enough to knock a few years off, make her feel better than she did.

She bent over a machine and ran my card, handing me something to sign. I had to think for a moment to recall the name on that particular piece of plastic. It was my usual alias: Liam Hunter. I made certain to add a generous gratuity.

"You're number 651," she told me. "We'll call you to the counter when your order is ready."

"Thank you." I settled into a chair beneath the front window. Didn't take more than five minutes before I heard 651 and trotted to collect our breakfast. Food in hand, I left the *Daily Grind* and started along Court Street. Another fifteen minutes, and I'd be back in the houseboat.

So far, I'd avoided calling up images of Cait in the shower or dressing for the day. They'd only get me in trouble. I'd discovered how weak I was when it came to her the other night. Had she gotten caught up in the sexual heat rolling off me? I'd be embarrassed if she'd figured things out, but it wasn't likely. She'd been asleep.

The unpleasant prickly feeling I'd felt earlier returned with a vengeance. No longer vague, it had moved up the scale until it commanded my full attention. I ducked into a nearby doorway. It belonged to a bookstore that wasn't open yet. Needing my hands for defense, I plopped the bag on a window ledge and cracked my magic open a teensy bit.

Surely, the miniscule amount of magic I'd gifted the waitress wouldn't have attracted anyone's attention. Something was up, though. Whatever this was, it was heading right for me. My Earth-eyes were useless, so I jettisoned subtle and threw my magic wide open. My psychic view illuminated Sidhe, Leanan-Sidhe. I recognized each one. Ha. Meant I didn't have to track them down since they'd found me.

I wasn't laboring under any illusions, though. I'd never be able to herd them back to their subterranean holding cell by myself, and help was an ocean away.

Why did their magic have such a rotten, decayed quality to it?

They hadn't felt this way when I'd locked them up.

Court Street was still full of unsuspecting humans. The Leanan didn't have me in their gunsights to invite me to tea. Whatever unfolded wouldn't be pretty. I suppose I should have worried about being outnumbered, but it never occurred to me. I'm Sidhe royalty. No matter how bad things got, they couldn't touch me. My power would always outstrip theirs by a comfortable margin. If not for Cait, I'd have teleported a long way away, but I couldn't leave her in the middle of what was shaping up to be a first class mess.

A series of overlapping liminal spaces span Earth. Leaving the breakfast bag behind, I teleported to a nearby one to move the confrontation away from all those hapless mortals.

By the time my erstwhile kin punched through, I was as ready as I could be.

"You've led us on a merry chase," Burke growled, but he stopped a few meters from me.

Good. He still recognized he owed me fealty and respect.

Conan and the others flanked Burke on both sides. Five of them. Where were the rest? I didn't recall the exact number we'd tucked away, but it wasn't important.

"Why have you joined forces with mortal Vampires?" I cut to the chase. I wasn't strong enough to bring this bunch in, but I could gather information.

Burke shrugged. Like the others, he had a ragged appearance. Things such as bathing seemed to have gone the way of the Dodo bird. Black hair straggled around his unshaven face. Bits of dried blood dotted his mouth. The lot of them wore faded dungarees topped by a variety of dirt-crusted shirts. No wonder they stank.

"You didn't want us, and they did." Burke shrugged.

All right. One question down. "Are you who taught them how to defeat sunlight?"

"Who else?" Conan sounded pleased with himself. His fair good looks were in just as bad a shape as Burke's darker ones.

"What's the link between you and Humans Rule?" I draped a truth net over all of them and waited.

"You always were too bright for your own good." Burke skinned his lips back from his teeth.

"We traded," Timothy smirked. I angled my gaze his way. Brown curls had once given him an altar-boy patina. No more.

"A wee bit of minor magic in exchange for food," Burke said.

"Handy to have blood when we need it." Timothy tried to smile but it came out more pitiful than anything else.

Part of me was suspicious. Why were they answering my questions so readily? I'd expected them to put up way more of a fight. "Any specific reason you were hunting for me?" I let my gaze rest on one of the fallen Sidhe after another.

And didn't dismantle my truth net.

No one said a word. They couldn't lie, but they could remain silent.

I turned my hands palms upward. "Fine. I'm leaving. You're welcome back into the fold. You always were, but you must agree to purification."

"The ritual to strip us of being Vampires?" Burke snarled again.

I nodded. "Same proposal you refused seven centuries ago. It still stands. You're still Sidhe."

Would three-quarters of a millennium of being either imprisoned or on the run make a difference? I rather doubted it, but I'd felt compelled to make the offer.

No more need to waste magic on my truth spell, so I reeled it in.

The same odd power that had snagged my attention unfolded almost lazily. A Sidhe to Burke's right liquified as magic danced around him. What the unholy hell? I raised my hands and summoned lethal magic, letting it arc back and forth between my hands.

If the Sidhe hadn't been William, who was he? We command a lot of magic, but shapeshifting has never been on the menu. If the construct I'd thought was William could change form, it had never been him at all.

A tall, beautiful man stepped out of the mist that had blown in when the faux Sidhe opted to reveal himself. Long hair so black it had a bluish cast was braided close against a finely-boned head. Clear coppery eyes shone out of a perfect face with chiseled features. He wore hunting leathers that encased his muscled shoulders and slim hips like a glove.

Crap. No wonder the Sidhe had been so accommodating. This was a trap.

I eyed the newcomer. "D'Chel," I presume.

"The same." He mock bowed. "You're coming with us."

"I think not." Loosing the power I'd been hoarding, I aimed right for his perfect face. Except he wasn't there anymore. My magic shot by the spot he'd occupied, igniting a clump of bushes.

He shifted to a field mouse and then back to a man with a few other forms in between that flashed by so quickly I couldn't identify them. "Save your magic, Sidhe," he hissed.

"Excellent advice," I purred to distract him as I quietly built a teleport spell. I was confident the Leanan couldn't stop me, but the dark gods had a different brand of magic altogether. A blend of Celtic and Norse strains so old no one understood it well.

A lack I'd do my damnedest to correct. Once I got myself out of this predicament.

"We have plans for you," D'Chel informed me. "And your girlfriend. The one who tricked all those poor Vampires."

"Really? Do tell? Poor Vampires, my ass." My spell was almost there. Almost. I had to make certain of it before I loosed it. There'd be a couple of seconds when D'Chel could dismantle my efforts—if he intuited my intent.

"Why, you'll join the Leanan. They've missed their prince, haven't you all?" D'Chel showed a mouthful of teeth at Burke and the others.

"Not exactly," Conan muttered.

"And my girlfriend?" I pressed. "Except she really isn't. Not being Sidhe and all."

D'Chel shrugged eloquently. "Depends if she behaves herself."

"Eh, she can be a mouthy one. What's in it for me?" I displayed my teeth as well. Two could play that game.

Topped out and ready, my spell took off. Screams buffeted me as I teleported the fuck out of there. Searing heat tracked down one leg. Goddamn D'Chel and his illusions. Something with claws had found enough of my molecules to leave a mark.

I'd selected the Quonset hut as my destination. Closer than Ireland by a good big bunch, but not a direct threat to Cait if D'Chel managed to follow me. I have to visualize something to feed it into a teleport spell. So far, the only places I knew in Seattle were near the houseboat and *Carrick Sky Sports*. I wouldn't be able to remain at Cait's office very long, but I could communicate with her and let her know she and I would be leaving.

As soon as I popped into her houseboat, I was taking us back to Ireland.

She might not want to go, but too bad.

The danger was real, and it was out to get us both.

My spell tracked true, and the walls of the Quonset hut formed around me. I hoped the protections I'd built to keep D'Chel from following had held. Blood sheeted down the side of my right leg, and I eyed my shredded trousers. In the interest of preserving my magic, I headed for a first aid kit attached to one wall and dragged out a bottle of disinfectant.

After I'd done what I could to treat the wound—not much I could do for my ruined trousers—it occurred to me that D'Chel had my blood. Meant he could track me with almost 100 percent accuracy.

Maybe dragging Cait back to Ireland wasn't the best plan, but she had a target painted on her back too. I tapped into telepathy channels. *"Cait?"*

"Where the fuck are you?" Worry seeped through even in mind speech.

"*Your office. I'm teleporting to the houseboat, and then we have to leave. I understand you won't want to join me, but the safest place for us is in the Old Country.*"

Silence stretched until I expected her to tell me to go fuck myself.

"*If it's that dangerous, don't come back here for me,*" she said firmly. "*I'll meet you in Ireland.*"

The connection went dead. I had to trust her, but not shielding her with my magic grated. After a glance at my healing leg, I visualized my home in the Sidhe compound and loosed another journey spell.

Cait wouldn't have lied about meeting me in Ireland. She wasn't the lying type. If she didn't show, and damned soon, I'd rustle up Death—and more Sidhe. Somewhere in betwixt and between, I'd find out everything I could about the dark gods and their magic.

I'd escaped by the skin of my teeth. D'Chel may have lost this round, but he'd be much sharper next time. And there would be a next time. The bastard had my blood.

CHAPTER THIRTEEN, CAIT

_I_'d been half out of my mind with worry when Liam's telepathy reached me. He'd been gone for the better part of two hours, way longer than a simple fetch-breakfast jaunt should have taken. I actually had my coat on, ready to go hunt for him when his strained voice reached me.

What the hell was he doing at _Carrick Sky Sports_?

Now wasn't a time for questions, but something must have gone horribly wrong. He was returning us to the safest place he knew: the Sidhe stronghold, but I didn't see any reason for him to detour to grab me. My first teleport spell had had a few rough spots I hadn't bothered to tell either him or Death about, but I understood what I'd done wrong.

I slung my shoulder bag across my chest and shut my eyes intent on avoiding a repeat of the mishaps when I'd summoned my initial journey spell. Liam had sounded damned worried—a significant departure from his usual unflappable demeanor—but I couldn't focus on that. If I did, my teleport effort would turn to shit.

I had to make this work.

Liam would bend the world into a pretzel hunting for me if I didn't show up in his home soon, so I spoke out loud as I constructed my spell, waiting until the last minute to pull down the wards around my houseboat. I had a feeling I couldn't teleport through them, and I didn't want to have to start over from scratch if the casting boomeranged back in my face.

My confidence in a cockpit was absolute. Not so much with my newly unearthed magic.

Shouts of, "She is too in there. Told you," faded right along with me as my spell propelled me through a time-space weave. Could whoever was doing the shouting follow me?

I had no idea.

Gah. Would they tumble out on my heels? If that happened, what would I do? I was a Reaper, not a warrior. Every one of my tricks to force Vampires across the veil required planning. Lots of it since I had to set snares at intervals. When one tripped, it sent the Vamp squarely into the center of the next one. My complicated strings of booby traps were one more reason why I'd been so short on sleep. I'd spent big portions of each day planning for the coming night.

The edges of my channel—or whatever the fuck it was— started to unravel. Damn! Damn! Damn! Magic was a relentless taskmaster. This casting required my absolute concentration, or who knew where I'd end up. I clutched my bag closer to my body for comfort.

At least I had a passport.

I rolled my mental eyes. If my second teleport attempt slewed sideways, I'd be lucky to end up somewhere that even recognized legal travel documents. One spot to my right did worse than unravel. A hole developed in its weave. Pinhole-sized at first, it was developing a life of its own. I slapped my hand over it.

"Believe," I told myself sternly.

Visualization and belief in outcomes were the cornerstone of everything magical. I knew this, but I'd let fear get the better of me. My heart was thumping like a tripwire. Breath steamed through my open mouth as I forced more air into my lungs.

I got a grip on my teleport spell. If I focused on how spun out I was, the spell would shatter around me. I repeated the last two steps, the ones where I held a clear image of my destination, and urged my mix of 90 percent earth and 10 percent air to take me there. Power crackled around the palm I'd covered the hole with. It burned, but I didn't remove my hand.

I reached deep within me, kept magic flowing.

It seemed like forever passed before my efforts bore fruit, but it probably wasn't much more than a couple of minutes. The waves of searing pain shooting through my hand backed off. I blinked hard and stared at the places that had begun to come apart. They were intact once again.

Excellent. I could celebrate later. If I got to Ireland.

"When I get to Ireland," I corrected myself, still talking out loud.

Since the spell had canted back onto its proper track, I worked on my breathing. I'd made a series of neophyte mistakes, traps I hadn't fallen into since I was a child and the dead circled me so thickly I panicked. Instead of telling them to form a line and use me one at a time, I'd dissolved into a puddle of shrieks.

Death had swooped in—back in those days, she'd favored black capes and looked like a goddamned bat—and marshaled the dead into better order. But then, she'd dragged me to my feet and stood by my side. Together, we'd offered a gateway.

Once we were alone, she'd squatted in front of me and put her hands on my shoulders. "It's not usually this bad, child," she'd said, "but a plague is sweeping through the land. Hundreds are dead with more coming."

I'd nodded solemnly.

"We are gatekeepers," Death had continued. "It means we hold the gates to the nether world. The dead can access them one at a time. Sometimes it takes many hours or days before everyone passes through."

"What happens once they've gone beyond us?" I'd asked.

"Not our problem." Death had dusted her hands together. "Make no promises. The destinies of the dead are out of our hands." She'd paused, perhaps for emphasis, and repeated the bit about us being gatekeepers.

Because I'd thought about something besides how terrified I was, my heart had slowed somewhat, and I'd stopped gasping for breath. When I'd vaulted out of Liam's home during my first teleport attempt, I'd been driven by determination. How bad could it be? Others teleported without a second thought.

I'd missed a few critical steps. Oh I'd read them, right enough, but assumed I could hit the high points and make things work for me. I'd cobbled plenty of near-misses together in the air. Never had a plane crash on me. Not even one, but I'd had my fair share of close calls.

Riding on hubris, I'd skittered out of Liam's second floor not knowing what to expect.

My initial attempt had plunked me down in the lush fields outside of Carlisle, a smallish town in northern England. The spell had barely gotten rolling before it ejected me squarely atop the spot I'd been born. Of course the cottage wasn't there any longer. Nothing remained but a few of the foundation stones.

Before I could pick myself up and give teleporting another go, two spirits shot toward me as if they'd been launched from a canon. I'd opened my grave-vision to see them better, and the half-light of the realm of the dead pulsed softly. Intent on flowing through me, the ghosts hadn't bother with words. I understood why. They wore clothing from hundreds of years ago, except it hung off them in tatters.

The stench of rot and the grave clung to the couple.

"Where have you been all this time?" I asked and got to my feet.

The man had looked at me through haunted eyes. I felt a familiar psychic alteration as he stepped through me. Clearly, he and the woman who followed right behind him had been waiting for a Reaper for centuries. The sense where I was straddling two worlds faded, and I shook myself from head to toe.

My vision had snapped back to normal.

Too late, I'd remembered my reservations about examining ghosts carefully before serving as a portal. Hell, I couldn't have held these two off if I'd wanted. Their passage through me hadn't done any harm. Before any more errant spirits homed in on me, I'd started from bedrock and rebuilt the teleport spell from memory.

Step by step. No more skipped ones.

This time, it had worked, and I ended up at home.

Remembering my earlier success had a stabilizing effect. I pushed one picture after the next of Liam's flat into the spell. Finally, after it seemed forever had passed—but it couldn't have been more than a quarter hour—the edges of my casting took on a silvery glow.

Breath caught in my chest. Win, lose, or draw, I was almost somewhere.

"No," I said in stern tones, "I'm almost at Liam's, and then I can find out what happened to him."

Maybe concentrating on him rather than my doubts did the trick because the walls of his living room shimmered around me. The fine points of making grand entrances have never been important to me, but I'd have to figure out how to manage so I didn't plop down like a rag dolly tossed from the top of a building.

"Oomph." I hit hard enough to push the air from my lungs before rolling to my hands and knees.

"Thank all the gods you're safe." Liam hooked an arm around my waist.

"Been here for a while?" I tried for jaunty, but jaunty is hard to pull off from a sprawled position.

"A few minutes." He hauled me upright and raked me from head to toe with his gaze. Today, his eyes shone more golden than green.

Extricating myself from his grip, I tugged the strap of my bag over my head and set it on a nearby chair. "What happened?"

"The Leanan-Sidhe showed up. I could have dealt with them—if one hadn't been D'Chel adopting one of his endless disguises."

I thought back to Liam's description of the various dark gods. "D'Chel, huh? He's the one who can manipulate how he appears?"

"Aye, he shapeshifts. Unlike other shifters, his transitions are fast and apparently effortless. Regardless, he's intent on turning me to his purposes. And now he has my blood."

I fell back a pace. "Awk. Did they turn you?" I blurted.

Liam held up his hands. "Nay, nothing like that. Christ, lass, have a wee bit of faith in me." He plucked a shredded pair of blood-streaked trousers from where they'd been puddled on the floor. I glanced from them to the spotless pair he'd apparently changed into.

My eyes widened. "Damn it, Liam. What does your leg look like?" I started forward, intent on assessing what had to be a serious wound.

"It's fine. I'm fine. I dumped half a bottle of disinfectant from your first aid kit on it, along with a dollop of healing magic. My injury isn't important. D'Chel turned into something with claws. He wasn't aiming for anything beyond a hearty sample of my blood."

"He can track you now, right?" A shudder crawled down my back. I glanced around the room half expecting the dark gods to seep through the walls like Vamps had in my shop.

"Aye. But they want you too. You've pissed off more than a few Vampires."

"Goes with the territory," I muttered and narrowed my eyes. Wisps of evil buffeted me, turning my blood to ice. My imagination was probably working overtime, and everything made me jumpy. Adopting a casual tone, I murmured, "What was that? I thought I felt something."

Liam's head snapped up; his nostrils flared as he scented the air. With zero warning, he closed a hand around my wrist and dragged me toward the door.

"Let go." I struggled against his grip, but I may as well have been attached to a building.

"You didn't mask your journey path." He yanked the door open and pulled me through.

Fuck. I'd been afraid of that. But I'd been at Liam's for a few minutes. Surely, if whoever had been outside the houseboat had been on top of things, they'd be here by now.

"How can you know?" I'd stopped fighting him. Together we sprinted across the narrow cobblestone byway.

Liam laid a hand across a locking mechanism, and a heavy wooden door sprang open, swooshing shut the moment we were through. Not bothering with telepathy, he shouted in Gaelic. "To arms. We are under attack."

We passed through halls and up staircases. Each had

imposing wooden doors that sealed behind us. Was the structure sentient, magical? Did it know what to do to guard its occupants?

Nothing was beyond the reach of possibility.

By the time we'd reached the large room where I'd been once before, the one that looked as if it had held jury trials back in the day, the chamber teemed with Sidhe.

A man with worried-looking dark eyes and red-gold hair hurried to Liam. "Tell us what we face." Khaki pants covered his legs, and he'd donned a pale blue linen shirt topped by a silvery hauberk that looked as if it were woven of stuff right out of *The Hobbit*.

"I had a run-in with the Leanan-Sidhe," Liam replied.

"Convenient," someone shouted.

"Aye, means we don't have to hunt them down," another agreed.

I scanned the crowded room. At least fifty Sidhe had rallied to Liam's call. Men and women, they were garbed in everything from jeans and sweatshirts to armor tossed over god only knows what.

"We still have to search for the Leanan," Liam corrected the speaker. "I wasn't strong enough by myself to do more than solicit information. They're truly in league with Earth's Vampires. And the dark gods. Beyond those alliances, the Leanan have done a spot of trading."

"Aye, and what might that be?" someone called out.

"All the Vampires have been dangling magic, trading it for a ready supply of blood from the Humans Rule crowd," Liam replied.

My mouth gaped. I closed it with a clack. Liam's

suspicions had been spot on. I'd been an idiot to discount them the other night. "So Humans Rule truly is a front?" I choked out the words. "A smokescreen to hide their alliance with Vampires."

"Appears so," Liam said in grim tones. "It gets worse, though. I'm afraid D'Chel got a taste of my blood."

"Is his fell magic what I sense without?" the man with red-gold hair asked.

"Aye. Him or another of the dark gods. Probably more than one of them. Does anyone recall the warp and weave of their magic?" Liam's sharp gaze scanned the crowd.

"How in Danu's name did they locate us?" a Sidhe yelled from somewhere near the back of the room.

Liam opened his mouth. Before he could cover for me and tell his kin it must have been his blood, I swallowed hard and took a step forward. "I'm afraid it was me. Apologies. I'm a Reaper. Teleport magic wasn't part of my repertoire until quite recently."

A woman strode forward and said, "It's all right, Reaper. You had no way of knowing. We're relatively safe for the moment since they can't get inside." Gorgeous like all the Sidhe, she had dark skin, flashing black eyes, and a regal bearing. Swathed in leather and armor, she could have been a Medieval huntress. Black hair formed tight curls, falling almost to knee level. Her attention skewered me, made me stand straighter.

"I am Dena." She never took her gaze from me.

"Cait." I nodded, offering my name in return.

A barrage of names from every corner of the room

washed over me. I'd never remember a quarter of them. The Sidhe with red-gold hair was Krin, though.

"I understand they can't get inside," Liam told Dena, "but it's not our way to huddle behind magical gates like a bunch of old women. What do any of you recall about how their magic works?"

"It's all different." A wizened Sidhe stepped out of a shadowed alcove. I did a double take. I'd believed them impervious to the ravages of time, yet this man was bent over and supported himself with the assistance of an intricately carved walking stick. Wisps of white hair were scattered over his mostly bald head. Despite his obvious age, his blue eyes retained a shrewd brilliance.

Liam hurried forward and sank to one knee. "Nemed, leader of the Third Race."

"Och, get up. We haven't time for such things."

My body tingled with the familiar transition where I had one foot in this world and one in the world of the dead. My eyes took on the half-light of graves and spirits. I narrowed them, understanding Nemed had to be a ghost, but one who'd neatly sidestepped leaving the mortal plane.

No wonder he wasn't ageless. He wasn't Sidhe. They had souls but were immortal. Did Nemed have anything to do with the ones who'd flowed through me the day before?

I waited, fully expecting him to hurry toward the pull of my Reaper beacon.

It didn't happen. He never even glanced my way. Fascinating. A dead mortal immune to the scent of a Reaper.

"The dark ones came to power during my time," Nemed was saying. "Because the Celts and Norsemen argued about their making, they hold varying blends of both brands of magic."

Dena strode close. She too bowed her head and murmured, "Thank you for any assistance."

"The best thanks would be you restoring me to life."

Dena attempted to pat his arm, but her hand went right through it. "If I could raise the dead, you'd be the first."

"Eh. Figured as much." He shrugged and rocked from foot to foot. "Listen and listen well, for I shall only say this once. Slototh can be distracted by filth. Bury him in a garbage pile, and he shan't pose a threat. Tokhots is dangerous. He is Loki's creation and his magic is stronger than the others."

"How can we defeat him?" Liam asked.

"You can't. His blood contains a deadly poison. Ridding yourselves of the others is your best line of defense with Tokhots. Perrikus and D'Chel are creatures of fire and air. Water will extinguish them for a time. Majestron Zelia's weakness is her son, Perrikus. If you capture him, she will do anything to save him."

"Adva is the last," Dena said.

"Aye." Nemed nodded. "God of portals. He's a slippery one. If he builds a gateway, follow him at your peril. His favorite trick is to lead his prey into a vast hall lined with mirrors. Each of the mirrors leads somewhere; all but one trap the unsuspecting deeper in the maze."

"How do you determine which mirror leads out?" Krin asked.

Nemed raised one hand and shook an index finger at Krin. "Excellent question, Sidhe. It's a subtle thing, but read the edges. The mirror with a faint blue glow leads to freedom, the others to everlasting doom."

What was Nemed to the Sidhe? Death probably knew, but her lessons had been strictly focused on how to make us effective Reapers. Items like the history of the various magical races had played only a cursory part in her curriculum.

"That is all I know." Nemed dropped his arm to his side and zeroed in on Dena again. "You're certain you can't restore me to life?"

I still straddled worlds. Stepping forward, I opened my arms. "I offer surcease and passage across the veil. Will you avail yourself of it?"

The Sidhe all stared at me. What? Had they never seen a Reaper at her job before? I shrugged it off and sent warm waves of Reaper magic Nemed's way. He'd done us a good turn. Seeing him safely on his journey was the least I could do to return his generosity.

After a long pause, he took a step toward me. And then one more. "I've avoided your type," he told me.

"Why?"

"Because then there'd be no coming back."

I smiled softly. "Maybe what comes next will be better."

"How can you know?"

"I don't. My job is simple. I am the gatekeeper and I offer you passage." Following a hunch, I added, "Two of your kin passed through me only a day or so ago."

"So they truly are gone. I wondered about that. Maybe it's time," he murmured.

The next part happened fast. One moment he stood a

couple of feet away; the next he passed through me. As soon as he was gone, I gradually released my core magic. The large chamber swam back into focus.

"You did him a great kindness," Dena said.

"Thank you," I replied.

Liam strode to the front of the crowd. "I'm going outside. Who stands with me?"

Shouts of *me* and *I do*, filled the hall.

In less time than I'd have believed possible, Liam, Krin, and Dena had mapped out several alternate strategies depending on who was rattling our gates. Despite our headlong dash from Liam's home to this building, the dark gods still stood at the outer gates unable to breach them.

I hoped the citizenry of Malin wouldn't turn into a bunch of casualties. They'd taken it up the ass during the Vampire attack, and they deserved better.

We divided into groups. I ended up with Liam and several Sidhe I recognized by sight but whose names had been lost in the many tossed my way. I'd work things out. It felt far more critical for me to fill my brain with Liam's specific instructions about what we'd do once we got outside.

Familiar energy flickered and bloomed until Death stood in our midst. She turned until she faced me and rubbed her hands together. "I adore battles. Wouldn't want to miss this one."

I waited for her to chide me about Reaping. Instead, she strode to me and dropped a hand on my shoulder. "Nice piece of work, Cait. Nemed's been an outlier for far too long."

"On our way," Liam shouted.

I'd have loved to have basked in Death's praise. Goddess knows it was a rare enough event, but we had work ahead of us. Even now, the dark gods might be mowing through mortals. "Out there"—I jerked my chin in the direction of a stairway—"what comes first? Reaping or fighting?"

"I don't see why we can't manage both," Death replied. "Come on. We'll have fun. Those dark fuckers have been a thorn in my side since the Celts and Norsemen haggled over the manner of their making."

I'd have asked why, but Liam and the Sidhe needed us. Answers could come later. Assuming I had a later. I wasn't quite as immortal as my battle companions. Should I tell them?

Nah. I didn't want any special dispensations or anyone worrying about me. Grateful this was unfolding quickly— before I could get cold feet or a bad case of the what-ifs—I ran lightly after the departing throng.

They were clearly pumped up as hell, and I did my damnedest to piggyback onto their battle lust.

CHAPTER FOURTEEN, LIAM

I'd paid close attention while Cait opened her arms to Nemed. I'd seen her dispatch Vampires, but today's use of her Reaper power was totally different. Love flowed from her, along with compassion. It had resonated deep in Nemed's soul. At first, I'd thought he'd resist, but the siren call of a Reaper in full bloom had been too much for him to say no to.

I didn't blame him. He'd died maybe nine centuries ago —possibly even longer than that. He'd originally led a band from Iberia. They'd settled in Ireland and had welcomed the Sidhe and our magic. Nine years and many battles later, plague overran the British Isles. Nemed died along with over 3000 others. Unfortunately, the close relationship between the Sidhe and the Nemedians never rekindled. It's often like that when a great leader dies. After a few more years, his group had returned to Iberia.

I silently blessed Nemed. He'd provided exactly what we

needed, and I wished him peace. By Danu, he'd earned it and then some.

What came next was familiar ground. Krin, Dena, and I had led our people into battle many times. Along with Hollis. Damn him, anyway. Maybe eventually, I'd wish him peace, but I was still too angry.

Magical warfare has petered out over the past couple of centuries, but it wasn't exactly a skill you forgot. I welcomed Death's presence. She'd make sure nothing happened to Cait.

I would too. Between us, we'd make certain she was safe.

We'd formed groups, not because I expected our enemy would be numerous—although there might be more than I expected if Vampires jumped into the fray—but because each of our cadres held specific abilities. Mine would take the lead if Perrikus or D'Chel showed up because I was skilled manipulating water. Krin's group would make short work of Slototh. We lacked a method to deal with Tokhots, Adva, or Majestron Zelia, but my kinsmen would make a good-faith effort. Sidhe have always been quick thinkers. It might be enough.

I ran down many flights of stairs with everyone strung out behind me. The stout wooden doors that had shut behind Cait and me opened once they sensed my presence. The building contained its own type of power. I trusted it to hold evil at bay, which was why I'd hustled Cait into it.

Once we got past today's little wrinkle, one of my first tasks would be to make certain she understood how to shield her teleport destinations from others. In this instance, whoever had followed her didn't make much difference.

Given my involuntary blood donation, they'd have located me anyway.

It wasn't a quantum leap to assume Cait and I had the same enemies.

I waited until everyone had cleared the stairs before passing through the illusion that kept us hidden from Malin. Eager to launch an offensive against the dark gods or the Vampires or whoever had the temerity to show their faces in the center of Sidhe power, I hurried forward.

My vision works differently in mortal-land than within the Sidhe stronghold. It takes time for Earth's harsh wavelengths to sort themselves into a cohesive pattern. Much like my experience a few days ago, the first thing I saw after my sight cleared were bodies. Humans sprawled at unnatural angles, some tossed atop others. From the looks on their faces, they'd died in agony.

"Why kill people?" Outrage ran beneath Cait's question.

"Because they're scum." Perrikus pranced into view. Bright auburn hair flowed to his waist and fluttered in the morning breeze. Eyes clear as fine emeralds one moment, shifting to another alluring shade the next, were set in a classically handsome face with sharp cheekbones and a chiseled jawline. His broad shoulders and chest tapered to narrow hips under a gossamer robe.

"Took you long enough to get out here," D'Chel sneered. "Peri and I grew bored. This"—he swung an arm wide—"kept us entertained until your fashionably late arrival."

"Most people would stop by the pub for a brew." I adopted a conversational tone.

"We're not *most people*." D'Chel mimicked my inflection. "By the way, how's your leg?"

"Healed."

"Mmph. Too bad. Next time I'll have to add poison to the mix. I do a great snake imitation."

"Who came with you?" Cait asked.

Perrikus offered a disingenuous smile. "That's for us to know." He narrowed his eyes her way. "So you're the bitch causing all the ruckus with our pet Vamps."

"Actually, that would be me." Death pushed between Cait and the two dark mages, a deceptively tolerant expression on her face.

"You! Ha!" Laughter erupted from D'Chel. "How's your boyfriend? I thought the two of you never left Hell. Too busy fucking."

The pleasant mien never left Death's face. Even though nothing had changed on the surface, her entire appearance shifted from her college ingenue look to that of an ancient deity. One who'd stood watch over dangerous narrows as ships foundered and sailors died.

Power erupted around Perrikus and D'Chel until they were encased in a fiery circle. I screamed at Death to stand down. The mages were creatures of fire. Surely, more of it would strengthen their magic. Another glance at Death told me she'd moved beyond where she could hear me. Even if my words had registered, she didn't answer to the Sidhe.

I mind-linked with the ten Sidhe in my cadre and Cait. Incorporating her wasn't easy. Different magical wavelengths and all. Once we were unbreakable, I guided our shared power as we dug deep into the Earth seeking water. Rivers, cascades, waterfalls.

Perrikus and D'Chel were playing with the fire around them. Laughing and jumping like two children who'd just been gifted the best toy of all, they chucked gouts of burning material this way and that. Mostly, they guttered on Ireland's perennially wet ground and turned into smoldering lumps that couldn't have harmed anyone.

Somehow, their wasted labor didn't sink in—or didn't bother them—because the dark mages kept right on wallowing in their fiery playground. Guess they'd never gotten the memo about switching things up if your efforts foundered.

Death hadn't moved. She was so still, she might have quit breathing, but maybe she didn't have to. Power swirled around her, turning the air incandescent as it crackled with electricity. Her strength impressed me, but then it was rare when any of the gods joined ranks with us, so I lacked examples for comparison.

I felt movement beneath my feet. Water would be here soon. Would it be enough to vanquish Perrikus and D'Chel? We couldn't kill them, but maybe we could make them so miserable they'd think twice before rattling our cage again. Oblivious—almost as if they'd forgotten we existed—they kicked fire this way and that. They'd moved several meters apart; the fire enclosing them had expanded to accommodate their altered position.

Not the least bit gentle, understanding smacked me between the eyes. Death's strategy was so obvious, I was chagrined it had taken me this long to realize her fire was a diversion. A shiny object to keep the mages from doing more damage to Malin township.

The ground rippled and heaved. *"Get ready,"* I sent through my link to the others. Water burst upward amid ripping and tearing that roared in my ears. Working together, we sent it crashing over Perrikus and D'Chel in waves and buckets and glistening cascades. The fire guttered and extinguished, leaving clouds of greasy black smoke.

"What a bunch of lousy sports," Perrikus shouted and raised a fist our way. His robe hung about him in sodden clumps.

D'Chel squeezed water out of his hair and barked a word I'd never heard before. A summons of some type, the very sound of it hurt my ears and my Sidhe soul.

"They've sent for something," Dena yelled in a clear, ringing voice. "Be ready."

It was tough to see through the smoky air, but I scanned Kilkenny Green. After the earlier slaughter, not a mortal remained. No one alive, that is. Those lucky enough not to be caught up in the carnage had made a run for it.

Good.

One less problem to worry about. I had no idea what troops the dark gods commanded—who they'd rustled up. It scarcely mattered. We were in this up to our eyeballs, and we'd fight until no enemy remained. Magical wars were different from human ones. No white flags. No compromises. No treaties. No prisoners.

The Sidhe moved closer until we stood in rough formation.

"What are we doing?" Cait asked softly.

"Calm before the storm. Hold tight," I told her.

Her face was scrunched into worried lines, and her hands had curled into fists. "The dead. They need me."

"We have a Reaper," I reminded her.

She rolled her eyes. "Yeah. Maxwell is a total wimp. No way he'll poke his nose out if he senses trouble."

I wanted to order her inside, but she'd never have gone. Arguing about it would have diverted my attention from the sense of vast evil bearing down on us. The pleasant morning had yielded to clouds; a fine rain spit from them.

Without a word to me, Cait darted forward, her intent clear as she loped toward the dead with their souls hovering near them. Death broke her statue pose and bolted after her, catching her before she reached the first of the corpses.

"But they need to cross," Cait cried.

"Not your territory," Death told her firmly.

"You didn't intervene with Nemed."

"That one was different. Get back to Liam." Death snapped her fingers twice. Maxwell staggered through a gash in the ether and stared at the green as if he'd never seen a dead body before in his life.

The rain had ratcheted up a few notches, drenching him as he sent a beseeching look Death's way. "Do your job," she shouted. "Now."

Without waiting to see if he'd comply or run the other way, Death dragged Cait back up the incline to where the rest of us stood. Somewhere between the killing field and me, Cait escaped Death's clutches and returned to her spot by my side.

"At least I'm not the only one she bullies," Cait muttered.

A shiver ran through her.

The touch of raw evil was expanding. It made my eyes sting and my nose run. My skin felt abraded, exposed. Several meters away, Maxwell set up shop in the center of the bodies. Arms spread and a pained look on his face that I interpreted as abject terror, he invited the newly departed souls to pass through the portal formed by his body and his magic.

Perrikus and D'Chel stood shoulder to shoulder, heads bent as they talked.

I tried to listen in, but an annoying buzzing grew in intensity until my ears ached. Coating them with magic helped a little. The whining, whirring drone ceded to a ripping noise that reminded me of someone tearing the earth in two. Rocks crashed and grated against each other. The ground bucked and heaved beneath my feet until standing was a challenge.

The dirt split, and Vampires surged through. Not Leanan. They knew better than to venture this close to their old stomping ground. I wasn't worried about the Vampires. They weren't much more than an annoyance. I wasn't certain how I knew, but the real enemy had yet to show themselves.

Shrieks and roars exploded from above. Harpies and Griffons formed from nothing. One moment the skies were empty, the next they were filled with winged horrors.

Death tossed back her head and laughed uproariously. Fire flew from her upraised hands. The same fire that had turned into a sandbox for the dark mages was death to anything with wings. Except Harpies. Part bird, part woman, Aello, Celaeno, and Ocypete were immortal just like us. I still held the reins of my group's shared power, and I focused it skyward, intent on taking down anything that crossed our path.

Fire was a real hog. It pigged up way too much magic for us to use much of it. Instead, I sought out individual beasts and stopped their hearts. Around me, the other Sidhe groups were doing the same.

Two of the Harpies swooped lower. D'Chel and Perrikus vaulted to their backs. The third closed on Maxwell who'd frozen in place. No longer holding any kind of gateway, he had a deer-in-the-headlights look about him. Eyes wide and staring, mouth open in a silent scream.

"Maxwell!" Death screeched and sent a blast of magic at the Harpy hovering above him. Neither effort bore fruit. Maxwell didn't even look her way; neither did the Harpy. Everything quieted, slowed to a snail's pace as I watched the Harpy land in front of Maxwell.

"Run!" I shouted. "Maxwell. Do something."

But the Harpy had him in thrall. By that point, it was always too late to intervene.

"What's happening?" Cait shrieked. "Why's he just sitting there like an idiot?"

Leisurely, almost lovingly, the Harpy placed her lips next to Maxwell's. His soul shimmered as she sucked it into her mouth with a little popping sound. The Reaper's body swayed before he crumpled onto the ground.

Death launched herself at the Harpy, but she was a shade too slow. The creature spread her wings and hovered just out of reach. "Thank you," she cried. "Reapers have the sweetest souls."

"I'll get you for this." Death shook both fists skyward, but the Harpy just flew higher. Death gathered her Reaper's lifeless body against her, crooning to him as if she could reanimate him with her will. Pain cut furrows into her face, and her eyes sheened with tears.

I looked away, unwilling to intrude on such a personal moment.

She'd ordered her minion to the front lines, and now he was dead.

"I finally remembered what I learned about Harpies," Cait said. "They're soul stealers. I've never seen one before."

"If the goddess is good to you, you'll never see one again," I muttered. I'd had more than one run-in with them back when they weren't so deadly.

The Vampires were milling about, rudderless. When I searched the green, I wasn't surprised to see Perrikus and D'Chel had teleported out of there along with their Harpy steeds. No reason for them to remain. They'd stirred up a total shitstorm. It was kind of their specialty.

The ground was littered with dead Griffons. Beautiful with their lion bodies and eagle heads, their senseless deaths made me sad. Once they'd been part of good magic. I had no idea when they'd fallen off the wagon and signed up with the other side.

Death placed Maxwell's body on the ground. The air around her developed a red haze as Vampires walked creakily toward her, one by one. I could tell they didn't want to, that they were fighting her pull, but she was Death.

And they were already dead.

This wasn't a battle they could win, and they understood as much.

Cait moved a few meters away and turned in a circle, surveying the green. "Still a few souls," she told me and walked toward where Death was still drawing Vampires into her unavoidable clutches.

Giving Death and the Vamps a wide berth, Cait set up her own vigil, arms open as she invited the remainder of the souls to enter the realms of the dead.

Krin and Dena made their way to me, somber expressions on their faces. "We need to move out of Malin for a while," Krin said.

"Aye, it's not fair to the mortals," Dena seconded.

"What did you have in mind?" I asked as I shuffled through possibilities. There weren't many, and all posed their own set of problems.

"Our old stronghold on the Scottish coast," Dena said.

"It's the only spot well-removed from mortals," Krin added.

"But half of it has fallen into the sea," I reminded them.

"If you have any better ideas, out with them," Dena said briskly. "I don't care if the whole Humans Rule group is a sham. After today, we've given magic-haters more grist for their mill."

"Only a matter of time before a real Humans Rule Forever type of faction shows up," Krin said.

"We could move off-world," I muttered.

"Nay. No defensible positions." Krin shook his head. "We'd be out in the open. At least with the old castle outside Scourie we won't have to watch our backs every moment."

I nodded reluctantly, mostly because I hated leaving the spot we'd carved out for ourselves here. Death walked toward us, Maxwell's body in her arms. Cait trailed behind her. The two of them were engaged in what sounded like an angry conversation. I focused magic to eavesdrop on the tail end of it.

"That bargain," Death said dully.

"Which one?" Cait asked.

"The one where I told you I'd release you from herding Vampires if you spent thirty days with the Sidhe."

"I recall." Cait's tone was uncharacteristically brittle.

"Aye, well, I rescind it."

"Wait a fucking minute. Why?"

Death didn't answer. Rain cascaded from skies so gray they looked bruised. Should I intervene? Drop my opinion into the mix? One look at Death's face told me it was a very bad idea.

"We should clear the bodies," I told the other Sidhe. The sooner we were done out here, the sooner I could talk with Cait. Death was upset. Surely, she hadn't meant what she said.

"Aye. We can at least move the Griffons out of plain view." Breath whistled through Dena's teeth. "What in the goddess's name has evil so riled up?"

"Been thinking about that," Krin said. "The best I can come up with is humans dabbling in magic shifted the dynamic balance a long way off its centering point. Their misuse of power has made it easier for wicked things to come out to play."

"Makes sense to me," I told him. "Question is what shall we do about it?"

"Only one thing comes to mind," Cait said as she joined us. Her face was drawn; sorrow rimmed her green eyes.

"What's that?" I asked her.

"Mortals were never meant to experiment with magic. Each time they have, the consequences have been disastrous. Either it drives them mad or kills them." She stopped to take a measured breath. "All we have to do is encourage a few mortals to take bigger bites of power…"

"Let them serve as an example?" Dena raised a coal-black brow.

"Why encourage them?" I countered. "It will happen on its own."

"Maybe not soon enough," Krin said. "Those Humans Rule members are eminently expendable from where I sit."

While we'd been talking, Death had built a portal. Without a word to any of us, she walked through still carrying Maxwell. "Do you know where she's taking him?" I asked Cait.

"To bury him. She has a compound in the Arctic northlands far from everything. It's where I went to Reaper school."

Water ran down my head and my neck. I was soaked from the skin out, so everyone else had to be as well. When I stepped outside our small circle and gazed at the field, the dead Griffons were gone. "That's odd," I said.

"What's odd?" Dena asked before she whistled long and low. "It's not like the enemy to clean up after themselves."

"Must have been something about the Griffons they

didn't want us to discover," Krin said in gruff tones. "Like maybe they're cloned or something."

"Don't make things worse than they already are, mate," I said in sharper tones than I'd meant.

"Can you come up with a better explanation?" He nailed me with his dark eyes.

"No." I bit off the word because I hated the implications of Krin's suggestion. Maybe Griffons hadn't jumped the fence, but it scarcely mattered if the dark mages had figured out how to create their own.

"I'm going to pay the village elder a visit," Dena said. "To apologize, reassure him we are leaving until this blows over, and ask if he wishes help burying their dead."

"I'll come with you," Krin told her.

It should have been my job, but I didn't lodge a protest. "I'll make sure everyone knows about Scotland," I said.

"No need," Dena told me. "I already took care of it. Where will the two of you be?"

I glanced at Cait. "What do you want to do?"

She moved her shoulders in what might have been a weary shrug. "I need to go home. I've missed several appointments. I have to call my clients, see if they want to reschedule."

"Putting some distance between yourselves and here is probably a good decision." Dena offered a terse nod. "You two seem to be in the eye of the storm. See you in Scotland when you get there, but no rush."

I bristled at her *no rush* comment. "We still have to round up the Leanan-Sidhe."

"Indeed, we do," Krin agreed. "But it's not going to

happen today. Or tomorrow, either." He turned to Cait. "Death was quite effective ridding the green of Vampires. Do you suppose she'd be willing to do that for all of them? Not the Leanan, of course. They're our problem. But for the rest of the Undead?"

"Ask her next time you see her," Cait replied. "Until I hear otherwise, Vamps are still my problem."

Krin lowered his brows into what might have been a disapproving line but didn't say anything.

I draped an arm around Cait's soaking-wet shoulders and said, "Come on. Not much more for us to do here. Let's go inside and dry off. And then I'll take you back to Seattle."

"Ha! Don't trust me to teleport on my own, huh?" The small return of her usual spirit heartened me.

"Not until I teach you to ward your destination."

"Oh yeah. Huh. That. I am sorry, and—"

I sliced a hand downward to short-circuit her apology. It was an abrupt gesture, but today had been difficult. "D'Chel has my blood. Remember? What you did—or didn't do—wasn't important. Not in this instance, but it might be in another."

I guided us through the veil and to my front door. It stood partway open. I was certain I'd shut and locked it, so I stepped in front of Cait.

"What?" she asked tiredly and craned her neck to peer around me.

"I don't know, but you stay put until I find out."

Puddles formed around where we stood. When I raised my arms and summoned power, the air crackled with static electricity. Ready as I was likely to be, I strode inside.

CHAPTER FIFTEEN, CAIT

Watching the Harpy suck Maxwell's soul out of him had shaken me. Badly. Damn. He hadn't even fought back. Not that he was much more of a fighter than I am, but he had feet. He could have run. Instead, he'd just sat there. Even before the creature set her sights on him, he'd been frozen by fear.

I couldn't imagine what Death must be going through. Maybe nothing, but I suspected guilt was gnawing a hole in her guts. A big one. Perhaps I was naïve, but it had never occurred to me her assignments would be the end of any of us—until my Vampire assignment. Reaping was part of the circle of life. As natural as the sun coming up every day.

Had other Reapers died carrying out her orders? The answer pretty much had to be yes.

The compound above the Arctic Circle had a small graveyard. I'd never asked who was buried there. It hadn't been like a normal cemetery. No headstones or other markers broke its icy vista. I wouldn't even have been certain what it was, if I hadn't sensed corpses deep beneath semi-frozen tundra.

No one else had questioned it, either. But that's no excuse. During my stint in Reaper school, I couldn't wait to be done. I'd been Reaping since my earliest memories, but Death had been quite clear. No one Reaped even one more soul until they passed every class in her curriculum. Some of us spent a protracted time at the compound, but I wanted to be finished and gone from there.

No long-drawn-out journeys through Academia for me.

No spare time to snoop around mysterious graveyards, either.

I shut my mind down. Reliving Maxwell's death would only upset me further. Between the Vampires and the dark mages and the Harpies and Griffons, I'd had about as much as I could stomach for one day. The only bright spot had been the souls I'd helped cross over. They'd heartened me, reinforced the life I'd been born into.

They're drawn to me, but I'm just as attracted to them. The moment they pass through me is one of purity, of light, of love, of a promise offered and kept. I've always felt a bit squirmy about the ones who ended up claimed by Hell's halls, but no one is stupid enough to believe the alternatives they chose throughout a lifetime won't come home to roost.

Besides, that part of the process was way above my pay grade. I held the gates open. Nothing more. Nothing less.

It was raining so hard, even my underwear was wet. I was grateful when Liam guided us away from the green. All the souls had found safe passage, but their bodies remained, and my heart ached at the meaningless slaughter.

Chilly and cruel, the dark gods weren't at all what I'd expected. I gave myself a brisk mental slap. I was worse than a fool if I'd presumed they'd waltz out of the pages of Marvel Comics intact. The Marvel characters had been good for at least an occasional laugh, but Perrikus and D'Chel exuded an evil miasma that made me feel like I'd taken a bath in slime.

Lost in thoughts, I trudged next to Liam. Maybe I could direct magic to dry myself. There had to be a way to accomplish that. I wasn't paying much attention to anything except not replaying Maxwell's grisly death when Liam pushed me behind him.

At first I didn't get it. Annoyance soured my stomach. I wasn't some brainless twit who needed protection. We were right in front of his damn door. Why not go inside? And then it registered the door stood partly open. I was absolutely certain we hadn't left it that way. I remembered Liam sealing it with magic. Before I could gather my scattered resources and tell him we were a team, in this together, he instructed me to stay put and strode inside.

I might be heartsick and wet to my skin, but no way in fucking hell would I cringe out here like a shrinking violet and let him deal with whatever had waltzed through his warding.

Maxwell had let fear get the better of him, and just look at how he'd ended up. At some point, when I wasn't feeling quite so raw, I'd be angry with him for being such a coward. Fear could stop you in your tracks, but only if you let it.

"What are you doing here?" Liam's deep voice boomed.

It drove me into action, and I barged through the door, kicking it shut behind me. One of the Harpies stood—squatted?—in the center of Liam's living area. Close to six feet tall, her upper torso resembled a human woman. Long, tangled blonde hair partially hid her naked breasts. Feathers began around stomach level, and her lower body was birdlike, with long curved red talons tipping each foot. Coal-black wings were neatly folded over her naked back.

She turned spinning silver eyes my way and opened her mouth.

"Aello! Leave her alone," Liam thundered. He didn't rebuke me for not staying where he'd left me, but he would once we were alone. I could tell by how he'd clamped his jaws together.

The Harpy made a gagging sound, and a glowing blue blob popped out of her mouth. Joy punched me in the ribs so hard I doubled over before I raced to gather Maxwell's soul into my arms.

"Thank you," I told the Harpy. "Thank you so much."

She never took her whirling gaze off me. I wanted to know why she'd changed her mind, but I had other priorities. If she was still here when I was done—and in a chatty mood—maybe I'd find out why Maxwell's soul was in my care and not hers.

I moved us both to the back of the large room, intent on soothing him as best I could before I released his spirit from Earth. "Hush," I crooned. "Hush. It will be all right now."

I cracked my Reaper magic open and took up my usual position, both feet firmly in the realms of the dead.

He slithered from my grasp and regained a shimmery outline of his human body. "Nay, Cait. 'Tis kind of you, but I showed myself for the miserable craven I am. I deserved what happened. I made no effort to save myself. Death is crying over me, and I can't even tell her I'm sorry, that none of this is her fault."

"I'll tell her." I met his dark eyes. "Promise. In fact, I'll use telepathy to make certain she knows right away. Just as soon as you've passed over."

He backed up a step—if a ghost could be described as walking—closer to the wall. "That's just it. I'm, uh, not quite ready."

"I understand." I projected as much empathy as I could muster into my words, eyes, and body posture. "No one wants to leave everything familiar, but you don't have a choice. I mean, you do, but wandering ghosts don't have much of a life. Sooner or later, you'll find a gatekeeper. I'm here, so you may as well choose me."

I opened my arms and waited. I'd been in this place before. Lots of times. The ghosts almost always welcomed my embrace, but I'd never offered passage to one of my own kind. Behind me, the hum of conversation rose and fell as Liam and the Harpy talked. From the sound of things, they knew one another.

Another curious development. I should have paid closer attention in school when Death glossed over the various types of magic-wielders and their histories.

Maxwell's form was becoming more and more insubstantial. He was leaving, and there wasn't a damned thing I could do about it. I considered threatening him with not telling Death a bloody thing if he didn't act like a good ghost and walk through me, but I couldn't force him.

Bargains and inducements were forbidden—except for Vampires. None of the normal rules applied in that arena. I gave it one last shot and turned up the spigot on my Reaper magic. "Whatever you're looking for," I told him, "you won't find it."

"I have to try." Even his voice was fading. "Before I go, I need to figure out how to be a man, not a failure."

My heart hurt for him. "We are who we are." My voice cracked, and I swallowed around a thick place in my throat. "You did your best."

"Did I now?" His words held a mocking quality. When I blinked at the spot he'd stood, he was gone.

Breath swooshed from my lungs, and I curled one hand into a fist. Poor sod. He wouldn't find the peace he sought. It didn't work that way. He'd drift from one spot to the next, looking in on places he'd lived, people he'd loved. He wouldn't be able to talk with them, only with another Reaper. We were the only ones who could see him in his spectral form.

Us and Death. And others with magic tuned to ghost energy.

Feeling just as much a failure as Maxwell viewed himself, I reeled in my grave vision. The realm of the dead fought back so hard, I gave up before I'd sealed off the gateway. I was barely hanging on as it was. I'd finish shutting the portal once I was dry. Nothing more to do in the corner where I'd planted myself, so I walked toward Liam and the Harpy.

They stopped talking as I drew near. "I have no idea why you did that," I told the Harpy, "but it was kind to release him."

The Harpy raised her blonde brows. "Was it? I'm not in the habit of being kind. He was a bit of a bitter mouthful after all. A seething mass of misery. Secrets were eating him up until naught but a shell remained."

"Was that why you let him go?" I held her spinning gaze.

She shook her head; curls danced around her shoulders. "Nay. As I said, I don't have a generous bone in my body. Liam and I, we go back many a long year. I owed him a favor, and now it has been discharged."

Before I could mine for details, she spread her wings. A gray mist rose around where she stood. When it cleared, she was gone.

"Maxwell didn't pass over, did he?" Liam asked.

"Nope. I did everything I could, but he's spinning in the wind." A shiver tracked down my body. I needed to communicate with Death, but first I needed dry clothes.

"Let me get you something else to wear," Liam murmured, "before your teeth chatter right out of your head."

"Can't we dry what I have with magic?"

He snorted. "Aye, but changing clothes is a whole lot quicker. Some of my things will fit you." He narrowed his eyes my way. "We may need whatever power remains to us. When you've used a fair amount, it pays to think twice before running your stores down further."

I resisted rolling my eyes. "Yes, Professor."

He opened his mouth but then must have changed his

mind because he turned on his heel and headed for the stairs. I was shivering in earnest now, and I stared after him unsure what to do. Would he toss some garments down here for me?

"Cait!" The sound of my name cut through the fog my brain was turning into. I wrapped my arms around myself, but my jacket had soaked in water like a sponge. Leather was great—until it got wet. My half-frozen fingers squished against the icy cow hide. I could barely feel them.

"What?" I managed.

"Follow me. We've got to get those wet clothes off you."

"Just throw something down here. I'll, uh, change in the b-b-bathroom." I did my damnedest to clamp my jaws together so my teeth wouldn't knock against each other, but it was a losing battle. A big part of the problem was I hadn't closed off the gateway. A portion of me remained in the cold, sere realm of the dead.

Before I crumpled into a heap and wasn't able to do anything, I slid the sodden jacket off my shoulders. It splatted to the floor. I picked it up—shocked by how much it weighed—and tossed it over the ledge in front of the kitchen sink.

Moving helped some. I couldn't feel my feet, but at least Liam wasn't ordering me about. I turned on the hot tap and held my hands beneath its flow. My fingers first tingled and then burned as blood roared back into them. I was still standing with my hands under the tap when Liam materialized behind me.

Had he teleported? I sure as hell hadn't heard his footsteps.

He wrapped a large fluffy towel around me and held me against his body, my back to his front. "Stubborn, stubborn woman," he muttered.

I sagged against him, reveling in the towel and the warmth of his body seeping through its weave. Letting him hold me was a bad idea, but I was fresh out of spunk. I turned off the spigot. No reason to blow through all his hot water. My hands were all right.

He dried me with a towel end and tucked my hands inside the fleecy terrycloth. Magic flooded into me—his magic. I glommed onto it and sealed the gateway. The alteration in my temperature was immediate.

"Better?" he asked. At my nod, he went on, "I sensed the portal wasn't shut, but my magic wouldn't touch it. I tried."

"Only for Reapers." My teeth weren't quite done chattering, but their involuntary spasms were better.

He tightened his grip on me, turned me in his arms, and then swept one beneath my knees. He'd lifted me as if I were a child before, and I intuited what he was about. I started to protest, but he said, "Ssht. All I'm doing is carrying you to a chair so we can get your wet boots off. I drew you a bath. It's waiting upstairs."

"But the bathroom is there." I glanced at the door off the kitchen.

"I had another installed one floor up. My home has a few luxuries it lacked when this part of Malin was built."

"Ha! Back then the only warm water came courtesy of kettles heated over a fire."

"So you remember those days too?" The corners of his eyes crinkled before he smiled. "Are you truly going to refuse a hot bath? You were quick enough to take advantage of the kitchen sink to thaw your hands."

He set me on one of the couches and knelt in front of me.

"I can take my own boots off." I reached for them, but he batted my hands away.

"I know you can." Liam tugged at the laces, loosening them. His deep voice developed a lyrical quality, and I figured he'd imbued compulsion or calming or a combination to anchor his words. "Nothing you can't do for yourself, but let me take care of you. Not forever, but for now."

I could have fought him—and his magic. But I didn't want to. Not really.

"What happened with the gateway?" he asked and levered one boot off before working on the other one. Somewhere along the line, he'd stripped off my sock and wrapped my newly bare foot in a trailing end of the towel that was still wrapped around me.

"Not sure. I was feeling pretty low about Maxwell. When I tried to shut it, it fought me. The combination of cold from the nether realm and being wet to my skin didn't help. By the time I realized I didn't have enough power to shut the gate, I was too tapped out to do anything about it—until you gave me a shot of your magic."

"Glad it helped. I wasn't certain it would. There." He plonked my other boot on the floor. Behind him, a fireplace crackled to life, and the boots traveled to sit in front of it.

"You weren't even looking in that direction," I said.

"It's my home. It responds to my magic with very little

effort on my part. Let's see how close the fire comes to drying your boots. They were soaked clear through."

He caught my gaze with his, and I had to hold myself back. No man had a right to be that gorgeous. Even with water still dripping off the ends of his fair hair, he had an ethereal grace. From his high forehead to his square chin and stark cheekbones, everything fit together creating amazing synergy. His mouth was eminently kissable with its well-shaped lips. I could drown in his eyes, lose myself and never look back.

"Do you want to walk upstairs?" He quirked a fair brow. "Or shall I carry you?"

My cheeks grew hot. He must have noticed how fixated I'd been on his face. Thank Christ I'd stopped there. His body was another study in masculine perfection. It took very little for me to reconstruct the feel of his hard, muscled chest against my side after he'd scooped me into his arms.

"I'll walk."

He grinned up at me. Not throwing my arms around his neck turned into a pitched battle.

I couldn't block out the few moments I'd been pressed against his body. My heart did a funny little flip-flop in my chest, but I ignored it. After a tussle with the towel that nearly sent me sprawling, I made it to my feet and walked toward the stairs. I hadn't seen a bathroom up there, but it didn't mean there wasn't one.

"I'll put on some tea," he called after me. "And find something dry for myself."

My fickle heart did the thumpity thing again. Was he going to follow me upstairs? Surely all those dressers and armoires were repositories for his clothes. What about garments for me?

Part of me wanted him to join me. Another part recognized what folly that would be. Even though I wasn't shivering any longer, I was still chilled to my bones. Nothing like a hot tryst with an even hotter male body to make me forget…everything.

"Not a good idea," I mumbled and reached the landing that branched into his bed chamber and study. I'd begun smelling fragrant herbs midway up the staircase. A door I hadn't noticed my first time up here had been propped open. A lush, steamy scent wafted through it.

Liam was thorough. I'll hand it to him. Folded neatly on a chair just inside the bathroom door were black trousers, a pale-blue woolen shirt, and an oversized ivory sweater. I pushed the door closed behind me and stripped out of my wet clothes. Surely a clothes dryer lurked somewhere downstairs. He had every other modern convenience here.

The herbal mix he'd scented the water with was heavy on mint and vanilla with overtones of something sweet like cherries or strawberries. I gripped the edges of the old-fashioned clawfoot tub and sank into it. The water reached my chest.

Maybe he'd spelled the water—in addition to scenting it. The knots in my muscles started to relax. The tangled places in my soul weren't as cooperative. I'd been blindly pushing forward, figuring eventually my life would get back to normal. Either the Vampires would go away, or Death would assign them to another Reaper.

Once that happened, I'd pick up the tatters of *Carrick Sky*

Sports and rebuild my business. From the ground up if need be. I'd done it before with other ventures. I could do it again. As I lolled in the tub, truth surfaced along with a few key realizations I'd been doing my level best to ignore.

"Buck up, Carrick," I told myself. "This is the new normal."

I winced and bent forward to sluice steaming water over my face. No getting around it. My life had turned a corner when Death assigned Vampires to me. No reason for her to drop them in anyone else's lap. I was doing a bang-up job by comparison.

That was why she'd rethought freeing me after a month of Sidhe duty.

I tried to recall who'd had Vampires before Jake, the unfortunate bastard who'd gone before me. Nothing came to mind. Jake had done basically nothing for a couple of hundred years. And then I remembered, he'd been the first to be assigned exclusively to Vampires.

Death had admitted as much.

A couple of Reapers before him had the job, but they Reaped other souls as well.

We'd all run into the occasional Vampire. If it wasn't too much trouble, we shunted them through the gateway. My successes had mostly been humans who'd been drained to the point of death with a Vamp still attached to their necks. The Vamp in question was punch-drunk on blood, so they'd never put up too much of a fuss.

Until it was too late.

The water was starting to cool. I grabbed a cake of

sandalwood-scented soap and washed myself. My hair wasn't particularly dirty, so I didn't bother with it.

"Tea is ready," wafted up the stairs.

I pulled the plug and got out of the bathtub. A few minutes later, I was dry and dressed with a towel wrapped around my wet hair to soak up the water. I did feel better. More like me, but I wasn't fooled.

The me who'd gloried in the rush of air beneath an airplane's wings would soon become a distant memory. Fuck. Maybe there wasn't any reason to hustle back to Seattle. Why reschedule clients only to no-show on them again?

I unwound the towel from my head and used it to wipe steam off the mirror. The woman who stared back at me looked familiar, yet not. A few more lines scrolled around my eyes. My mouth held a grim aspect. I relaxed my jaw muscles. It made a difference. A positive one.

I took a moment to hang my damp towels on racks.

Determined to put the best face on this that I could, I snatched up my wet clothes, and walked out of the bathroom and down the stairs. I remembered my promise to Maxwell, but he hadn't crossed over. Death was about the last person I wanted to talk with. I was still smarting from her commuting my sentence—and then taking it back.

Hard to lose something I didn't have, but it still felt like she'd ridden roughshod over me.

Food smells rose, making my nostrils twitch and my stomach tighten with hunger. Liam had made more than tea. It felt as if several lifetimes had passed since he'd run out to get us breakfast much earlier today.

I crossed the living room, passing a table that held a scrumptious looking meal. Eggs, toast, sausage, tomatoes, mushrooms. "Clothes dryer?"

He pointed. "Behind that curtain. Your stockings are already in there, along with what I was wearing."

After adding the sodden garments I'd draped over one arm to a surprisingly new looking General Electric dryer, I joined Liam at the table. Unexpected emotion rocked me. No one had cooked for me—or taken care of me in any way at all—for so long, I couldn't remember the last time.

"Thank you." I took a sip of scalding black tea with Chai herbs in it.

"My pleasure." He turned a million-watt smile my way.

"You're making it very tough to walk away from you. Men who can cook are a rare commodity."

"We are, eh?"

"Indeed. Damn, this is good." I chewed and swallowed, trying to savor the food and not just choke it down.

He set his fork aside and reached across the table to capture one of my hands in his. "We have a lot to deal with, but I hope you never walk away from me." His coppery skin took on even deeper color before he released my hand and went back to working on the contents of his plate.

My cheeks warmed, along with the rest of me. He hadn't asked anything of me, but he'd just offered the greatest gift of all. I was important to him. Important enough, he wanted me by his side.

A million thoughts crowded my mind, but the one that sprang to the fore was what a crappy bet I was as a love interest. Among my friends, I was famous for my one-night stands. The sex part was great, but I was the original commitment-phobe.

Of course I was. How could I even consider a relationship with a mortal? They'd be dead before we even got rolling. Liam wasn't mortal, though...

I clamped a lid on my busy brain. Maybe romance hadn't been what he meant. Perhaps he simply viewed me as a valued colleague in the Vampire war that was crashing down around us.

I liked that interpretation better because it was far less complicated.

"About Seattle," I began. "Maybe it's not such a good idea."

"I disagree," he said, "but tell me what you're thinking."

CHAPTER SIXTEEN, LIAM

Remaining downstairs while Cait bathed was far harder than I'd imagined. Images of her naked and floating in the oversized tub bombarded me from all sides. My groin developed the dull ache it gets when I'm aroused with no hope of slaking my desire. I considered bringing myself off, but it felt perverse with her so near. I'd done it once before, but I'd assumed she was sleeping.

Somehow that had made it a wee bit less deviant.

I settled for tossing clothes in the dryer and getting a meal together. By the time I was dishing up food, my desire was more or less under wraps. At least the front of my trousers wasn't tented like a sail in a brisk wind.

Once we'd eaten, we needed to be on our way. The other Sidhe had already left. I'd felt their magic as they teleported away from Malin. As I'd cooked, I prioritized our tasks. The Leanan-Sidhe sat squarely atop of the list. There'd be no getting control of the Earth-bound Vampires until we herded the Sidhe Vamps back behind iron bars.

Also, if anyone was teaching magic to humans, it had to be the Leanan—or the dark mages. The Earth-bound version of the Undead didn't have enough magic to shake a stick at, let alone share.

Two solid reasons to get the Leanan out of the way.

I'd meant what I said when I restated an offer I'd made to them long ago. If they recanted their blood-linked ways, we would welcome they back into the Sidhe fold. Eh, maybe welcome is too strong a word. But we wouldn't turn them away. Many of them had been perhaps not friends, but acquaintances. I'd never understood the allure of adding blood—and domination—to their diet, but then I'd never actually asked, either.

I still didn't recall the precise number who'd defected. It didn't matter. They'd been operating outside Sidhe strictures for long enough, they could have produced children. Whether they'd been born Leanan remained to be seen. I didn't believe such a thing had occurred in our long history, though. Sidhe produced Sidhe children.

End of story. I hoped.

The thought of the Leanan producing baby Sidhe Vampires made my skin crawl.

I set the bar low. If even a scant handful of my erstwhile kinsmen rethought their love affair with being Vampires, I'd consider it a win. They were clearly located somewhere not terribly far from Seattle. The band who'd stalked me proved as much. I wasn't a betting man, but if I were, I'd have placed big money on all of them being in the same vicinity.

I needed to rustle up at least a dozen Sidhe to meet us in Seattle. Not much sense ending up with insufficient firepower to do more than ask questions. I'd already been in that predicament. It might have ended better if D'Chel hadn't intruded.

D'Chel. I hadn't exactly forgotten about him, but his association with anything Sidhe—Leanan or not—left a rotten taste in my mouth. Fifty Sidhe would be a better bet than twelve if we had to deal with the dark mages.

Humans Rule wasn't much more than an annoyance. Even with an infusion of forbidden magic, they'd never pose a significant threat.

I called up the stairs to let Cait know our meal was ready. She must have been nearly done with her bath because she walked into the kitchen a few minutes later. Her dark hair was just starting to dry, and tendrils curled around her face. Her green eyes had regained some of their sparkle. The trousers and shirt I'd selected fit her well enough. She'd rolled up the bottoms of the pants and tossed the sweater over everything.

Even with oversized clothes on, she was unbelievably stunning. Far deeper than her looks, though, she possessed a beautiful soul. Warm, compassionate, and spunky, she wasn't one to sidestep what needed doing. With a shock, I understood I'd fallen hard for her, and it was too late to instigate damage control. Feelings weren't like that. Once loosed, they developed a rhythm and cadence all their own.

Without being too obvious about it, I scanned her with magic, relieved her power was mostly back to acceptable levels. We chatted of this and that as we ate. I could tell she was both surprised and delighted by the food. It was far from a feast, but it would provide fuel for our next steps.

At one point she said my skills in the kitchen were making it damned difficult for her to leave. My response slipped past the safety of my throat, and I told her I hoped she never did. It was far too personal a thing to give voice to. My face heated, and I refocused on my meal.

I would have preferred it if she was drawn to me because of some of my other talents, but if cooking was too personal, the kisses we had yet to share were off the charts.

Out of the blue she said, "About Seattle. Maybe it's not such a good idea."

I didn't agree, but I urged her to tell me what she was thinking.

She tipped more tea from the pot into her mug and buttered another slice of bread. Seemed to me she was buying time to organize her thoughts, and her words clinched my impression.

"There's no easy way to say this," she began, "but I had one of those epiphanies you get in a bathtub."

"Mostly, I'm afraid they've bypassed me, but go on." I smiled encouragingly.

A small, breathy sigh burbled past her lips. "I only wanted to go back to Seattle to pretend I still have a life there. I don't. So maybe it's wasted magic and time when we could be taking a bite out of our other problems. The real ones. God knows we've got a piss pot of them."

She looked so desolate, I reached for her hand, but she shook her head. "I'll be all right. I admit I'm feeling sorry for myself, but I'll get over it."

"Magical wars don't generally last very long," I said. "Maybe you're—"

"Throwing the baby out with the bathwater?" She furled her brows. "As in overreacting? I don't believe so. These last six months have been hell. I've barely slept. It's a wonder I haven't dropped a plane out of the air." She shifted her gaze to the table and drank more from her mug.

"Nope. My inescapable conclusion is I can either Reap Vampires or run *Carrick Sky Sports.* I cannot do both. I've damn near torn myself in two trying."

"Any idea why Death zeroed out her offer to release you after a month of helping us?" I asked.

"Because she's a bitch?" Cait rolled her shoulders back and shook hair out of her face. "Scratch that. It was mean of me. Maxwell's death did something to her. I'm not sure quite what, but she wasn't in a place where I could have argued the point. Damn it."

"What?"

"I promised Maxwell I'd let Death know the Harpy freed his soul. Even though he refused passage, I'm still bound by my word." She shut her eyes, and I felt more than saw Reaper magic flicker around her as she reached for Death.

Cait nodded once briskly. "Okay. That's done. Back to our Seattle discussion." She snagged my gaze with her own.

"We do need to go there," I said. "It's where I saw a band of Leanan Sidhe."

"Do you believe all of them are in the same place?"

I nodded. "Probably. I'd thought to put out a call to Dena and Krin and maybe fifty others. We'll need to choreograph an attack that's quick and effective and ends with the Leanan back underground."

"I'm all for capturing them," Cait muttered. "I have a feeling most of our problems with the Earth-bound Undead began when their Sidhe cousins joined forces with them."

"Not just Vamps," I said. "The usual type of Undead has very little magic. They have superhuman speed and strength, and the ability to hypnotize their victims, but that's about all. Our problem with humans trying to manipulate power they have no business with should decrease substantially, but only if we can cut the Leanan-Sidhe out of the picture. And the dark gods, but they're another story."

"Excellent reasons to go after the Leanan. Guess we can tackle the Marvel Comics goons later."

"It's a mistake to underestimate them," I cautioned. "A big one."

"Yeah. I know, but they're easier to deal with as caricatures." She shut her eyes for a moment. When she opened them again, she said, "Even if we're successful, I'll still be the Reaper assigned to Vampires."

"Have you considered quitting?"

She burst out laughing. "Yeah. Right. I'm one step up from an indentured servant. At least they could buy their freedom after umty-ump years."

"What could Death do to you if you told her you were done?"

"Um, feed me to the Vamps in Hell just like she did with Jake."

I shook my head. "I didn't believe her when she said it, and I still don't. Jake may be out of the way somewhere, but I don't see the goddess who was weeping over her dead Reaper earlier being quite so callous."

"Only because you don't know her," Cait mumbled.

"Maybe you don't, either. If you're done eating, let's toss the dishes in the magical half of the sink. I'll get hold of Krin and Dena to see if they can float a small regiment, and then we'll be on our way."

Cait nodded and pushed her chair back. After carting an armload of dishes to the sink, she ducked into the laundry room. By the time she emerged with a stack of neatly folded clothes, I'd confirmed our plans with the other Sidhe.

"Hang on. Let me get my boots back on," Cait said and handed me a pair of dry stockings. My guess was her boots had to be nearly dry by now. The fire was putting out decent heat.

"I need to do the same." I knelt to stuff my feet into my tattered trail runners. They hadn't been anywhere near the fire, so they were still quite wet. I sent a jot of magic their way; a cloud of steam and droplets rose from the saturated fabric.

After pushing upright, I walked to Cait's side. She'd slung her bag around her body and said. "Ready when you are."

"Where do you want to go?"

A furrow grew between her brows. "Probably home. I'm curious to see if they sacked the place."

First I'd heard of it. "What are you talking about?" I asked, followed by, "Who?"

She shook herself impatiently. "Right before I left, I had

to dismantle the wards, right? I didn't think I could teleport through them."

"Sometimes you can," I said, "but it was a prudent call on your part."

"Yeah, well anyway, right before my spell took off I heard a bunch of shouting outside. Men's voices saying they'd been right about me being inside."

I didn't like the sound of that at all. "How about if we aim for your office?" I suggested. "You have a car there, right?"

"I do."

"All right. We'll go to your office, and you can check for email and messages. Surely, if your houseboat was sacked—or scuttled—someone would have let you know. Assuming it's still floating, we'll take your car and park a few blocks from the houseboat. It will give us a chance to scope things out. By the time we're done, the other Sidhe should have arrived."

Cait's frown deepened. "Probably smarter than my plan. We could have plopped into the middle of a trap."

After today's run-in with two of the dark mages, I wasn't in a big rush to lay eyes on them again anytime soon. We'd confront them soon enough when we tackled the Leanan. No reason to give voice to negative thoughts, though.

Cait's head snapped up. Telepathic magic formed a nimbus around her. This time, I listened in. "We're leaving," Cait told Death. "If you want me, find me in Seattle."

"What did she want?" I asked.

Cait shrugged. "Who knows? Her opening gambit was I'd failed because Maxwell is loose. I didn't want to hear any more."

"Why would she care? There are lots of ghosts kicking around. I run into them regularly."

"You can ask her when you see her. I have a feeling she'll be waiting for us wherever we pop out. Where will we meet the other Sidhe?"

Krin and I had hashed that out. "A protected location a couple of hundred kilometers north of Seattle."

"But that's in Canada. Not that it matters. Never mind. Should have kept my mouth shut."

"When the Sidhe fortified an abandoned Inuit village, there was no Canada. No United States, either. The risk is the Leanan may have chosen that exact same spot, which means our battle strategy won't be quite as cohesive."

"Of course they'd know about it," she murmured. "Maybe we could overfly it. You know, check it out."

I'd assumed we'd accomplish the same thing with magic, but if anyone was paying attention, they'd notice even a subtle thread of seeking power. Cait was smiling, clearly pleased with her suggestion.

I glommed onto it. "Grand idea. We'll accomplish two things since I'd love to fly with you."

Her cheeks developed a rosy glow. "You're just saying that."

"Nay. I'm not. I've always wondered what it would be like. I've avoided commercial air travel since I can teleport, which is quicker and cleaner, but—"

She flapped her hands my way. "Come on. Let's get moving. Death loved flying. If she's there, you might have to fight her for who rides shotgun. Besides, I'll have to file a flight plan. It might take a while since we'll be crossing an international border, but so long as we're not landing I'm not expecting any issues."

Cait's enthusiasm was contagious. Being a pilot clearly made her happier than Reaping. I cracked a grin and built a journey spell. Once it reached full strength, I wrapped it around both of us and kindled it. The walls of my home fell away.

"You really enjoy flying," I said.

She nodded and leaned into the arm I'd slung around her shoulder. "My life was damn near perfect before the whole Vampire thing. Flying fed my heart and mind. Reaping kept my soul alive." She hesitated for a beat. "I've had a whole lot of jobs. When you live as long as we do, it's inescapable. But the first job that captured my heart was flying airplanes."

"Did you go to some kind of school?" I was curious how she'd ended up owning an aeronautic business.

"Eventually, sure. At the beginning, back in the 1920s and 30s, I kicked around airfields. I washed airplanes and worked on them and begged rides whenever I could talk someone into it. The guys taught me how to fly and loaned me a plane to go on a check ride so I could get licensed. The whole process wasn't nearly as organized as it is today. And the requirements were pretty loose."

"You must have faked your death and started over at some point," I said and checked the trajectory of my teleport spell. We were right on course.

She nodded. "My next go round, I had to go to pilot school and take a written test and one in the air. I picked up an old junker plane for a song and rebuilt it so it was airworthy. From there, I started flying freight and saving my money. It took a few years—and a lot of lucky breaks—but *Carrick Sky Sports* was the result."

"How long ago was that?"

She chewed her lower lip. "Let's see. Maybe twenty years. I figure I have another twenty or so before I need to start planning my next death. For a while, I was excited about magic wielders being outed. It meant I didn't have to conceal how long-lived I am, but with this whole Humans Rule thing..."

"Don't give up yet," I told her. "It's not as if they can stuff the cat back into the sack."

"No, but if prejudice against us keeps on growing, I won't have any customers. Not that I've told much of anyone about what I am, but not looking older is a dead giveaway." She rolled her eyes. "I've been expecting Humans Rule to start handing out armbands any day and enforcing us wearing them."

"Nah. They aren't nearly as well organized as the Nazis were."

"Not yet," she countered solemnly.

"We can mask what we are," I pointed out. "Discovering who has magic isn't that much of a slam dunk."

"Yeah, but better magical detectors are right around the corner. The technology is—"

"Stop borrowing trouble," I hugged her tighter against my side.

She nodded. "It's good advice. Not sure quite what's wrong with me. Usually, I'm more optimistic."

"Wading through carnage would dull anyone's optimism.

We'll figure things out as we go." The edges of my spell developed a silvery glow. I fashioned air to cushion our descent, and we popped out inside Cait's office. Death stood in front of the desk, arms folded beneath her breasts, clearly waiting for us.

Rather than holding back until Death revealed what she was doing here, Cait grabbed the point and planted herself in front of her mistress. "What do you need?"

Death had jettisoned the glamour that made her look about twenty-five. She was in full goddess mode: ancient eyes, stern demeanor, and attitude to burn. "Why didn't you force Maxwell across?"

Cait regarded Death from beneath lowered brows. "And how could I have done that? Passage through me has always been voluntary—except for Vampires. Nothing about that has changed." She continued in a singsong voice, probably quoting from something. "No Reaper shall coerce or otherwise force—"

"I know the regulations. I wrote them," Death cut her off in icy tones and pressed her lips together. "If he crosses your path again, he must leave Earth."

"Unlikely I'll see him again," Cait said. "What's your interest in a dead Reaper?"

"He cut a deal with the Vampires. Rather than showing up at the point of a mortal's death, he'd wait a while. Long enough for a Vampire to lure their soul." Death skinned her lips back, baring her teeth.

"Why?" Cait demanded. "What was in it for him?"

"The Vampires probably left him alone," I tossed out.

"Exactly." Death glanced my way.

"Fine." Cait angled her head to one side. "Anything else?"

"What are the two of you doing here?" Death answered Cait's question with one of her own.

I hastily constructed a ward and tossed it over the three of us. It wasn't absolute, but it would deter casual eavesdroppers. "The Leanan-Sidhe are my problem," I told Death. "Mine and the rest of the Sidhe. We have ideas about how to recapture them."

She shook her head. "It will never work. Not with the dark mages to contend with."

"Why not?" I narrowed my eyes. Being told no isn't pleasant to hear.

Death let her arms drop to her sides. "Even if all of you were involved, there are too many different magics. Tokhots is an enormous distraction when he bounces in and out of sight. You never know where he'll show up next, and his bite is lethal—even to those like you."

I'd never known about that little tidbit. It ran deeper than his poison blood.

"Adva with his portals is nearly as deadly," Death went on. "Never, never follow him. His favorite trick is running like a mad thing, but slow enough you believe you can nab him. You can't. What he's doing is leading you into a liminal space lined with mirrors."

"We heard about that part," Cait cut in. "The one with bluish edges is the way out."

Death nodded approvingly. "It is, indeed." She turned her image-laden eyes on Cait. "The 'anything else' is this. For the next couple of days, I and others like me will...distract the dark gods. If you're quick and thorough, you should be able to deal with the Leanan-Sidhe."

I rolled the information around before I said anything. "First off, many thanks," I ventured. "You've offered us a great boon, but there is a downside. A big one."

"Aye, true enough. Most gifts come with crappy underpinnings." One corner of her mouth turned downward. "The dark mages will be furious, and they will seek retribution."

"Too bad we can't sic them on Humans Rule," Cait muttered.

"A group of mortals ripe for corruption would be an attractive target," Death agreed, "but let's focus on the short game. Do you wish our aid?"

"Aye. Without it, we may fail at our first objective," I told her.

"Don't you want to see if we can manage on our own?" Cait asked.

She hated to be beholden to Death. I understood that part loud and clear, but capturing the Leanan had to happen before we could accomplish anything else.

I blew out a tight breath. "If we try—and fail—our next attempt will require still more of us. We will have shown our hand and many of our tactics, and—"

"Never mind," Cait spoke over me.

"'Tis settled, then," Death said. "Don't forget about Maxwell. I'll be in touch." The place she'd stood turned into empty air.

"Sorry," I murmured. "I know you would have made a different choice, but—"

"You were being practical. I get it. Sometimes I trip myself up standing on principle." Cait had moved in front of her monitor and dragged a phone from her bag, plugging it into a charger. The screen flared to life, and she scrolled through mail and punched a few keys.

Apparently, we were done talking about Death's visit and her offer. I positioned myself to look over Cait's shoulder. "Is your home still afloat?"

She cracked a weak smile. "Appears so. Just let me answer a couple of these. I filed a flight plan. Need to wait till it's approved, anyway."

A staunch knock sounded on the door. "It's just my friend, Kiko," Cait said.

I strode across the room and unlocked the door. A diminutive Asian woman with clouds of black hair hurried inside and made a beeline for Cait. "Where in the hell have you been?" she demanded. "I've been worried half out of my mind. Couldn't find you at home, and you haven't been here, and—"

Cait hadn't bothered to drag the desk chair over or sit down. She turned and hugged Kiko tight. "It's good to have friends like you, but I'm fine. Thanks for worrying, though."

Kiko extricated herself and turned toward me. "Who are you?" She winced. "Sorry. Probably none of my business."

"Liam Warwick." I strode close enough to extend a hand.

Kiko shook it briefly. "Kiko Tanaka." She glanced from Cait to me, and a knowing look washed over her face. "Aha. Suddenly, I understand why you've been traveling under the radar."

Cait offered an enigmatic smile that could have meant

anything. "I'll call you, but don't be concerned if a few more days elapse."

"Oh, honey," Kiko lowered her voice. "Take whatever time you need, but I do want to know where you found him." She smiled at me. "You don't happen to have a brother, do you? Or maybe a cousin?"

"Lots of cousins." I smiled back.

"Mostly, I was joking," she replied. "Just brought a plane back. Need to hangar it and get to work. I'm on the late shift at the pharmacy. Let's fly sometime next week."

"Of course," Cait responded warmly. After another hug, Kiko trotted out the door, pulling it shut behind her.

Cait's computer chimed. "Bingo!" She fist-pumped the air. "Flight plan is approved. We're good to go."

I ran through a preflight on the Seneca. We were going far enough, it made sense to take the faster plane. Liam stuck by my side like a limpet asking questions as I checked the fuel, made certain nothing was falling off the plane and all the control surfaces were functional.

After alerting the tower, I followed their instructions. We were third for takeoff, but the queue always goes fast. Because Liam had asked, I walked through what I was doing until we were airborne and circling to head north. The usual sense of peace I found in the air surrounded me. It was one of those unusual days in the Pacific Northwest when the sun was shining. It glinted off Lake Union and Lake Washington to our right and the snow-capped Olympic range to our left.

"I can see why you enjoy this," Liam said. "It's amazing. What keeps this thing in the air?"

I'd love to have chatted about flying and planes—hangar

talk—but it wasn't why we were up here. "We can talk about flight dynamics later. Have you heard from the other Sidhe?"

He nodded. "They're waiting on what we find."

I'd pulled up charts on the computer back in my office. "There's a primitive airstrip not far from our destination. We might be able to land there."

"Instead of returning the plane and teleporting?" Liam quirked a fair brow.

I nodded. "It would be a deviation from the flight plan I filed, but I can amend it once we're back."

"Forgiveness rather than permission, eh?" Liam grinned.

"Exactly." I smiled back.

I was still blown away by what Death had told me about Maxwell. No wonder he hadn't wanted to cross over. He had sins to expiate. Lots of them. Or was that even why he'd resisted the pull of the gateway? Was he hoping Vamps could somehow resuscitate him? Not likely since Death had probably burned his remains.

Vampires needed a body, last I'd checked. Given what Death knew, she'd have opted for immolation rather than burial.

"You're quiet," Liam observed.

"The Maxwell-thing bothers me, but I can pick it to shreds later. What's our plan for the Leanan?"

"Simple enough. Surround them. Overpower them. Immobilize them with magic and transport them back to their cells. Unless some would rather return to the Sidhe fold—minus the Vampire part."

"I assume they'll resist." I fed a course correction into the autopilot. It had a tendency to drift to the east, but I'd never gone to the expense of having it recalibrated. Easy enough to just keep an eye on it.

"Aye, but they traded some of their magic." He shook his head. "Not exactly right. Their power is different now, more attuned to seducing mortals and becoming irresistible to them."

"Will it make them easier or harder to deal with?"

"In truth, I'm not sure. It wasn't all that difficult to round them up the first time because some were ashamed."

I added another two thousand feet to keep us on our assigned flight path. "If they were so ashamed, why'd they sign on to become Vampires?"

"The forbidden has an allure." Liam hesitated. "When you live a long time, finding things you care about becomes harder and harder."

"Yeah. I understand. There's always this feeling of having been there and done that. Multiple times. It's why I latched onto flying. It holds my attention, and every flight is a brand new game."

"Does your friend know what you are?" Liam's question came out of the blue.

"Kiko? She does." I scanned the duplicate gauges—one for each engine—before continuing. "I avoided having friends until magic came out from under wraps. And I knew Kiko for a while before I told her. She caught me walking through the airfield after a big airliner had crashed and wanted to know why I was there."

"Do you talk about Reaping with her?"

I shook my head. "It makes her uncomfortable, but not so uncomfortable she walked out of my life. It was a chance, an experiment. If I ever get close to someone else…"

"We're becoming close."

It was true. We were, but hearing him say it scared the stuffing out of me. "We're different," I said. "Because we both have magic."

"Does it make being close mean less?"

He was playing devil's advocate, but it was a thorny question. "Not exactly, but I can be myself with you and not worry about damaging your sensibilities."

"Och, lassie." He'd switched to Gaelic. "I can be quite sensitive."

"Aye," I replied in kind, "but not because my magic terrifies you. Look." I dipped the nose of the plane to better display thick forests passing beneath us. "We're nearly there."

"Our transit went quickly." Liam was back to English.

I patted the yoke. "She's a good old girl. I was lucky to be in the right place when she went up for sale."

A few more minutes, and we passed over a clearing. I could see its appeal to the Sidhe. Since no roads led in or out, it was an eminently defensible position and quite well hidden. Flipping off the autopilot, I said, "All right. I'm going to circle lower. See what you can because I don't want to be here long enough to create suspicion if anyone is down there."

"Will do." Liam gave me a thumbs-up.

I banked the plane to give him a decent view out both the windscreen and his side window and scribed large, lazy circles in the sky until we were about 1500 feet above the surface. No one showed up in the clearing, but it might not mean anything. I'd taken my time on the way down, but I laid into the throttle getting us out of there. It wouldn't take much magic to toss something—like a passing bird—into one of my propellers.

"What do you think?" I asked.

"Seemed deserted."

"Only seemed? Are we going home, or are we landing?"

After a pause that felt longer than it was, he said, "Let's land and get this over with."

I nosed the plane to the west where my charts had shown a strip. When I saw it, I pursed my lips together. "Not going to work, "I said. "Maybe if someone had cleared the debris off it, but it was barely long enough to start with."

"Circle for a bit. I'll handle it." Power flared around Liam, and he was gone. Moments later, I saw him on the ground. The chunks of wood and rocks that had littered the runway were flying to one side or the other.

I chuckled to myself. Magic came in handy for a whole lot of things. Would there have been a way to tap into my brand-new, enhanced power spectrum to do the same thing from the air? I'd have to ask him.

As I got set up to fly a pattern and land, I reflected on Death and her offer to divert the dark mages. She and at least a few other deities also thought making a dent in the Vampire population was a priority. The question was why. Clearly, she was privy to information she wasn't sharing.

Like Maxwell, for instance. How long had she known he was batting for the other team? Was that why she'd dragged him front and center and forced him into action? Had she been banking on someone killing him—and then been saddled by a heaping dose of remorse?

I shoved everything about Maxwell aside. He wasn't my problem. Unless he crossed my path, and I had to come up with a way to Reap him.

Always responsive, the Seneca jumped to my pressure on rudders and yoke. Her wheels kissed the rutted dirt strip moments after Liam had moved the last rock out of the way.

I stood on the toe brakes. No margin on this strip. I had to be proactive if I was going to get the plane stopped before it slewed off the end of the runway. We'd have to be facing the other way to take off, so I used the plane's momentum— and a shot of magic—to get us turned around before I rolled to a halt.

Wasn't perfect, but we could drag her into position before we left. Taking off would be a whole lot harder than landing had been, but I'd dealt with worse situations. Maybe Liam could teleport into the plane once it was airborne. Not having to deal with his weight would compensate for the uneven runway. All those lumps and bumps would make getting up to the speed I needed to leave the ground harder.

I grabbed my bag, got out, and joined Liam. A journey spell was already bubbling around him. "Thanks for the help," I said. "The next strip was over fifty miles from here."

"I heard from Krin," he told me. "They should be at the clearing when we arrive."

"Sounds good."

Liam stopped his spell preparations and dropped his hands onto my shoulders. "You're vulnerable to the Leanan, not the Sidhe part of their power, but the Vampire portion."

"No more than any other Vampire." I tried to evade his grip, but he didn't let go.

"Yes, much more than the Vamps you're used to. Their paltry attempts aren't backed by much magic. Do not make eye contact. Don't talk with them."

"Didn't you say I was immune to some of your magics?"

He nodded slowly. "Aye, but their magic isn't quite like mine. It's keyed to seducing mortals. I have no idea how susceptible you'll be to their...charms. Until we know, your best bet is to exercise caution."

"It sounds as if you're expecting us to walk into an ambush. We were just there, and—"

"Cait. Stand down. I'm making certain you have information—in case you need it. Our old compound appeared deserted to me too, but then Sidhe never have paid much attention to anything mechanical." He tapped my shoulder bag. "Do you need anything in there?"

I shrugged. "Probably not. I always keep it with me, though."

"It might get in the way. How about if you leave it in the plane?"

The odds of either planes or cars showing up at this remote location were slight. I compromised and tucked my bag out of view between two thick bushes.

Liam's spell caught me up, and we traded one wooded location for another. The sounds of raised voices reached me before the dregs of Liam's spell cleared. After a string of curses in Gaelic, he said, "Ward yourself."

So the clearing hadn't been empty after all. Telling myself it would be good to get this part behind us didn't do a thing for my skyrocketing heartrate, my dry mouth, or my sour stomach.

I understood flying, but fighting still felt as if it belonged in someone else's wheelhouse. Yeah, I damn well had to get over that. Just like I'd have to suck up Reaping Vampires. Maybe Death would show me how she simply slurped them through her gateway.

Now that my magical game had taken a great leap forward, perhaps I could do the same thing. High-pitched whistling was the only warning I had before a blast of power missed me by half an inch.

Crap. Shit. Fuck.

Would my warding have held? It was smoldering. I patched it up damned quick and focused on the unbelievable scene stretched around me. Other than a few Sidhe I recognized from Malin, the others could be anybody.

With a sinking feeling, I understood I had no idea which of these fuckers were the enemy. Sidhe magic felt like, well, Sidhe magic. And the Leanan were just as Sidhe as the rest of them. I hadn't anticipated that little wrinkle, but then I hadn't anticipated a whole lot of shit.

Like falling in love with Liam.

Maybe not love, but for sure lust and wanting and craving and all the rest of it that went along with me longing to throw my arms around him and explore every inch of skin underneath his clothes.

Pay attention, Carrick. My inner voice sounded horrified I was thinking about fucking while a battle raged around me. Yeah. Pretty dumb of me. I edged closer to Liam. "I can't tell who's who."

"The Leanan's auras are darker. Dial in your psychic vision." Bolts of power flew from his upraised hands. They wouldn't do much more than slow the Leanan down—if that.

Our surround-and-capture strategy wasn't looking promising. Bunches of Sidhe poured out of gaps in the ether, but most of them were Leanan. Damn. How big was the compound here? I hadn't seen much in the way of buildings. Was it underground?

So many things I didn't know, but they weren't critical bits of intel, either. We'd fight until either we'd won. Or lost. At the moment, the outcome was anybody's guess.

"Cait?" Liam's tone held a tense edge.

"Darker auras. Got it. Thanks." Would I always need his help for every little thing? Didn't make me very attractive partner material. I've always been keen to pull my weight. So far, other than flying the plane close to here—which had been mostly a waste of time—I hadn't done a whole hell of a lot.

That was about to change. I took stock of my magical reservoir. It was mostly full. Good. I mixed earth with fire and air until the combination crackled between my raised hands. Light on my feet, I danced into the midst of the throng. Sidhe squared off against each other, power sizzling between them. Now that I knew what to look for, at least I had the field sorted into friend and foe.

"Where'd you come from?" A man with dark hair longer than mine glided close. Leather pants and a wool shirt hugged his tall frame. "I don't remember you, but you're a pretty one."

Liam had said not to look at the Leanan, but it was impossible not to. Movie-star striking just like all the Sidhe, something about the Vampire addition only added lumens to his gorgeousness. When it sank in that I wasn't just looking, I was outright staring, I made good use of my faux pas and released the power I'd been hoarding between my upraised hands.

It crackled in a blue arc and glanced off his shoulder. His silvery eyes widened. "Reaper, eh? I didn't think your kind did aught but collect souls."

Too late not to look at him again. I'd fallen off that pedestal a while back. "Nope. Don't even do that," I told him. "I'm just a gateway. What happens to the souls once they cross over isn't my affair."

"You're such a lissome creature, Reaper. Come closer."

To my absolute horror, my feet took a step nearer without my permission. Did the bastard have me in some kind of thrall? Was that why Liam had said not to look at them? He'd said not to talk with them, either.

Meanwhile, one foot wanted to kick forward. I kept both planted firmly beneath me. "Uh-uh. I'm not the patsy you think I am."

"Not a patsy at all," he crooned in hypnotic tones that held multiple levels. If I listened with my Earth-ears, I would have believed all was well, that he would love me, take care of me, that I'd never want for anything. My psychic hearing was a whole other ballgame. The honeyed tones were calculated to lure me.

Even knowing he was planning on adding me to his blood stable wasn't enough to keep my feet in one place. I forced them sideways, backward, any direction but closer to the smiling Sidhe.

Power crackled through me, and I loosed another volley. My aim was better this time. It hit the Sidhe square in the chest and did nothing but roll off him. What the fuck? I was only a few feet away. Surely, all that electricity should have at least set his garments aflame. Leather burned handily once it got going.

Shouts and curses and the sizzle of magic running into other magic surrounded me, but it was as if the Sidhe and I stood on some kind of island that was only loosely attached to the remainder of the clearing.

I cracked my Reaper magic open, not knowing what to expect, but I was fast running out of options. The Sidhe's glamour dropped away. No wonder his clothing hadn't ignited. It wasn't real. Beneath the illusion, he was garbed in ancient-looking brown hunting leathers. Creased and greasy with dirt caked into the cracked places, they looked as if he'd been wearing them for months if not years. The gray-black perimeter Liam had described was far more obvious. Under it, I could see several broken places the Leanan affiliation had chewed in the Sidhe's soul. No longer beautiful, he looked haggard and worn.

He reached for me, but I'd moved to a place that defeated his magic: the realm of the dead. The overwhelming desire to walk into his embrace abated, but he wasn't going anywhere. The minute I closed off my death vision, I'd have to deal with him again.

The world of the dead, cold and sere, replaced the vista spreading around me. Mortals had died here. Lots of them.

Ghosts streamed out of everywhere and nowhere, drawn by my scent. Their spectral forms were decorated with wounds that looked as if they'd come from arrows.

What the hell had happened here? I hadn't seen so many shades in one place since plague decimated half of Europe's population.

Probably not many Reapers passed through this spot, but the call of so many dead should have alerted someone. Plus, it wasn't as if ghosts were stuck where they'd died. The spirits cried and yelped and screamed as they flowed in and around and through one another. The sound reminded me of a herd of coyotes on the hunt.

Did all of them want passage? I swallowed hard and fought my side of the Reaping equation. I didn't have enough power to hold myself back from Reaping and keep the Leanan at bay. He hadn't gone anywhere, and he'd upped the magic powering his compulsion spell. Fragments of it stretched toward me. So far, the nether regions had a dampening effect.

Would it last? Or would the Sidhe switch things up until he found a way through?

"Take me," a spirit cried as he sped toward me. Half his neck was a gaping hole.

"How long have you been here?" I asked, still not believing so many ghosts could have congregated in this deserted spot. They were mobile. If they'd wanted to cross, they could have sought out a Reaper.

Realization slapped me hard. Much like the ghosts in Malin, these wanted me, specifically. Meant Vampires had to be behind everything. It made sense. The Leanan-Sidhe and the Earth-bound Vamps were in league with one another. Maybe my comparison of the shades to a pack of coyotes wasn't so far off the mark.

Both were predators, but in this instance, I was the prey.

The first wave of ghosts was almost upon me. Shouts of, "Open the gate," battered my ears. Every Reaping cell in my body longed to comply. It was what I did. Held the gateway for souls to find eternal something-or-other. Rest for some, torture for others.

I looked from one choice to the other. The Sidhe shimmered behind the veil of the realm of the dead. The phalanx of ghosts were crystal clear. Did I fight one or many? The shades would do the same thing as the ones in Malin had. I was certain of it. They'd chip away at me as they passed through. It would burn and sting like liquid fire.

After more than two or three used me for a gateway, I'd be lost. Probably forever, unless Death had lied about that too.

No choice. Not really. The Sidhe was a fucker, but the shades would be the end of everything I'd ever known. I voiced a sharp command to close off my Reaper magic. Usually, withdrawing the flow of power had an immediate effect.

Not this time.

Nothing changed, and the ghosts just kept on coming. The first ones had reached me now, and they clawed at me, running spectral fingers through my body. They couldn't hurt me unless I established a portal, but I didn't want to have to dig my way out from beneath a heap of quivering, slithering, jellylike protoplasm.

There's no substance to the dead, but a lot of them can form an annoying barrier. Even though these shades had to have been dead for a long while, they stank of rot.

The reek was the least of my problems.

I cleared my mind as best I could and tried again to pull the edges of my Reaper magic together. This time, I didn't aim for totally shut. Movement in the right direction would be a win.

Still nothing.

To compound matters, flickers from the Sidhe's continuing efforts were growing brighter. I twisted my mouth into a sour expression. Nothing wrong with his magic. Why the fuck had mine turned into a balky mule?

Once more, I told myself, and started from the ground up, building my Reaper magic one thread at a time and weaving the strands together. I checked the warp and weft at intervals and tightened things up as much as I could. This time, the edges did move.

I was certain of it.

Remaining on my feet was growing harder. The shades had packed up. Between clawing at me and throwing themselves against me, they were making it hard to maintain the concentration I needed to block out the world of the dead. If I stumbled, I'd go down.

And then, I'd have to give up what I was doing to crawl out from under the heap. They couldn't force me to open a portal, although that particular bit of power pulsed within me, doing its damnedest to break through. If it had a voice, it would have been shouting at me to open the fucking gate.

"No." I spoke out loud. "Not this time. These aren't ordinary shades."

The words had a stabilizing effect, and for a moment everything got a whole lot clearer. But then, the shades started shouting again. I was wrong. Nothing wrong with them. Why was I so mean? They deserved to cross. I was the gateway, and—

"Shut up!" I shrieked. "Shut the fuck up."

Driven by the panic I'd tried—and failed—to marshal, I slammed the gates shut. Finally. The realm of the dead vanished with a loud crash.

"I'm so honored." Sidhe-boy was back. "You chose me."

I whirled, intent on ripping his head off, but I wasn't warded. I can't maintain wards in the nether world. If I did, what kind of gateway would I be? The dead would throw themselves against me and not be able to break through.

He closed a hand over my forearm in a viselike grip and leered at me.

Too late for wards.

I yanked my arm back but couldn't shake him. "Let. Me. Go."

"Really? You think to defeat me with words?" His fangs dropped, and he opened his mouth. "You're mine, darling. You could have remained with all those lovely dead things, but—"

"Don't talk to me," I shouted and put every ounce of strength into trying to break his grip. His words were seeded with magic—compulsion. The less I listened to him, the better chance I had.

I glommed onto my thoughts. I did have a chance so long

as I believed I did. If I gave up, I'd be just as lost as the mass of ghosts who'd accosted me in the nether world.

Had they even been real?

Some of them, sure, but others had to have been illusion.

"You're special," Sidhe-man went on. "We have to get rid of you, but I'm not into wasting...anything. I told the others we could turn you. That other Reaper was a disappointment, but I bet you won't be."

That other Reaper? "Maxwell?" I gritted his name out.

The Sidhe shrugged. "He may have had a name. Mostly, we called him boy. And he never answered very well."

"Guess what?" Riding on hope, I funneled fire through my body, making my skin hot to the touch, and heaved away from the Sidhe with all my strength. It worked. He yelped and loosened his hold just enough for me to jump back a couple of feet.

From my newly free vantage point, I finished my sentence. "I don't answer well, either. To anyone." Skinning my lips back from my teeth, I drew magic from the Earth beneath me.

If wanting someone dead was a prerequisite for success, the Sidhe was two steps from a slagheap. I rocked from foot to foot. Power crackled from my fingertips.

Just let him try again. I was ready.

CHAPTER EIGHTEEN, LIAM

When Cait loped into the thick of the fight, I started to go after her, but a quartet of Leanan surrounded me. It might have been coincidental, but I didn't believe so. They wanted her off by herself. It made me frantic to break free, but the four Leanan turned into eight and then into sixteen.

What in the unholy hell? Were they cloning themselves? A quick check told me they were real enough. Power sizzled, turning the air blue-white with a static charge. After exchanging volleys that weren't more than a diversion, I changed things up and focused my power into a funnel that cut through the bodies massed around me.

Maybe because they weren't expecting me to modify my tactics, it worked, and I charged through the gap before it crashed shut. Not to say they couldn't regroup, but I'd be far more alert. Warding myself was pointless. Their power stung when it hit me, but it couldn't do any damage.

Unfortunately, that cut both ways. I couldn't do much to them, either. We'd counted on superior numbers, but there were far more Leanan than I'd remembered. Time has a way of softening things like mass defections.

I scanned the field for Cait and her characteristic magic. No dice. And then I looked again with the same result. She was either gone or cloaking herself behind something so absolute I couldn't sense her.

My chest tightened with frustration—and concern. Had a group of Leanan made off with her? I didn't sense the other type of Vampire nearby, so they weren't responsible for her disappearance.

Krin loped to my side, looking as if he'd just chewed through a roll of barbed wire. "Those bastards!" He fisted a hand and punched the air in front of him. "I'm ashamed we were ever related."

"Skip that part," I said sourly. "Cait's missing, and we have to come up with something foolproof to deal with our kin. Or all this will be naught but a waste of time and magic."

"Aye, and then we'll have to start over from the beginning. Except now, they'll know we're out for blood. Eh, poor choice of words."

I agreed with his assessment. It was make this work, or back away from the problem. Backing away wasn't on the table. It left us vulnerable on so many fronts. Getting rid of the Leanan was the first step to dealing with the other Vamps and Humans Rule. I raked the field with magic again, intent on locating Cait.

My first pass, she wasn't there. Determined bastard that I

am, I tried again. This time, she popped up from somewhere. Relief washed through me, so heady I caught a quick breath and unclenched my jaw.

Krin bent his head close to my ear. Wise of him. Telepathy was easy to intercept. "Goes against the grain," he was saying, "and everything in our covenant, but we have no choice."

"No choice in what? I missed the first part," I hissed back.

"We have to levy the power of the liminal space. Only way to trap them."

My eyes widened. "It's forbidden, and for good reason. That wavelength is lethal to humans."

"None of those around that I can see," he countered. "Do you have a better plan?"

I didn't. I'd been keeping watch over Cait out of the corners of my eyes. Padhraic, one of the Leanan, had grabbed her, but she'd broken free. Good for her. Meant she had resources to defeat their mesmerism. I wouldn't have guessed as much, but it was one less problem. I'd take my gifts any way they arrived.

"Five minutes," Krin said. "We'll begin the casting and then form a ring around the clearing."

"That will trap the Leanan here, not in our dungeons," I cautioned as I recalled what I knew about our version of the Doomsday spell. A highly flammable blend of mineral-imbued earth, fire, and electrically charged air, it would blow a hole halfway through the Earth's crust. Presumably, the Leanan would fall into it. Once we'd sealed it over, we'd be done.

Krin shrugged. "They escaped before. They might again,

but whoever helped them will have to figure out where they are. Hundreds of meters of rock and dirt are bound to be a deterrent. Before, the dark gods—or whoever—could simply waltz into the dungeons and break the magic powering the locks on the Leanans' cells. This will be harder."

"Aye. Maybe hard enough to make it not worthwhile." I hated to admit it, but using the illicit power was sounding more and more appealing. Cait had squared off against Padhraic, and the two were snarling at each other. She must be getting to him because his usual glamour had fallen away revealing a shell of who he'd once been.

Damn it, anyway. The Leanan were nothing better than a pack of addicts. They'd gotten a taste of Paradise and couldn't recognize it for the false god it was. Too many blood rituals, and they moved beyond redemption. I'd been a fool to believe they could be salvaged. For a fraction of a minute, I felt sorry for them, but I ripped the feeling out by its roots. I needed to be front and center, 110 percent present.

We were about to consign the Leanan to a new kind of Hell. I wasn't certain I could keep up my end if I got sidetracked wondering if we weren't making a mistake.

"Clock starts now," Krin told me. "I'll alert everyone."

I hustled to Cait and hooked a hand beneath her arm. "Padhraic." I tipped my chin his way. "Apologies, but the lady is spoken for."

"Not leaving until I kill him," Cait snarled.

"No worries on that front. You'll get your shot."

She shifted her gaze from Padhraic long enough to send an incredulous look my way. "What the fuck is that supposed to mean? Let go of me. I'll join you once I'm done here."

"There is no done," I reminded her. "Why do you think bodies aren't sprawled this way and that across the clearing?"

Laughter rumbled from Padhraic's throat. "Finally," he said. "Well, met, Liam. Does this mean you're leaving off this foolishness and going back to Ireland?"

I lifted my shoulders. "So far we've squandered a whole lot of magic with zero results. Do you think we should keep slugging it out?"

"Of course not, but then we didn't invite you to drop by in the first place."

Cait narrowed her eyes. "What a bunch of lily-livered cowards. Are you in the habit of snatching defeat from the jaws of victory?"

"I'll explain later. We're out of time."

"No explanation could—" She shut her mouth with an audible clack.

She looked so fierce, dark hair swirling around her and emerald eyes snapping with anger, it touched places deep within me. Places I'd never have guessed existed. Protectiveness surged, savage and absolute, obliterating everything but the need to make certain she never wanted for anything.

Even if she spurned me, I'd care for her, protect her.

I locked gazes with her and read both determination and confusion. Why was I demanding she stand down? She'd barely gotten started. "Come on," I urged. "The others are waiting for us."

She jerked her arm out of my hand. Her upper lip curled into a sneer, but perhaps she knew me well enough to understand now wasn't the time to pitch a fit. Not in front of our enemy. Or maybe it had nothing to do with knowing me and everything to do with preserving her dignity. Without waiting for me, she stalked toward the edge of the clearing where the Sidhe were bunched into a group.

The Leanan would know immediately what we were about if we'd formed our circle first. Smart of Krin and the others. We'd kindle the spell and do quick teleports until our perimeter was unbreakable. The one piece that bothered the hell out of me was not knowing if Cait would be immune to the power that held the liminal space together.

Another problem was that Earth would be vulnerable to damn near anything waltzing through its weakened barrier. That segment wouldn't last long, but the high frequency magic fried mortal brains, turned them to mush.

Cait should be solid. She passed through the liminal boundary to Reap souls, but I'd have liked to be more certain than I was. I ran to catch up with her. Her face held a closed-off expression, but I had to talk with her. Before I could come up with a supportive opening line, she twisted to face me.

"I had a plan." She spat the words my way.

"I'm sure you did," I adopted a bland tone.

"I'm not a child. Stop patronizing me." She stopped a few meters from Krin and Dena.

I bent my head until my mouth rested very near her ear. "The others require our magic."

She drew her brows together until they formed a dark line carving across her forehead. Understanding kindled in the depths of her eyes, but she didn't ask what we were doing. Since she wasn't fighting me—thank Danu—I plastered my mouth against her ear. "How do you protect yourself when you construct a gateway?"

"I don't."

"Just to be on the safe side, once this gets rolling, remain near me and ward yourself. We have to hurry."

"Once what gets rolling?"

I didn't answer her. Couldn't risk one of the Leanan overhearing. Instead, I ran toward Dena, Krin, and the others. After a slight hesitation, Cait ran after me. I'd have gone back for her, but it was better this way. For her to do the choosing and be mistress of her fate. Plenty of rebukes about how idiotic it had been for her to race into the midst of the melee were on the tip of my tongue, but I quashed them.

Loving her meant trusting her instincts, not lecturing the crap out of her if she did something I didn't agree with.

We reached the others. The muted simmer of their combined magic heated the air, but it could have been anything. I was certain the Leanan were keeping a close eye on us, and I made a few adjustments, so our nascent spell resembled a teleport casting.

"Let's give it one more minute," Dena muttered.

Our magic had begun to spiral, growing with an energy all its own. I felt it pressing against me as it leached from the liminal space holding Earth separate from other worlds. A faint burnt smell was rapidly increasing.

"We don't have another minute," I told everyone. "Let's ride this pony before it breaks its halter."

Amid nods, the Sidhe who'd been ranged around us

vanished. We'd planned it this way on purpose to offer a temporary sense of victory for the Leanan. They were still watching us with all the subtlety of hawks keeping an eye on field mice.

I swathed Cait in my teleport spell. When we touched down, it was on the far side of the clearing. "I don't require explanations right now," she murmured. "They'll keep till later. Let me know what I need to do."

"Open your magic to me."

That she complied immediately pleased me. Sharing magic is almost as intimate as having sex. She'd taken power from me before when I'd offered it, though. So it wasn't as if this was our first time.

Our spell was done flirting with us. The liminal boundary held untold energy, and it lived for opportunities like this, times when it could get up and romp. Cait couldn't both ward herself and share power with me, so I constructed a partial ward around her.

As we'd disappeared, ostensibly teleporting back to the Old Country, the Leanan had headed toward what was left of the caves and structures that had once belonged to an Inuit settlement. The feel of our casting rolled toward them, and they stopped dead. Outraged yelps were testament to their knowledge they'd been had.

They broke and ran toward the perimeter we'd formed, but we'd reinforced it with magic. Cait sent a blast of fiery air at a woman who got too close to us. She flew backward and landed on her ass. Undaunted, she sprang to her feet for another go.

Screeches and cries rose in intensity as panic set in. The

ones who tried to teleport—and splatted onto the ground—understood we'd locked that exit route. Not us, actually, but the liminal space's power was so robust, no one could have punched a journey spell through its weave.

My heart hurt for the Leanan. They were still Sidhe, and we were slaughtering our own. The thought was so unnerving, I shoved it ten meters under and focused on the task ahead. We'd taken a risk unleashing the arcane magic. If we couldn't shape it, control it, we'd never leave here, either.

Too late now. We'd picked our poison. Magic released from the liminal space dug deep into the ground. Clods of dirt and huge rocks rained down on the Leanan. Made it harder for them to run—not that there was anywhere to go. Beneath my feet, the earth rocked and rolled and shook.

"I know what you did," Cait shouted. "Death said never to do that."

"It is prohibited," I agreed, "but we've manipulated the liminal space before. It settles down after a while." I hoped I was right about that.

"Damn it!" Crackling heat shot from Cait's hands, and two more Leanan crashed backward.

"You're doing great," I called over the cacophony of the Earth ripping itself asunder. The hole had expanded to maybe five meters and was digging itself even deeper as we watched. Almost as if the magic sensed its progress and was proud as hell, the excavation went faster with each passing second.

"Not about me," Cait shouted. "It's Death. How many

things did she lie to me about? Me and all the other Reapers."

"Using the liminal space and its magic was our last resort," I told her. Whirling at the last minute, I stymied two Leanan trying to sneak past me by punching one, and then tossing both of them backward and into the spreading pit. "It's forbidden for the best of reasons. Our covenant with humans says we do no harm. These wavelengths would kill any mortals close enough to feel them."

And thank all the fucking gods they weren't affecting Cait.

Our circle was tightening as we moved inward until we stood at the edge of the hole. As we went, we drove the Leanan into its maw. They'd moved beyond screams and curses, but their stoic silence was almost harder to take than their yelps had been.

Guess I'm not the hard-hearted bastard I saw myself as.

Heat spewed from the abyss, which told me it must be deep enough. We'd drilled through the earth's crust to the molten rock below. Step one was accomplished. Once loosed, though, the untamed magic came alive. It wouldn't fold itself back into the liminal space easily or without pushback.

"Look!" Cait pointed. "That one who almost had me. He's getting away."

I followed the line of her arm. Padhraic had swathed himself in an invisibility glamour, but it was slipping and revealed his outline. Was he the only one, or had others escaped our net?

If so, it couldn't be very many.

Curses damning me and the other Sidhe to eternal misery billowed from the depths of the chasm. Once someone was trapped, the magic wouldn't let them leave. Dena leaned over the edge. "Silence! The only eternal misery will be your own." Power flowed from her upraised hands.

I've always believed the liminal space borrowed energy from dead humans as they passed through. If it were true, Sidhe power would be like ambrosia to the liminal's magic stores.

"I'm going after him," Cait yelled to me and took off running. Her feet barely skimmed the ground. Either she was high on our near victory, or she was employing magic to move faster.

"Time to close it up," I yelled at Dena.

"I'm trying," she yelled back.

After making certain the Sidhe on both sides of me combined their magic so my absence wouldn't break our circle, I sprinted after Cait.

She threw her body atop Padhraic and drove him to the rolling ground. He bucked and writhed, trying to throw her off. When sheer strength didn't cut it, he hit her with magic.

I wanted to kill him. No one raised magic against Cait, not on my watch. I dove on top of the heap, doubled up a fist and punched Padhraic in the side of the head. The satisfying crunch of small bones in his cheek breaking delighted me, so I did it again.

"She is mine," I shouted. "Mine. If you hurt her, you'll pay for the rest of forever."

"Wasn't that what you had in mind, anyway?" he asked in

a droll tone I remembered from before he'd thrown his lot in with the Leanan.

"Aye, but I can make it worse for you."

"Why are we even talking with him?" Cait demanded. "Let's toss him into the pit before it's sealed."

"Let me up," Padhraic said. "You have my word I won't run."

I rolled off him and got an arm around Cait. She struggled. "We can't trust him," she protested.

"Aye, he is bound by his word, just like all Sidhe," I told her.

"Thank you." Padhraic's words held a simple dignity. He flipped over and crossed his legs beneath him. Absent a glamour, he looked as if he'd racked up some hard miles.

"Make it quick." I nodded tersely. "She's right about the chasm closing."

"I don't have much to say. I'm tired. I'd be lying if I said I don't crave blood, and an endless supply of mortals to drink from and fuck, but I'm ready to give all that up and come home. If you'll have me."

I tossed a truth net over him. "Say it again."

He did, and his words pinged neatly off my casting.

May as well take advantage of my truth spell, so I asked, "Where were you sneaking off to when we caught you?"

"Back to the compound. From there, I had no idea." He blew out a long ragged breath. "All of us were here. I'd have been the last, and I'll be goddess damned if I knew what to do with myself."

I reeled in my spell. Sidhe can be high-handed and cold, but we're not liars.

Cait looked at me, and then at Padhraic. And I looked within myself, a quick, harsh soul-search. I'd offered mercy. How could I go back on a bargain of my own making and still live with myself?

Padhraic hadn't been in the group who'd accosted me that morning near Cait's houseboat, but it didn't matter. Even if he hadn't heard the words from my lips, it didn't mean I hadn't said them.

Krin hustled to where we crouched. "Hole is nearly shut," he said tersely. "What do you want to do with him?"

Padhraic bowed his head. "I surrender. I want to come home."

"Pfft. I don't fucking think so," Krin sneered. "Now, when being buried alive is your only option, you've had an epiphany? Forgive me if I have a hard time believing you're sincere."

I got to my feet and faced Krin. "I made the offer. Not to him, but to other Leanan. I say we give him a chance."

"If I fail, I will seal myself back in the dungeon," Padhraic said. "I offer my word as a Sidhe. It binds me, as well you know."

Krin's gaze traveled from Padhraic to me and back again. "So be it," he said at length and called, "Seal the hole," over one shoulder.

"Do you need help with the liminal power?" I asked him.

"It's being its usual bitchy self, but we're on top of it." He set his mouth in a grim line. "No solo travel," he told Padhraic. "One of us must accompany you at all times."

"That's fair." He rolled his shoulders straighter. "This... transition won't be easy. I'll have a lot of rough moments. It would help if someone kept an eye on me for the first few months."

"We'd do that even without you asking," I said. At least for now, Padhraic was saying the right words. Whether he'd still be whistling the same tune when the blood hunger struck remained to be seen.

Cait scrambled to her feet and stood by my side regarding Padhraic. He'd made no move to get up. "Earlier," she said, "who orchestrated all those shades?"

"Earth-bound Vampires," he said.

"But I didn't sense any of them here," I spoke up.

"Cait—and aye, I know her name—finalized the death of many Vampires," Padraic said. "Hellbent on retribution, they've mustered mortals they've drained, who wander Earth like wraiths. There are a lot of them, and because of how they died they're not like regular souls."

"I've been a gateway for many humans who died at Vampire hands," Cait said. "None of them felt different until the ones who were out for my hide in Malin. And the pack demanding a gateway today."

"Aye, you've helped those newly dead. The difference is death by Vampire chews holes in mortal souls. The longer they drift, the more corrupt they become until most of them never leave." Padhraic turned his hands palms up. "Why would they? Naught awaits them but Hellfire."

"Let me make sure I understood you." I loomed squarely over Padhraic. "Earth-bound Vampires are incensed because Cait tricked many of them into permanent death." Once he nodded, I went on. "So they've rustled up whatever is left of the ghosts of their prey—the ones they didn't turn—and sicced them on her."

"Close enough," Padhraic agreed.

"Why did the Leanan align themselves with the other Undead?" Krin asked.

Padhraic looked away. "Promise of blood. What else would lure us?"

"They gave you humans to feed from in exchange for?" Krin leaned a little closer, clearly not willing to let Padhraic wriggle off the hook.

"Teaching them certain, um, skills."

"What exactly did you teach?" I pressed.

"We know some of it." Cait skewered Padhraic with her green eyes. "You taught the Undead how to walk under the sun and how to enter dwellings without an invitation."

"Guilty," Padhraic said. "We also taught humans how to work with primitive magics, nothing that could ever harm them. Just enough so they'd be full of themselves—and provide us with a ready food supply."

The crashing and booming had settled out. I wasn't surprised to see that the abyss in the clearing was sealed, the ground as smooth as if nothing had ever disturbed it.

Padhraic got slowly to his feet and bowed his head before Cait. "Words don't mean much, but I apologize for my attempt to turn you."

She made a snorting sound. "You wouldn't have gotten far. We Reapers are tough. Did you think you'd just make a dive for my neck and I wouldn't fight back?"

"I figured I was stronger than you. Reaper magic has never been a threat." He straightened. "I misjudged you, but

I'm glad I did." His gaze skittered in my direction. "Liam is in love with you. If I'd gotten my fangs into your neck, he'd have turned the world upside down hunting me."

"You know me too well," I growled. "Once I found you, I'd have staked you out on rocks and let the birds eat your liver over and over again. It was good enough punishment for Prometheus, and you wouldn't have had Hercules to save you."

"No one to save me," he agreed. "I'm the last of the Leanan. Once we're back in Ireland, please cast the spell to strip me of my fangs."

"We'll strip you of more than that, and we're actually returning to Scourie. We've done enough damage in Malin." Krin raised an arm; a bolt of magic wrapped around Padhraic's waist. "Get moving. We have work to do."

"We'll see you in Scotland," I told Krin.

"He will, but I'll be a while," Cait said. "I have a few items I have to attend to first."

We stood next to each other as Krin and Padhraic joined the other Sidhe. "Shall I teleport us back to the plane?" I asked.

She nodded. "You don't have to come with me. Looks as if your kin have their hands full. They probably need you more than I do."

I wrapped an arm around her shoulders. "What if I want to come with you?"

She looked up at me, and her full mouth curved into a soft smile. "Well then, I'd appreciate the company."

"You do know we won today," I said.

She screwed her face into a grimace. "Today was a start.

We have a shit ton of work to do. And I'm still the Reaper assigned to Vampires. They hate me, and they're not going to go away." She exhaled briskly. "They're not all that bright, but even they will figure out I had something to do with the Leanans' demise. It will be one more nail in the coffin they want to chuck me into."

"You could quit." My words took me back to an earlier conversation we'd had.

"I'm considering it."

"Before you said it was impossible. What changed?"

"Me. I've changed. Let's go."

I was curious what had happened to her in the nether world, but it could wait. She'd get around to telling me in her own time. A quick shot of power returned us to where the plane sat patiently waiting for us. A combination of magic and brute force got her headed straight down the runway.

Just like the clearing had smoothed over, the airstrip had as well. No longer pockmarked with holes, it stretched flat and clean before us.

Cait retrieved her bag and crawled into the cockpit with me right behind her. After she'd kicked the ignition on, I placed a hand over hers. "Could you teach me to do this?"

Her eyes widened with surprise. "To fly?"

"Aye, I'd like to learn."

A smile began in her eyes and spread to her mouth. "That could be arranged, but I warn you I'm expensive and a total bitch of a taskmistress."

"I can live with that. Tell me what these dials mean."

She ran two fingers down a vertical row of matching gauges. "Someone smart decided it would be wise to place all the important instruments for each engine next to one another. That way, you can tell at a glance if one if misbehaving."

"Will this thing fly with only one engine."

She nodded. "Yeah, but they're difficult to control if that happens. You compensate with the rudders and ailerons..."

CHAPTER NINETEEN, CAIT

adhraic had said Liam was in love with me. The revelation sent a blinding flash of joy to every cell in my body, but I'd tried not to do anything obvious. Like shriek or throw my arms around his neck—Liam's not Padrhaic's—or squeal like a teenaged girl.

I wanted to turn to him, ask if it were true, but first we had loose ends to address in the clearing. And maybe it was rotten timing to talk about love or relationships or anything mushy. Liam must be feeling...something. He'd known all the Leanan we'd marched into the pit. Once upon a time, he'd broken bread with them.

And now, they were as good as dead. It had to be a bitter pill to swallow. It was a wonder it wasn't choking him.

I'd let him know I was a good listener—if he felt like talking—but now wasn't the time for that, either.

I hadn't known any of the Leanan Sidhe. To me, they

were just one more brand of Vampire. It would have been easy to indulge in today's victory, lap it up like nectar.

Except nothing in my life had changed.

Not really. Scratch that. Something had. And it was major. No matter how much I didn't want to face up to it, I now knew for certain how much the Undead loathed me. They were ready and willing to go that extra mile to ensure I never Reaped another of them. I could have another sit-down with Death, but it wouldn't alter anything. She might pat me on the shoulder and coo a little, but in the end she'd send me right back out there.

In her mind, I was still one of her soldiers. And soldiers obeyed orders.

On that sobering note, my brain backpedaled to the whole love thing. Maybe I shouldn't say anything. It wasn't as if I was certain how I felt. I cared about Liam, but whether it was love or not was anyone's guess. Certainly not mine. As a candidate for poster girl of one-night stands, I had no idea what love—or commitment—entailed.

It was one reason Kiko and I were such good friends. She was just as much of a commitment-phobe as me, but for entirely different reasons. She planned to settle down after she hit thirty. I'd never told her how old I was, and I never would.

I'd offered Liam an out when I'd suggested he run along with the other Sidhe. He hadn't taken it, and that weird little dance my heart did was back in spades.

I wasn't sure what to expect when we teleported back to the plane. What had probably been off the Richter scale as far as earthquakes went could have obliterated the airstrip. Instead, it had made it far more useable. So much so, I didn't worry about getting off the ground with us both in the cabin.

When Liam first said he wanted to learn to fly, and then asked about the instrument panel, my spirits soared. I muffled a snort as I got us set up to take off while explaining things as if he were a student taking his first lesson. Of course, first lessons never happen in a twin engine aircraft, but the same basic principles apply.

Some women might be lured by perfume or diamonds. For me, it was airplanes. Was Liam genuinely intrigued by flying, or was he hunting for common ground with me? I nursed the plane skyward and decided it didn't matter. He cared about me enough to at least pretend to be interested in flying.

It was good enough for me.

Once we were in the air, I let hm get a feel for how the control surfaces—rudders and ailerons—changed our flight path. And I squared things up with Air Traffic Control. Told them we'd run into a spot of engine trouble and had landed at a remote strip where I'd fixed a loose hydraulic line. After a few admonitions to make certain I had a certified aircraft mechanic sign off on whatever I'd done, ATC had disconnected.

"My airplane," I told Liam. "It's time to land."

He laughed. "I know it's your plane."

I laughed too. "That's pilot talk for take your fucking hands off the yoke and your feet off the rudders."

"Got it." He folded his hands in his lap. "Have you

thought about where we'll go once we're back on terra firma?"

I had, but it was more of a conversation than a done deal. "Why don't we talk about it once we're down."

"I figured we would," he replied.

The next half hour we got the plane on the ground, back in the hangar, and buttoned up for whenever her next flight might be. Liam caught on quick and was really helpful. My last stop was my logbook hanging from its nail on the wall next to the door. I scribbled in details about this flight and hung it back in place.

"I'm surprised all that isn't electronic," Liam commented.

"It could be." I grinned at him. "But I'm an old-fashioned kind of pilot."

"When's my next lesson?" he asked.

"Whenever we can work it in," I told him and pointed at the Cessna 152 off to our right. "This is what you'll learn in. For one thing, it costs a fraction of the twin to keep it in the air. For another, it flies slower, so you have more of a margin if something turns to shit."

"What? I can't just teleport out of the plane?"

His delivery was so deadpan, at first I thought he was serious, but then I saw crinkles in the corners of his eyes. In the muted light of the hangar, they appeared almost violet.

"You could," I said, equally deadpan, "but then you'd have to buy me another one. Plus, you'd be stuck explaining what happened to the Federal Aviation Association."

He wrapped an arm around my shoulders. It felt good and natural for him to touch me like that, so I didn't duck from beneath his arm. We walked out of the hangar and covered the few feet to my office. I skipped digging my keys out of my bag and focused a beam of magic to disengage the deadlock. Everything looked exactly the way we'd left it.

Part of me had expected Vamps to show up and wreck the place.

I dipped out of Liam's embrace and dropped my shoulder bag next to my desk. The message light was lit up on my landline. Lights blinked on my computer monitor as well. Maybe *Carrick Sky Sports* wasn't quite dead yet. I bent and fished out my cell phone, mostly to plug it in, but it, too, had messages. Lots of them.

They could be from bill collectors, but they might be from clients. No way to know until I retrieved them, but they weren't my primary concern. The realization was freeing in an odd kind of way. If you'd asked me even a couple of weeks back, I'd have pegged my business as the most important thing in my life.

And I would have nosedived into those blinking lights, eager to connect with my clients. Despite my precarious financial position, only part of that intense focus was money. I loved flying, and this gave me a way to indulge my passion and get paid for it.

Another epiphany crowded on the heels of the first. Death expected me to put Reaping above everything. It was why she hated *Carrick Sky Sports*. To her way of thinking, it competed with what I was supposed to be fully engaged in: Reaping.

Liam moved until he faced me, and he dropped both hands on my shoulders. "You're quiet."

I lifted my gaze to his face. No matter how many times I

looked at him, there was this initial breath-stealing moment when I fell into his beauty. "Lots to think about," I said.

He hooked a foot beneath the pedestal on my desk chair and spun it to face the desk. Then he cleared off a corner and perched on it. I understood he was settling us in for a chat and slid into the chair.

"What happens next is up to you," Liam began.

I shook my head. "No, not really. Nothing is simple." I held up one hand and extended my index finger. "One, the Vamps haven't gone anywhere, and I don't have any bigger or better bag of tricks to snare them. Two"—I held up another finger—"Humans Rule is a worldwide organization. We have no idea how widespread their use of magic is. Or how hard they'll fight to hang onto it."

Liam nodded slowly. "You're right about Humans Rule. I haven't actually thought much about that part of things. We can't allow any mortal to wield magic. It will interrupt the dynamic balance of this planet—and not in good ways."

"Since there are so many members of HR, it's unlikely all of them are dabbling with magic. Probably only some of the more highly placed ones," I murmured.

"I'd thought the same. They've managed to keep their forays into sorcery secret, which argues it can't be more than a handful of them."

I closed my teeth over my lower lip. What he'd said highlighted how little I knew about magic. My only information came from my stint in Reaper school, and Death had titrated what she wanted us to know. Watered it down until I wondered why I'd wasted three years there. Or had it been four?

"All those books and scrolls in your apartment, they contain information about things like that, huh?"

"About what specifically?" Liam arched a brow.

"Dynamic balance and humans with magic. That kind of stuff."

"Aye, those things and much more. Why?"

I offered a crooked grin. "I wish there was a way I could absorb all of it by osmosis or something. I've never been the swiftest student, but I can't let it hold me back. I have to educate myself. Death never told us anything that might have turned us into independent thinkers. Even a lot about Reaping fell into the 'we won't bother to mention that topic' category."

"You're welcome to my source materials, and the remainder of the Sidhe library, which puts my small collection to shame." Liam stopped and nailed me with the kind of look I couldn't squirm my way out of. "But that's a long-term project. What do you want to do right now?"

Tossing myself into his arms was high on my list, but it wasn't practical. My cheeks heated until I was certain I had to be bright red. I resisted rolling my eyes. He could help himself to my thoughts, so I may as well spit some of them out. Not about crawling up his body, but all the other jumbled, confused places.

"The way I see it," I said, "I don't have too many choices. I can go back to business as usual. Trying to keep *Carrick Sky Sports* from going under by day and Reaping Vampires at night."

"*Carrick Sky Sports* will be just fine." Liam's deep voice was comforting. "You just landed a new student, and he'll pay up front for a hundred lessons. Or a thousand. Just tell me what you need."

I stifled a laugh; it came out anyway. "I couldn't let you do that, but thanks for the thought."

"Beyond this place"—Liam patted the desk—"and Vampires, what else could you do?"

"Yeah. I was getting around to that. I could tell Death I'm done. What can she do to me? Thanks to you, I uncovered the rest of my magic, which is easily ten times the power I thought I had." I licked at suddenly dry lips. "But I can't quit Reaping. It's hardwired into me. The dead will always be drawn to me, but I'm attracted by them too."

I scrunched my forehead in thought. "This might not be the best comparison, but I have Vampires on the brain. You know how they're drawn to warm, pulsing jugulars?" At his nod, I went on. "Well, the dead hold the same type of attraction for me. There's nothing quite like the sensation as a soul slips through when I hold the gateway for them."

"No one said you have to stop Reaping," Liam said.

My eyes widened. I'd never considered freelancing. Reapers worked for Death—or they didn't Reap at all. End of story. Or was it?

"What?" Liam asked.

Still flummoxed by my discovery, I murmured, "You can read my thoughts, why ask?"

The corners of his mouth twitched into a smile. "Because I'm trying to be respectful."

Unexpected emotion flooded me. Gratitude. Love. Hope. With a heaping side order of conflict. It was the conflicted aspect that got to me, and I sorted through my new magic as I worked to create a ward around us. One Death couldn't listen through if she were so inclined.

"Let me," Liam said smoothly, and I felt the flow of his magic surround us. "What is it you have to say where you're worried about prying ears?"

"If I tell Death I'm done taking orders from her, but that I plan on continuing to Reap souls, I'll turn her into an enemy."

"You can't know that," he said.

"Yeah, I can. I've known her a long time. She's a jealous mistress, and she demands absolute allegiance from us."

He shrugged. "We all change. The world isn't the same place as it was when she decided she needed to create those like you to help with the burden of ferrying souls across the veil."

"She won't see it that way," I said. "She believes she has a system one that's working—"

"Except it's not," he interrupted me. "Not really. Vampires are out of control. Humans are dabbling in magic they have no right to."

"She won't see them as her problem," I pointed out. "They're not dead yet."

"The Vampires are." He frowned. "Look. Cait. It will take a long time, maybe as much as the next fifty years, to fix what the Leanan set in motion. Earth-bound Vamps won't suddenly forget how to walk in sunlight. Just like humans won't develop selective amnesia about how to deploy magic."

I propped an elbow on the arm of my chair and rested

my chin on my upraised hand. "What it comes down to is whether I continue Reaping under Death's aegis or go out on my own. I can't make that decision today. It's too monumental."

"Wouldn't expect you to. On a far more manageable level, do you want to go home? If so, which one? Yours or mine?"

I dipped my chin, but I'm certain he saw my lips curve into a smile. "Planning to stick with me, are you?"

"Only if you want me to."

I angled my head, trying to decipher what he'd meant, but then I gave it up. He didn't seem to be in any hurry to leave, and dissecting every nuance of his expression or voice tone might not yield much. Taking his words at face value was smarter.

"Would my houseboat work for now?" I asked. "Or do you need to catch up with the Sidhe in Scotland right away?"

He smiled, and something unreadable flickered in the depths of his eyes.

"What?" I asked.

"You're beginning to view us as friends. It makes me happy. For a while, you were skittish as a feral cat and circled around almost everything I did or said sniffing for ulterior motives."

I smiled back. "You are a friend," I told him. "And I don't have many."

"Neither do I. The houseboat is fine. We can eat and rest and then figure out what comes next."

"Can you give me maybe ten minutes to run through my messages?" I asked.

"Of course. Anything I can do to help?"

"No. I'll be quick." Warmth spilled through me as I brought my computer out of sleep mode and scrolled through email and messages. I returned the ones that needed attention and then checked both phones: landline and cell.

Liam had moved off the corner of my desk to offer me space to work. After a few minutes, he said, "I'm impressed."

I glanced at where he stood not far from me. "Why?"

"You've made the leap into the electronic age seamlessly."

The laughter I'd stifled earlier bubbled from me. "Ha! It was far from seamless, but if I wanted to run a business in the twenty-first century, I had no choice."

"I'm still impressed. My efforts to encourage computers to do anything haven't gone well, but I'm still trying."

I clicked a few keys, and the computer went back to sleep. "I'm ready to leave," I told Liam and pushed upright from my chair. "Mostly all the messages were good news. I've set up quite a few appointments over the next few days."

He narrowed his eyes. "Was that wise?"

I shrugged. "Not sure about wise, but necessary if I want to eat and pay my hangar fees and houseboat rent."

"We'll make it work." He held out a hand, and I laced my fingers with his.

I started to correct him, tell him making it work was my job, but I didn't. I loved the idea of us being a we, and for once I wasn't in a hurry to slam the door shut on a man who wanted to share my life.

Not that there had been many candidates. And none for the past century or so.

"Thanks," I murmured and leaned into him.

"Anytime," he said. "How about if we teleport to the houseboat. I'm not feeling like dealing with traffic."

"Do you drive?" I asked him. For some reason, I'd expected he used magic to get everywhere.

"Aye. One part of modern life I embraced, although not without a few hiccups."

"There's a lot I don't know about you," I said.

"The reverse would be true as well. How about if we do a wee bit of sharing over"—he glanced out my window, probably to judge what time it was—"dinner?"

"You show me yours if I show you mine?" I teased.

His fingers tightened around mine, and he swung me to face him. Before I knew what he had in mind, his mouth crashed down on mine. I should have protested, should have pulled away. We were having dinner, not sex, but I couldn't stop kissing him.

I'd dreamed about his lips on mine, and now it was finally happening.

I wrapped my free arm around his body and threaded my fingers through his thick, silky blond hair. His lips were firm and insistent, and he tasted of heat and promise. The scents of Sidhe magic rose around us, thickening the air with the smell of green, growing things and sandalwood. My own scents of heather and wildflowers mingled with his.

When he ran his tongue along the seam between my lips, I opened my mouth to him, welcoming his tongue. He threaded his free hand, the one that wasn't holding mine, around my back and ran his fingertips along my shoulder blades and down my spine.

I sparred with his tongue, and nibbled his lips in between kisses. Soft, sweet, his lips trailed across my cheek to my ear and then back to my mouth. I felt as if I were floating. Nothing in the world mattered except the man in my arms and his mouth crushed against mine.

The hand that had been exploring my spine came to rest on my neck. Liam lifted his mouth from mine and smiled softly. "I've wanted to do that for a long time."

My face grew even hotter than it already was. "Me too," I admitted.

He tilted my head. "About that dinner. Shall we find something to eat?"

Part of me was disappointed, but what did I have in mind? Dragging out a sleeping bag and ravishing him on the floor of my office? Probably not the most romantic surrounding.

"Dinner would be wonderful," I said.

Without letting go of me, he summoned the magic to take us home. I welcomed the feel of it, and of him.

"This was a good beginning," he said. "You're important to me, Cait. Too important to hurry things."

The walls of my office dissolved, replaced by my small living room. What he'd said had touched my heart. My soul. "You're important to me too," I began.

He placed two fingers over my mouth. "Probably a good place to stop."

It was because I had no idea what I'd say next. "It's kind of like with flying," I murmured.

He stepped away from me. "How so?"

"Well, when someone does an especially good landing, they always want to try again, but I tell them not to. When everything is perfect, it's tough to replicate, and it's best to stop when you're ahead."

He chuckled. "It is, indeed. I really like you, but I don't suppose you've been to the store since the last time I rustled through your cold box."

"When would I have had a chance? Between Vampires and—"

He waved me to silence. "We can go out. You pick the place. Something small, intimate, where we can take a bite out of that mutual show and tell you suggested."

I looked down at myself and realized I was still wearing Liam's clothes. "Give me a second to change, and then I know just the place."

"Excellent. I'll do the best I can with what I have on. If the restaurant requires a suit, I'll weave a glamour."

"Convenient." I hated to leave his side, but I trotted down the hallway to my bedroom closet.

"Magic is many things." His voice followed me. "The odd convenience makes up for what a pain in the arse it can be."

Damn. Was that ever true. It struck me as funnier than hell, and I was still chuckling after I'd changed into a long black skirt and teal tunic. I draped a woolen cloak over everything. It would probably start raining between now and when we were done with dinner, and my leather flight jacket didn't go well with anything but jeans.

And then I remembered it was draped over a chair at Liam's house in Malin.

I walked to the living room. Liam had "changed" into a gray woolen suit, cream-colored shirt, and art deco tie. He jumped up from the couch and offered me an arm. "You look lovely."

"So do you." I stroked the arm of his coat. "Feels real."

"Aye. It is. Until I disperse the magic powering the illusion."

"Can I learn to do that?" I asked as we strolled out the door.

"Probably. Your enhanced magic is different from mine, but we can experiment." We reached the street that faced the pier. "Shall I summon a cab?" he asked.

"Nah. It's only a couple of blocks. We can walk."

"I love that idea." Bending, he kissed my cheek.

Arms linked together, we strolled through the gathering dusk. I had a lot facing me, but for now, for tonight, I wanted to forget about everything except Liam.

"Aye, lassie. I approve." He winked at me.

I grinned back. "Harvesting thoughts again, eh?"

"Guilty as charged. Do you mind?"

"Not at all." And the odd part was I didn't. I had no idea what would happen tomorrow, or even later tonight, but I trusted Liam. He'd said we had a good beginning between us.

For now, it was enough.

You've reached the end of *Shadow Reaper*. Cait has some hard days ahead, but she has new resources at her disposal to deal with whatever crops up. *Rebel Reaper*, next book in this series will be along presently. Keep reading for a sample chapter.

Please take a few moments and leave a review for *Shadow Reaper*. Doesn't have to be fancy, a few lines will do. Reviews mean so much to authors. They're how you can let other readers just like you know why you loved a book.

Come fly with me. Catchy, huh? It works for airplanes. Maybe it will work for the dead once I launch my own Reaping business.

Back when my life was simpler, I thought all I had to do was hold gateways for the dead to pass through. Silly me, I actually enjoyed Reaping. Almost like a drug or fine, old whiskey, it made me high, filled me with delight, and left me glowing with the rightness of providing a last bit of compassion.

Good little Reaper that I am, I never examined any of it too deeply, just crafted portals, exactly as Death trained me. Ha! She neglected to mention I command way more magic than she'd let on in Reaper school.

Death smiled pretty to my face, and then lied to me. Used me.

Me and all the other Reapers.

I can't not Reap. It's hardwired into me. But I can tell Death I quit.

Big words. I have no idea if I've got the guts to follow through, or what Death will do about open insubordination.

I've always liked to live on the wild side, though, so I guess I'm about to find out.

Air rushed beneath the Citabria's wings. Normally, I don't borrow airplanes, but I needed something with aerobatic capability. My student would show up in about two hours, and I was upstairs putting the plane through her paces.

Most people would never guess airplanes have personalities. Even the same model from the same manufacturer has its idiosyncrasies and will fly differently. Luckily, one of my fellow pilots owed me a favor, or I'd have had to turn down a previous student who wanted to try his hand at aerobatic maneuvers.

By the time I paid to rent the Citabria, any profit from my lesson would go down the proverbial tubes. I flew figure eights and did a few rolls. The right rudder felt mushy, and one of the wing struts creaked alarmingly when I pulled out of the last roll.

A quick glance out my window was far from reassuring.

Bellanca, the company that made the Citabria, had gone out of business forty years back. All the Citabria models had issues, the worst being cracking struts. The original wood had been reinforced with a length of metal, but the bottom screws had pulled out of the body of the plane.

Crap.

So much for getting ahead of the stack of bills that had piled up since I got stuck Reaping Vampires. I couldn't use this plane for a lesson, knowing it had a mechanical issue. And Doug, the plane's owner, would probably insist I pay for repairs. I nosed the plane back toward the field. The gauges weren't reading what I wanted them to, either.

Damn it. Nothing I'd done during my short flight would have created this level of damage.

I slapped my forehead with my open palm. I'd been both gullible and a fool. None of the local pilots would willingly give me the time of day. I'd been pleasantly surprised when Doug had agreed to let me borrow the Citabria, thinking maybe my problems with him were over.

The other pilots tolerate me. Their antipathy isn't as "in my face" as it was when I first set up shop as *Carrick Sky Sports*. The bedrock problem is they still believe I belong in a kitchen or shackled to a bed. Flying is for men, and Amalia Earhart got what she deserved.

I am such a Pollyanna. Doug had known exactly what was wrong with his aircraft. And now he had someone to blame—and charge—for fixing it. I let go of the yoke and doubled up a fist. Yeah. Right. Punching the instrument panel wouldn't solve anything.

Doug must have added extra heavy hydraulic fluid, so

the plane's issues wouldn't become apparent until I was in the air. Ditto for the screws and the strut. I'd done a preflight. I always do. I walk around the plane jiggling things to make certain nothing is loose.

Apparently, I didn't jiggle hard enough.

I patted the yoke. None of this was the airplane's fault. "Come on, sweetie," I crooned. "We can do this."

And then I summoned magic and wove air beneath the wounded wing to keep the plane straight and level. More magic, heavy on water, kept the engine from overheating. Damn Doug to hell. I'd pitch nine kinds of fits if he opened his yap about sending any fixit bills my way. To hedge my bets, I opened a channel to Air Traffic Control. When they responded and cleared me to land, I told them the plane had a myriad of mechanical issues.

And listed them.

Nothing gets ATC's attention quite as fast as a plane that could turn into a danger to other aircraft. They directed me to land and taxi directly to one of the certified mechanics who maintain shops along the strip.

They didn't care which one, so long as I did not pass go or collect 200 bucks.

My headset crackled. "What in the hell did you do to my plane?" Doug demanded. He didn't identify himself, but he didn't have to. I recognized his voice.

"Nothing," I said succinctly, knowing we had ears listening in over on the ATC end of things. "Your plane was broken when you loaned it to me. It's a wonder I wasn't killed."

He shut up fast after that.

My wheels kissed the ground; I taxied to the shop I use. If I hadn't been so angry my blood was nearly molten, I'd have asked Doug which mechanic he preferred. As it was, I was determined to turn the Citabria over to someone I trusted.

I gathered up my shoulder bag with my logbook, phone, tablet, and flight computer and exited the plane. Most of the mechanics monitor radio channels, so Rick Dogris was waiting for me. Middle height and barrel chested, he wore his usual set of greasy gray coveralls. Bald as a pinball, he sported dark glasses that covered his shrewd blue eyes. I dropped the keys into his hand.

"Wouldn't fly it if I were you," I said and sketched out everything from the visibly busted strut to my mushy rudder and overheating problems.

Rick's worried expression deepened. "Christ, Cait. I'm glad you got her back on the ground. Did Doug authorize repairs?"

I shook my head. "Nope." I sucked in a breath and cut to the chase. "He must have known the plane had serious problems. I want to make certain he doesn't pin them on me."

Rick set his jaw in a tight line. "He's a slimy one. Wouldn't put it past him."

"Yeah. Which is why the plane is here and not with whoever signed her off as airworthy."

"Don't you worry. I'll chase that angle down too." Rick's nostrils flared with annoyance. "Until I hear from Doug, I'll taxi her out back and leave her."

"It's as good a plan as any."

Rick patted the fuselage. "I really like these planes, but they never were as reliable as, say, a Cessna."

Awk. With all the excitement of almost crashing, I'd forgotten the whole reason I'd had the Citabria in the air. "Hold up," I told Rick and fished my phone out of my bag. A bit of scrolling yielded my student's number.

Xavier picked up right away. "Yeah, Cait. What's up?"

"We don't have a plane. I took the one I'd planned on using for a test ride, and it's not safe."

"Damn it." He hesitated, and I visualized his dark eyes narrowing in thought. 'I'm already en route. Is there anything else we could do today?"

I thought about it. "Do you have any plans to get certified in a twin engine plane?"

"Not really, but I suppose I could give it a go."

I smiled. "It's a lot of work. Today would only be the tip of the iceberg. And it would be expensive."

"How about if I just rent the Cessna 172 and fly around for a bit?"

"Sure. We can do that. Normally, I don't rent out my planes, but I trained you."

He chuckled. "I'll do my best to bring your baby back in one piece."

Before I could respond, he'd disconnected. I dropped my phone back in my bag, swiped sweaty hair off my forehead with the back of one hand, and glanced at the sun. It was early afternoon. My lesson may have gone up in smoke, but I had plenty to do.

I quashed a wry grin at my choice of imagery. I was damned lucky the Citabria hadn't caught fire.

"Want a ride back to your office?" Rick asked.

I shook my head. "Nah. Good to get the kinks out. I'll walk."

"Do you want my report once I've checked out the Citabria?"

I chewed my lower lip and hefted my bag over one shoulder. "She's not my plane. How about we do it this way?"

"Which way would that be?" he quirked a brow.

"If you find anything that could conceivably be my fault, let me know. I'm not overly fond of Doug Printz, but if I damaged his plane, I'll pay my share."

Rick punched my upper arm lightly. "I like you, Cait. Will do."

Coming from him, the bit about liking me was high praise. Rick was known for being a dour son of a bitch, but being an airplane mechanic is considerably more nerve-wracking than, say, working on cars. If someone screws up a car, you can pull it to the side of a roadway.

Not so much with aircraft.

I set off toward the Quonset hut where my office is. It's right next door to a hangar that shelters my three planes. It did feel good to walk the half mile or so back to my shop. The day was chilly, but clear, and the air had a bite to it that reminded me winter was just around the corner.

The sky was full of fluffy clouds, but they had gray edges. Rain was never far away in the Pacific Northwest, and I wagered it would pour sometime before dark. The drone of airplanes coming and going filled my ears. I loved flying, and I was damned lucky to have built a viable aeronautics business.

Eh. It had been viable, but that was before Death assigned Vampires to me. I'm a Reaper, one of many, actually. We all report to Death. She sort of un-assigned me, but the damage was done. Plus, I'm kind of in limbo. The Vampires don't give a rat's ass I'm not plotting their downfall at the moment.

I'm still on their hit list—or more accurately, their "let's make her just like us" project roster.

Death had rescinded her No Reaping edict, and a few other promises, until I had no idea quite where I sat.

My breath made plumes in the frosty air. My long legs ate up distance quickly as I crossed in front of the hangars and small businesses that catered to pilots and our specific needs. A month had come—and gone—since I'd seen Death. Liam, a Sidhe I'd fought side-by-side with, had been absent as well.

He'd had to go back to the Old Country. He'd asked me to go with him, but unless I wanted *Carrick Sky Sports* to truly go into receivership, I'd had to remain here.

Probably for the best. I'd halfway fallen in love with him, but getting closer wasn't a good idea. He and I had both spent the entirety of our lives—his immortal and mine not quite so bombproof—by ourselves.

The familiar whine of an engine snapped my head upward. My mouth dropped open. The goddamned Citabria was back in the air. Why? She was a flying deathtrap. My phone started ringing, and I dug it out. Rick's number flared across my screen.

Before I could even say "hello," Rick was screeching in

my ear. "That bastard just up and grabbed his plane. How bad was it, Cait?"

"Bad enough to not be in the air. What the fuck do you suppose—?" The whine turned to a squeal. Metal scraped against metal, and something with all the subtlety of a sonic boom sent me to my knees. The wing with the broken strut fell off, and the Citabria turned into a fireball.

"Call the Fire Department," Rick yelled at someone.

I got my feet back under me. Phone still clutched in my hand, I did my best to judge the plane's trajectory. It was spinning, falling almost straight down. It would explode again on impact. Anything it touched would go up with it.

Humans don't trust anything magical. Usually, I sheathe my power. For most of my life, I didn't realize I could do anything beyond create and hold a gateway for the dead. Liam changed all that. He opened my eyes—and my magic —much to Death's annoyance.

She liked it better when her Reapers maintained their focus on Reaping. None of this fancy-schmancy magical shit. The plane was dropping fast. Not much time. Certainly not enough for me to make my next moves look accidental. I bolted closer to the touchdown spot and shot magic ahead of me to form shielding over people and cars.

I'm stronger than I believed I was, but magic has limits. Mine were rapidly stretching to their endpoints. I wheezed from effort and dug deeper. Half a dozen people were screaming and running, but there was no way for them to move fast enough. Satisfied my shielding was as robust as I could make it, I focused on the burning mess that was the plane I'd been in not an hour before.

The detached wing hit the tarmac and crumpled to matchsticks on impact.

Feet firmly planted on the ground, I drew Earth magic, mixed it with huge gouts of air and gave the Citabria a hefty shove to the north where nothing would be beneath it. I'd built the protective canopy first, in case my current maneuver failed.

Power arced from my extended hands. I wound it around the doomed plane and guided it to where it wouldn't hurt anyone. It smashed against the asphalt with enough force to dig a crater a couple of feet deep. More explosions rocked the ground.

For the second time in a few minutes, I staggered and fell. My mouth and throat were raw from panting, but the only casualty was Doug—and his poor airplane. I felt far worse for the Citabria than I did for the man stupid enough to take her upstairs.

Footsteps pounded toward me from all directions. The shrill beat of sirens filled the air. I cut the flow of my magic. It had done its job. Before anyone else reached me, I felt the chill of the grave descend. It had to be Doug.

I cracked my Reaper magic open, but only a little bit. Sure enough, he shambled into view. "If you think I'm going to help you cross," I hissed, "think again."

I'd be damned if I'd help Doug. Let him find another Reaper.

He barreled toward me, singed and stinking of greasy smoke. "You bitch," he snarled. "Everything was fine. Until you fucked it up."

"And just how did I do that?" Without waiting for an

answer, I kept chugging along. "Safety first, bud. Or did you forget that part? We don't fly planes that aren't safe. And we don't foist them off on our associates, either."

I could have said more. A whole lot more, but I didn't.

He launched himself at me, but he was dead, and so he passed through me. I slammed my grave vision shut and thinned my Reaper power to the barest glimmer. I'd meant the part about him finding another gatekeeper.

He threw himself at me again. And then a third time, ending up sprawled on the other side of me. "I have to get out of here," he yelped. "You're my ticket."

"Some people's," I agreed. "Not yours." With a flick of my hand, I dismantled the canopy I'd constructed. The people trapped beneath it had been panicking. I'd felt the stream of their horror and fear through my casting.

I had no idea what Doug would do next. "Be a good ghost," I purred, infusing my next words with compulsion. "Go away."

"I can't," he wailed.

"First ghost ever who couldn't leave the place they died." I mocked him, certain I was right. "You sidestepped the wrath of the FAA. They'd probably have stripped you of your certifications, but you'll have a lot of time to think about it."

"You don't get it." He was still snarling, but now he sounded more pathetic than anything. The transition to being, well, dead, takes a while. Ghosts don't exactly embrace a change that means they'll never be able to do anything again—except talk with a Reaper.

So long as I'd thought about it, I added, "Doesn't matter what I understand, no one but me can see you."

The first fire trunk squealed to a halt fifty yards from me. Men jumped down, hustled the hose off the truck, and sprayed fire retardant around the burning wreckage. It's astringent scent polished off what was left of my throat, leaving it even scratchier than it had been before.

Rick reached me and wound a big hand around my forearm. "Cait. Thank god you're all right. Who are you talking to?"

The old me would have demurred, said I was talking to myself, but I was done concealing who I was. Over a hundred people had witnessed me throwing magic about. Denying I could command power was disingenuous and stupid.

I twisted until I met his blue eyes. "I'm a Reaper. Doug was lobbying for a way through the veil. I refused."

Rick's fingers tightened around my arm. "Now is not a time for jokes, Cait. I know you've had a rough time here, but—"

"I'm not joking."

Something about my tone must have gotten through. He dropped my arm as if it had turned into something that would poison him and crooked two fingers into the sign against evil.

I screwed my mouth into a grimace. "Really? You drank the Kook-aid, huh?"

"What do you mean?" He was still looking at me as if I might suddenly sprout another head. Or horns.

"Did you sign on with Humans Rule?"

He looked at his feet. "I might have."

Meanwhile, Doug had switched to throwing himself through Rick's body. He was clawing at him, shouting in his face.

"What part about 'he can't hear you' didn't soak in?" I asked.

Rick shifted his gaze from side to side. "What's going on?"

"Nothing much. Doug just walked through you for maybe for sixth time, and—"

"Ick. Make him stop. I never liked him when he was alive, but this has a huge creep factor." Rick sounded freaked, his voice shrill, and jumped back a step.

"I have no control over him, but he can't hurt you. Or anyone else. He's a ghost. A spirit."

"Fine." Rick was doing his damnedest to appear stoic. I swear, being a man comes with a shit ton of baggage. I'd have sent a thread of calming magic his way if he hadn't admitted to being part of Humans Rule. On the surface of things, they're a bunch of bigots who want people like me locked away. If you dig deeper, they're a front for humans who want to sling illicit magic around.

I'm certain most HR members are like Rick, horrified by magic, but some of the more highly ranked folk are dabbling in magic. Vampires traded with them: magical tricks for blood. Humans were never meant to wield power, so it's a huge problem for the rest of us.

A crowd was gathering. At least Doug had faded from view. Maybe his new position at the sub bottom of the totem pole was sinking in. It always did.

"Ms. Carrick." A man called my name. Turning toward him, I recognized the airport manager. Tall, spare, and dressed in gray slacks and a wrinkled white shirt, he trained solemn brown eyes on me. His hair was black and cropped short.

I inclined my head. "Mr. Johnson."

He extended a hand, and I shook it. "That was incredibly brave of you," he told me. "Most people would have run the other way."

Pleasure at the compliment warmed me. I hadn't exchanged two words with him after signing contracts allowing *Carrick Sky Sports* use of the runway.

"She did something," a youngish woman with red hair shouted.

"Trapped us with magic," another yelled.

Bill Johnson turned his attention toward them. "She protected you while she made certain the plane came down where it couldn't hurt you or anyone else." Before others jumped into the fray, he raised his voice and said, "Everyone here owes Ms. Carrick a huge thank you."

"Not necessary." I projected my voice as well. Maybe it wasn't the smartest thing to do, but I rolled my shoulders back. "I used the magic that lives within me to make certain none of you were harmed. I'm a Reaper, and damn it feels good to stop hiding what I am."

"Why didn't you kill us?" someone called.

I swallowed back a sharp retort and jumped on my first opportunity to educate humans. "Reaping isn't like that. I hold the gates for newly dead to cross over. We don't kill anyone."

Except maybe Vampires, but I didn't feel compelled to add that part. Besides, they didn't count since they were already dead.

The adrenaline was fading. Being a hero has never been high on my list. Before anyone got any ideas about a longer conversation, I threaded my way through the crowd, still intent on at least stopping by my office. Xavier had probably come and gone by now. Or maybe the crash had been on the news, and he'd turned around and headed back into Seattle. The strip would be shut down for at least long enough to clear the wreckage from the Citabria and patch the hole it had made in the runway.

I'd broken a few rules, the biggest of which was revealing what I was. Death didn't want us outed. As I covered the few hundred yards to my Quonset hut, my thoughts were a jumbled mess.

I'd check my messages and head home. Probably, I'd teleport. The last thing I needed to deal with was rush hour traffic. I skipped hunting for my keys and sent a shot of magic at my locked door. It sprang open, showering me with the decayed, rotten stench of Vampires.

Fuck. Crap. Damn it all to hell. There should be a quota for how many bad things happen to one Reaper in a single day.

The air near me shimmered and glistened. I unclenched my fists and untangled my bag from around my neck. I knew who was coming, and at least her timing was good. Sure enough, Death sashayed through a silver-rimmed portal. Leather pants and a long leather tunic fit her like a second skin. Lace up high-heeled boots encased her lower legs. Her silver hair was loose and hung to knee level. A blood-red gemstone I hadn't seen before glittered from where it hung around her neck, and an ever-changing collage of the dead and dying played across her eyes.

"Come on." She clapped her hands smartly together.

"Come on, what?" I asked.

"Let's go get 'em." Without waiting to see if I'd follow like the obedient puppy she imagined me, Death surged into my office right into the middle of a pack of Vampires.

I might not want to Reap Vampires, but letting them run around free was far worse. Before Death could yell for me again, I warded myself and charged after her.

ABOUT THE AUTHOR

Ann Gimpel is a USA Today bestselling author. A lifelong aficionado of the unusual, she began writing speculative fiction a few years ago. Since then her short fiction has appeared in many webzines and anthologies. Her longer books run the gamut from urban fantasy to paranormal romance. Once upon a time, she nurtured clients. Now she nurtures dark, gritty fantasy stories that push hard against reality. When she's not writing, she's in the backcountry getting down and dirty with her camera. She's published over 70 books to date, with several more planned for 2019 and beyond. A husband, grown children, grandchildren, and wolf hybrids round out her family.

Keep up with her at www.anngimpel.com or http://anngimpel.blogspot.com

If you enjoyed what you read, get in line for special offers and pre-release special reads. Newsletter Signup!

Dragon's Call

Dragon's Blood

Dragon's Heir

Dragon Lore

Highland Secrets

To Love a Highland Dragon

Dragon Maid

Dragon's Dare

Dragon Fury

Earth Reclaimed

Earth's Requiem

Earth's Blood

Earth's Hope

Elemental Witch

Timespell

Time's Curse

Time's Hostage

Gatekeeper (Winter 2019 and spring 2020)

Shadow Reaper

Rebel Reaper

Untamed Reaper

GenTech Rebellion

Winning Glory

Honor Bound

Claiming Charity

Loving Hope

Keeping Faith

Ice Dragon

Feral Ice

Cursed Ice

Primal Ice

Rubicon International

Garen

Lars

Soul Dance

Tarnished Beginnings

Tarnished Legacy

Tarnished Prophecy

Tarnished Journey

Soul Storm

Dark Prophecy

Dark Pursuit

Dark Promise

Underground Heat

Roman's Gold

Wolf Born

Blood Bond

Wolf Clan Shifters

Alice's Alphas

Megan's Mates

Sophie's Shifters

Wylde Magick

Gemstone

Lion's Lair

Unbalanced

STANDALONE BOOKS

Branded, That Old Black Magic Romance (paranormal romance)

Edge of Night (short story collection, paranormal and horror)

Grit is a 4-Letter Word (nonfiction)

Heart's Flame (post-apocalyptic romance)

Icy Passage (science fiction romance)

Marked by Fortune (post-apocalyptic coming of age story)

Melis's Gambit (historical paranormal romance)

Midnight Magic (paranormal romance)

Red Dawn (post-apocalyptic paranormal romance)

Shadow Play (historical paranormal romance)

Shadows in Time (Highland time travel romance)

Since We Fell (contemporary romance)

Warin's War (paranormal romance)